LITTLE
GIRLS
SLEEPING

BOOKS BY JENNIFER CHASE

JENNIFER CHASE

LITTLE GIRLS SLEEPING

bookouture

Published by Bookouture in 2019

An imprint of StoryFire Ltd.

Carmelite House
50 Victoria Embankment
London EC4Y 0DZ

www.bookouture.com

ISBN: 978-1-78681-830-0
eBook ISBN: 978-1-78681-829-4

For Mark

PROLOGUE

The oversized tires obliterated the rural roadway before the large truck came to an abrupt stop. The driver stalled the engine. Dust rose in a curious flowering cloud, swirling in front of the vehicle's hood and creeping toward the back of the camper shell. When the surrounding vicinity finally cleared, a dense forest landscape emerged.

The truck overlooked the sheer cliff and rugged scenery that had become a permanent roadblock. The usual silence of the deserted region was interrupted by the incessant and rhythmic sound of a cooling engine.

Tick... Tick... Tick...

The vehicle remained parked. No one moved inside the cab or got out. The truck stayed immobile as if an unlikely statue in the vast wilderness—a distinct contrast between nature and manufactured steel.

The truck sat at the ideal vantage spot, which was both mesmerizing and terrifying for any spectator; but still the occupant chose to wait. The intense high beams pierced ahead into the picturesque hills, leaving a hazy view of the area above the massed trees.

When the driver's door finally opened, a man stepped out, his steel-toed leather work boots hitting the dirt. They were well-worn, reflecting the many miles he had walked and the many hours he had labored. Swiftly the door shut as the man, medium build and wearing only a plain dark T-shirt, walked to the back of the truck and, with a loud bang, released the lift gate. He moved with purpose and with a calm assertiveness, as if he had performed this particular task many times before. His weathered hands, calloused from years of working with heavy tools and machinery without the protection of leather gloves, had a certain agility and speed.

He grasped two well-used shovels, a large arching pick, and a bulky utility garbage bag. As he tossed the bag onto the ground, the top burst open and several medium-sized teddy bears spilled out. Their smiling faces accentuated the brightly colored ribbons tied around their necks, contrasting with the muted shades of their surroundings.

The man pushed the floppy bag aside with the toe of his boot. He worked in quiet solitude, no humming, no whistling, and no talk.

He flipped on the flashlight fixed to his baseball cap. Straight ahead and slightly arced, the large beam illuminated his path while he strode steadily toward a particular wooded area.

The surrounding thickets and trees remained still without any wind to rustle the leaves. The only audible sound was the man's quick footsteps—never with any hesitation. He walked with the gait of a young man, despite his stature of someone older.

He hesitated as if he had forgotten something, standing motionless with his arms down at his sides and his head hung forward as he shone the bright light at the ground and the tops of his boots. He still held firmly to the tools. He mumbled a few inaudible sentences of a memorized prayer, which sounded more like a warning than a passage from the Bible, then he raised his head and continued to walk into the dense forest.

Dropping his tools, he carefully pushed a pine branch aside and secured it with a worn piece of rope that had been left for the purpose. An opening was exposed—a tunnel barely large enough for a man to enter.

He grabbed his digging tools once again and proceeded. The flashlight on the front of his cap brightened the passageway as it veered to the right. He followed, only ducking his head twice before the path opened to an area with several boulders sticking out of the cliff. Clusters of unusual rock shapes, some sharp, some rounded, made the terrain appear more like a movie set or backdrop.

A narrow dirt path of crude, sloping man-made steps dropped fifteen feet to a landing jutting out from the rock formation. A small yellow flag was stuck into the earth, marking a spot. A slight evening breeze picked up, causing the flag to flutter.

The man balanced the shovels and pick against the hillside and pulled a hunting knife from a sheath attached to his belt. Pressing the bone handle tight against his palm, he drew the blade through the packed dirt to mark a rectangular pattern on the ground.

He stared intently at the soil, then retrieved the pick, gripping it tight, and swung it hard against the dry, heavily compacted earth. It dented the surface, spewing chips of dirt in every direction. A few small rocks buried in the soil since the beginning of time hampered his progress, but after several more arced swings, the ground began to crumble, exposing the fresh earth.

The heavy pick was exchanged for one of the shovels. Soon there was a small pile of California soil, comprised of sand, silt, clay, and small rock. The repeated movements of dig, scoop, and deposit continued for more than forty-five minutes at a brisk pace. The hard work of manual labor didn't deter him. It only made him more determined to create a work of genius—his ultimate masterpiece.

At last he stepped back and admired his handiwork, perspiring heavily through his shirt from the effort. Exhilaration filled his body, keeping his muscles flexed and his heart pumping hard. He leaned against the shovel, a smile forming on his lips as he waited for his pulse to return to normal, and marveled at the unmistakable outline of a freshly dug grave.

CHAPTER 1

Four years later

The enemy waits for the perfect moment to attack, when you least expect it.

An unknown force seems to decide whether it's time to die or time to move on—yet by the grace of God, I continue to survive.

*

The rattling overhead compartments and sudden roller-coaster drop in altitude shook Katie Scott awake. She sat straight up in her seat, absently wiping the slight perspiration from her forehead and upper lip. Her stiff muscles and sore back from sleeping in the same position for a couple of hours made her exhale loudly. She stretched her arms above her head, relieving some of the tension in her neck and shoulders.

With sleepy eyes, she glanced to her left and saw a dark-haired young man sitting next to her who looked as if he would vomit at any moment. His terrified fixed stare, ashen complexion, dry lips, and white fingers gripping the armrests were obvious characteristics of a fearful flyer.

Katie thought she might give him some gentle advice on how safe commercial flights were, especially compared to the flights she had experienced during the past two years, three months, twelve days, and nine hours in the army. In fact, all her military transportations had been dangerous, whether on foot or riding in military vehicles. Whereas it was highly unlikely that the young man would die on this particular flight—it was not his time, at least not today.

Taking a deep breath and settling back again, she decided to keep her comments to herself. She closed her eyes. She hadn't slept in a real bed with fluffy pillows in months and looked forward to going home to enjoy all the things most people took for granted. Her mind wandered to the loaded double cheeseburger with French fries, onion rings, and a double dark chocolate milkshake that was going to be one of her first meals.

But as much as she looked forward to going home, there was the dreaded question looming. What was she going to do now?

The airplane rattled and thumped with a little more intensity, but Katie remained comfortable and relaxed. It felt to her almost like a gentle movement designed to lull her to sleep. Still, murmurs from concerned passengers filtered through the cabin. She opened her eyes and casually scanned the people around her. A baby cried and fidgeted in its mother's arms. Two women sat up straight in their seats as if they were preparing for a crash landing. Flight attendants made sure everyone was comfortable, something they did a million times during their careers.

The seat-belt light appeared in bright letters to keep everyone secured in their seats until further notice. Katie adjusted her body and inched closer to the window in case her fellow passenger decided to puke up his last meal. She stared at the scattered clouds in the mid-morning sky as the early sun permeated the horizon. It never grew boring to watch the beginnings of a new day. Katie liked to think of each one as a blank script and a way to begin again; to make things right—or just better.

Her eyes grew heavy and she shut them again. Since joining the army, she had rarely slept more than a few hours at a time, never the luxury of seven or eight continuous hours, and was used to frequent catnaps to gain renewed energy. Most times after she closed her eyes, she relived the many patrols she had experienced over the past two years, the unmistakable sights and sounds ingrained in her memory.

Revving engines.

Gunfire leaving a foul taste in your mouth.

Extreme dust clouding your vision.

Every footstep in brutally hot conditions, and the long, exhausting hours of stress were permanently etched into her DNA. She had already recalled those days and weeks hundreds, if not thousands, of times.

After Katie's initial seventeen weeks of intensive training, she had become part of a working K9 team. Her primary duty was to find explosives. She usually took the point position and led the others forward to complete their assigned orders, which meant finding bombs and gathering intelligence, as well as searching out explosive devices.

Katie and Cisco, an eighty-five-pound black German shepherd, who was assigned his second tour with her, were the only thing keeping the soldiers from being blown up or ambushed. As such, they were often targeted specifically.

Being part of a military dog team was something Katie had always wanted to do. Even as a young girl she had trained her own dogs, and daydreamed of helping others someday—finding the bad guys, or locating missing people. It was so important to her that she took an open-ended leave of absence from the Sacramento Police Department to travel across the world into unknown enemy territory to fulfill that dream. The sudden death of her parents had left a raw void in her life, so it was more important than ever to step out and do something to serve others.

The airline pilot interrupted her thoughts, announcing in a deep, well-rehearsed voice over the intercom, "We should be out of this weather in another few minutes and begin making our descent into the Sacramento International Airport. Thank you for your patience. Please remain seated until we come to a complete stop. Our destination is a mild sixty-nine degrees, with winds at fifteen miles per hour."

Katie's excitement and enthusiasm for going home was mingled with growing anxiety the closer the plane got to the airport. She felt caught between two worlds—civilian and military—something she had never experienced before. Things were different, changed, and no matter how hard she tried to make herself believe it was okay, nothing would ever be the same.

The aircraft changed gears, the engines raced, and there was a grinding underneath the belly of the cabin before they began the steady descent toward the airport runway. Katie stared out the small window, watching the familiar landscape. Buildings, cars, and the outlines of recognizable geographical features came into focus.

She heard a sigh and looked at the passenger on her left. Now that he knew he was almost on the ground, he appeared to have managed to calm his nerves, leaning back and releasing his death grip on the armrests.

For the first time, Katie felt conspicuous wearing her army pants, combat boots, and olive-green T-shirt, even though everything was freshly laundered, with precise creases. It had never bothered her before, but now, as she looked at her masculine boots, she realized it made her an outcast. It represented being different—not in an empowering way, but in a distancing way.

The sudden urge to run to the exit to be the first to escape overwhelmed her. Instead, she smoothed her long dark hair back into a neat ponytail. Everything she had trained for and experienced counted for something, and she was determined to make her skills work in a positive way to move into the next aspect of her life.

The landing gear touched down with a quick, uneventful rumble as the aircraft decelerated along the long runway, the engines slowing its speed until the plane taxied to the appropriate gate. As it came to a complete stop, passengers readied themselves for the usual mass exodus. Katie remained seated, staying in the moment, as others grabbed their carry-on luggage and pushed their way into the aisle, forming a bottleneck in the process.

She was going to wait, happy to be one of the last to exit, but an older man with sparse gray hair stopped and smiled, then backed up a bit to allow her to merge into the line. She returned his smile and quickly grabbed her backpack from the overhead compartment. It was obvious that the man had served in some area of the military; it was common for those who had shared these experiences to extend polite courtesies.

Finally out of the plane, Katie followed the other passengers through the plastic tunnel towards the baggage area. Then, loaded up with her backpack and duffle bag, she made her way to the airport entrance, where crowds of people were rushing about in a myriad of directions.

Standing near the sidewalk, waiting patiently, was a tall, striking man of moderate muscular build, with a grayish speckled crew cut, and a neatly trimmed mustache. His face instantly lit up when he saw Katie exiting through the automatic doors, and he moved toward her, giving her a big bear hug.

"We've missed you so much," he whispered. "We prayed every day that you would be safe. Your parents would have been so proud. You know that, right?"

Katie nodded while emotions welled up inside her.

"We're *all* proud of you," he added.

"It's great to see you, Uncle Wayne," Katie said, relief filling her voice. It comforted her to be in her uncle's arms. "Where's Aunt Claire?" she asked, looking around.

"She wanted to be here to greet you, but she had an emergency with the women's auxiliary club. You'll see her later."

"So how did you get the department to let you come in person?" she asked curiously.

He picked up her duffle bag and said with some humor, "That's one of the perks of being the sheriff."

"Of course, I almost forgot," she said. She grabbed her backpack and followed her uncle to the short-term parking area. The fresh, crisp air and the familiar distant rolling hills soothed her. She was finally home.

Her uncle stopped suddenly. "Oh, I have a surprise for you."

Katie was puzzled. "What do you mean?"

"You know... a *surprise?*" he emphasized.

"Uncle Wayne, I'm not ten anymore. What is it?"

He smiled, and the lines crinkling around his eyes gave him a concerned, fatherly look. "I cannot begin to understand what you've been through, Katie. I know it was the toughest thing you could ever experience." He paused a moment before continuing. "So that's why I did everything I could to make this happen. I hoped it would be done before you came home. And as the good Lord is my witness, it is."

"Now you've really got me thinking..."

"C'mon," he ordered.

As they rounded a corner, passing several sedans and trucks, Katie saw her familiar black Jeep Wrangler. Inside, jumping from window to window and barking with pure joy, was a large black German shepherd.

She dropped her backpack, ran to the car, and opened the door. "Cisco!" she exclaimed, choking back tears. The dog whined, spun around several times, then licked her for several minutes, before repeating the whole process again. His joy was clearly evident.

"I don't understand," Katie said, looking at her uncle teary-eyed. "How did you get him home so quickly? I thought I was going to have to fight for months to have him released to me."

"I got started when you first told us that you were making arrangements to come home. I know about all the red tape and politics involved with the military. Cisco had already had two tours, so I just made a few calls, and then a few more, and the next thing you know, I received a phone call to pick him up at the military naval base in Concord."

"How? Why would they? Never mind. Thank you so much for bringing this guy home. He saved countless people, including me," she explained, still hugging the dog.

Wayne opened the back of the Jeep to load Katie's luggage. "Let's just say a friend of a friend knows someone in the White House administration. And it helps that they are all dog lovers," he laughed.

"I guess you'll never tell me the real details, but that's okay, because this is the best surprise I could ever hope to receive."

Her uncle shrugged his shoulders, grinning. "C'mon, get in. I'm driving. You just sit back and relax."

The drive to Pine Valley took more than an hour and a half. Katie gave her uncle some updates at first, but otherwise the ride was mostly a quiet one. The excitement of having Cisco home made Katie the happiest she thought she could be under the circumstances. Optimism crept in and she anticipated that things could get back to normal—maybe even better.

After an hour, she drifted off to sleep and allowed the gentle motion of the road to keep her relaxed and comfortable.

"Hey," her uncle said gently. "Wake up, Katie, we're here." He had parked next to his large white SUV.

Katie opened her eyes to see her familiar yellow house with its white trim. It always made her smile and reminisce about all the memories of growing up. It reminded her of long summer days and the many good times she had had with her friends and family.

Heavy breathing and several licks accosted the side of her face as Cisco seemed to pick up on her enthusiasm.

"Yeah, buddy, this is your home too," Katie said. "Sorry, Uncle Wayne, I really conked out."

"No apologies necessary. You'll need a few days to rest up and get back on Pacific Standard Time." Her uncle grabbed her bags out of the Jeep. "Oh," he said, and stopped.

"What?"

"Actually, I have a bit of bad news."

"What?" Katie repeated, this time with trepidation.

They walked up to the porch, and her uncle paused before inserting the key in the lock. "Last year we had some record rainfall, and…"

Dread overwhelmed Katie. "And?"

"Well, your house sprung a leak—actually, several leaks—in the roof. Before I checked on it that week, there'd already been a fair amount of water damage. I know you haven't had time to address home repairs, and I've been so busy…"

Katie's thoughts went to her things: her parents' furniture, the photographs, and her huge collection of crime and forensic books. "How bad?" she asked.

"Well, we've fixed everything and salvaged what we could." He opened the door.

To Katie's surprise, most of the furniture, except a couple of pieces, still sat in the usual places. The smell of fresh paint lingered in the air. She noticed a few new things: some throw rugs and artwork.

"There are still some things drying out at home, and other things being professionally restored," her uncle said. "The good news is that the roof is completely fixed. It should last you a good ten to fifteen years."

Cisco ran around the living room, sliding on the newly refinished wooden floors, then headed to the kitchen. Within seconds, she heard him noisily lapping up water.

"Well…" she managed to say. "What about—"

He finished her sentence. "Your books?"

Katie nodded, holding her breath.

"Believe it or not, most didn't get a drop of water on them."

She heard herself let out a sigh of relief.

Her uncle led the way to the kitchen. "We did do some updates," he explained, "and got you a new refrigerator and stove. Basically updated them into this century. And you'll love this, a safe area for Cisco to run and play. A bunch of the guys pitched in to help."

Katie went to the glass doors and saw that there was a huge dog enclosure. "Wow, that's really nice." She turned to her uncle. "Thank you, Uncle Wayne, for everything."

"It's our pleasure. Claire stocked up the fridge with some things you can just put in the oven, and some of that girlie food you like—fruits, veggies, and some kind of weird seeds." Motioning to a large basket on the counter, he added, "And she packed some soaps, lotions, toothpaste, and other stuff so you wouldn't have to immediately go to the store."

Katie laughed and kissed his cheek. "Thank you," she repeated softly.

"That reminds me. Art gallery and lunch next week?" he asked.

"Oh, of course. I look forward to it."

Katie and her uncle had an ongoing arrangement to enjoy a gallery and have lunch together at least once a month—just the two of them. It had long been their way of spending time together.

Wayne headed to the front door. "Sorry I have to run, but I want you to report to me at headquarters at 0730 hours sharp on Monday. We're going to keep you busy until you decide what you want to do. Nothing better than hard work…"

He gave a quick wave before he got into his SUV.

Cisco sat in his standard heel position next to Katie's left thigh, with his ears perked forward and his gaze targeted, actively searching for anything out of the ordinary.

Katie continued to stare out the window until her uncle's vehicle disappeared down the driveway.

Then she rubbed Cisco's head, scratched his ears, and sighed.

She was alone again.

CHAPTER 2

Every time I close my eyes, I see what people can do to one another—the destruction, the ugliness, the terror, the deep sadness—and when I wake, I know I will always carry those images with me. It's a part of who I am.

*

Katie drove her Jeep faster than the speed limit, the familiar buildings and roadways racing by her windows. At the last possible moment, she swerved away from the main road and took the more scenic route to the sheriff's headquarters to allow more time to get her thoughts together. She knew there would be tons of questions fired at her about the army, and she wasn't sure how she wanted to answer them.

After sleeping for a few days, she was looking forward to working with people again in a civilian setting. Police administrative work, even if it was only filing, was just a diversion for now; she didn't want to make any big decisions yet. In truth, she didn't know if she would return to Sacramento PD. She wanted to wait until she had more of a relaxed focus. Staying neutral and on autopilot sounded like a perfect option—at least for now.

As her car raced around a tight corner lined by trees, she almost careened into a large blue pickup truck blocking half the roadway with its front end facing down toward the ravine. Swerving to miss the truck's bumper, she came to a complete stop before easing her vehicle to a safe area a little ways up the road. Her first thought was that someone had crashed and was unconscious. She needed to make sure no other cars repeated her maneuver.

She grabbed several flares and quickly ignited them, then placed them strategically along the roadside to alert oncoming drivers to the accident. She checked her cell phone, but there was only a weak signal.

"Hey! Are you okay?" she yelled. She moved closer to the truck but couldn't see anyone inside. Confused, she carefully stepped around the vehicle; there was no sign of the driver or any passengers.

She opened the driver's door and peered inside. The keys were in the ignition, with two other ordinary house keys dangling from the keychain. There was a man's leather jacket lying on the seat. Overall, it was a tidy vehicle. She didn't notice anything unusual, like blood, or alcohol containers; nothing to indicate what might have happened.

"Where are you?" she said quietly to herself.

"Are you talking to me?" responded a man's voice from behind her.

Katie turned to find a sandy-haired man with intense blue eyes and a tanned, muscular build watching her with amusement. It was the unmistakable smiling face of Chad Ferguson. He had left town before she had.

Slightly embarrassed, she said, "Oh, hi. I wasn't expecting to see you here."

"Just who were you expecting?" he asked, still smiling.

"You don't seem surprised to see me," she said.

"Nope."

"Why?"

"The sheriff."

Katie gathered her wits. Of course her uncle would have told people she was back. "Is this your truck?"

"Yep."

"What happened?" she asked.

"This big brown-and-white dog—probably some type of St Bernard or mountain dog—ran out in front of me. I swerved to miss him and got stuck. I went to see if I could catch him and make sure he wasn't injured, but he was long gone. Little bastard."

"Did you call a tow?" she asked.

"Tried."

"No cell signal?"

"No, they won't be available for more than two hours—big wreck over on the 99."

Katie walked back towards her Jeep. "Well, do you want me to tow you out?" she said over her shoulder—almost as an afterthought.

"If I had to choose… yes."

"Got chains?" she asked.

"Sure."

"Make sure no one else comes barreling around the corner while I get my Jeep hooked up."

Chad jogged around the corner as Katie moved her Jeep into place. She took the chain from the truck bed and hitched the pickup to the Jeep, then climbed back into the driver's seat.

Chad gave her a dramatic thumbs-up sign.

She eased the Jeep into four-wheel drive and hit the gas pedal. At first the car didn't move, so she pressed the accelerator harder. The engine whined, and then suddenly she was able to pull the truck onto the roadway. She put her car in park and jumped out, but Chad had already unhitched the chains.

"Bravo," he said. "Quite impressive for a little Jeep. I have the bigger version at home."

"Yeah, it may be small, but it's definitely strong."

Chad moved closer and said casually, "So you haven't asked me what I'm doing back in town."

"I figured it's your business," she said coyly, though she was surprised that he had come back.

"Well, the forestry department needed some volunteer firefighters. And you know me."

Katie laughed. "Yes, I sure do. Not much has changed, I see. Always the guy ready to help in any type of situation."

"But you've changed," he said seriously.

Katie didn't answer and averted her gaze, feeling conspicuous and remembering the close relationship they had once shared.

"You have the determination and confidence to take on the world," Chad said. "I admire that."

"I don't know about that."

"What you did in Afghanistan took guts and heroism. Don't let anyone take that from you. You stepped up and followed a dream."

Katie smiled. "Well, I'm on my way to the SO. I'm filling in with some clerical work—for now." She walked to her Jeep and got in. "It was nice seeing you."

"Oh you'll be seeing me again, Katie Scott, and maybe I'll repay the favor," he replied.

As Katie drove away, she couldn't resist glancing in her rearview mirror, watching Chad climb into his pickup. Nothing had changed about him. His charm and good looks were his obvious attributes, but he had been a true friend to Katie, in every sense of the word. Throughout her childhood she could tell him anything—her dreams, fears, and anything else that came to mind. He was a part of her life that she'd thought was gone forever, the last person she'd expected to see back in town. Usually, once people left Pine Valley, they moved on to new things and never looked back. Chad had returned, and it changed everything.

CHAPTER 3

Katie found a parking spot at the administration building for the sheriff's office and cut the engine. She was still thinking about her chance encounter with Chad. She gazed into the mirror and was surprised to see makeup on her face. She had spent extra time applying mascara and eyeliner, and made many mistakes before she felt she looked decent. At this point, she felt more comfortable with an AR-15 in her hand than a mascara wand.

She opened her car door and stepped out. She was dressed in dark slacks and a crisp white blouse. She hadn't been quite sure what she should wear, but casual professional was a good selection and she was relieved that her old clothes still fit. She had dropped about eight pounds since she had been away.

Initiating the locking alarm for the car, she hurried to the main entrance.

She arrived in the administration lobby of the sheriff's department on time. The building housed the dispatchers, records clerks, accounting, and other miscellaneous functions—including the sheriff, undersheriff, and lieutenants. The detective division and forensics were located in an adjacent building.

Katie walked up to the young red-headed receptionist behind the glass. "Hi," she said. "I'm Katie Scott, here to see the sheriff."

"Of course, Ms. Scott, the sheriff said you were coming in. Welcome back," the girl said with a genuine smile. She moved from the window and came out a door. "Please, this way."

Katie followed her down a couple of narrow hallways until she reached the sheriff's office. The girl motioned for her to enter and then politely left.

Katie saw that her uncle was dressed in his usual uniform instead of a business suit. As he finished up a phone call, she gazed at photographs and various ribbons and medals won for all types of law-enforcement events. The photo situated in the middle was the image of Katie herself graduating from the police academy.

She stopped and stared at one particular photograph. It showed a smiling couple with a five-year-old girl. It stung her seeing her parents and how happy they had all been together. It had only needed a horrible storm on a fateful night to take them away from her forever. If only they hadn't rushed home, but had spent the night somewhere along the way, things might have been different.

"You look rested," stated the sheriff.

Katie turned to face him. "I feel pretty good. Eating a lot," she laughed.

"Are you and Cisco getting into a routine yet?"

"Definitely. There are no words to thank you, and your *special* friends, for bringing him home."

Sheriff Scott moved around the desk to face her. "Well, I have to use my political power once in a while."

"So where do you want me? I'm ready to work; just point me in the right direction."

The sheriff picked up the phone. "Denise, you have time to show Katie around now? Great." He hung up. "She'll be right in. We're short on administrative staff; two of our records clerks are on maternity leave. So if you know your ABCs, you can file, and if you know your way around a keyboard, you can enter data. It's actually really helping us out."

"Sounds good. Glad to help."

An attractive brunette with a pixie haircut poked her head around the doorway. "Katie? I'm Denise Ashton, the supervisor for the records division. It's nice to meet you." She moved inside the office and shook Katie's hand. She was dressed in a snug business suit and wore high heels.

"Nice to meet you too."

"Have fun," the sheriff said as the women left the room. He was already engrossed in paperwork.

Katie followed Denise down the narrow hallway, bypassing two doors until they came to a large room with several desks. There were three women working there, two entering data on computers, and one on the radio giving information to officers.

"This is the warrants area, where we receive all warrant checks from every police department in the county," Denise said. She led Katie through to another large room. "And this is where the other part of the records division is located." She motioned to one side. "Here, searches are conducted for current investigations: suspects' backgrounds, prison records, owners of vehicles, and so on. It's also where we enter all daily information from patrols and investigations, and collate everything from the department for the crime data that goes to the State Department of Justice and the Uniform Crime Reporting Statistics." She walked through to a smaller room, "All filing for the last twelve months is located here, and anything before that is in the vault."

"Vault?" Katie asked.

"Not a real vault," Denise laughed. "We just like to call it that."

Katie spotted three more women. They were lost in their repetitive work and didn't seem to have any interest in meeting her.

"C'mon," said Denise, smiling.

Katie followed her down a long, dimly lit hallway. They passed two uniformed officers, who nodded to them. When they reached an unmarked door, Denise inserted a key into the lock. "This is the office supply room. It's supposed to be locked and is only for administrative personnel—if any of the officers need anything, we have to get it for them. I guess it's for budget purposes and a tight inventory. Anything you might need is here."

Katie peered inside and saw metal shelves stacked with paper, pens, notebooks, and other items.

Denise locked the door and they continued to the next one, which she opened without a key. Stepping inside, she said, "This door remains unlocked during the day, but you'll need the key in the evening if you happen to be working late. This is where all the cases ultimately end up."

The room was the size of a small warehouse, with high shelves reminding Katie of a superstore. Boxes and sealed plastic containers lined the shelves, with identifying case numbers, year, and name. "Wow, you could get lost in here," she said.

"On the far wall are the filing cabinets, along with the cold cases," Denise explained. "Of course, all the actual evidence is stored in the forensic division." She studied Katie for a moment. "I'm really glad you're here. We need the help, but I'm afraid you'll probably get bored before the day is over."

"I doubt that. It's what I need right now. Work to keep me busy."

Denise smiled. "Great. I'll show you to your workstation."

Katie spent most of the morning entering data and issuing details for warrants. It was tedious but made her feel needed without worrying about bombs and gunfire. A few curious people approached her and asked what it had been like in Afghanistan. A few others, mostly women, just completely ignored her existence. Most people were polite, but it was obvious who felt that Katie was being treated special because she had spent two years in the armed forces and her uncle was the sheriff.

She sat at a corner workstation with a department-networked computer and a fairly comfortable chair. The desk was next to Denise's area, and Katie couldn't help but notice several framed photographs of a smiling boy about four years old, along with other knickknacks that helped her desk to appear personalized. Her screen saver was a big shaggy dog, and two small crystal vases with wildflowers sat along the edge of the desk.

Katie worked her way through two large stacks of files, making sure everything was entered into the mainframe, then collated, and returned to the folders ready for the final filing. When she'd finished, she went to her uncle's office to see if he was free for lunch. He wasn't there, and his assistant was also gone. She was just about to leave when she saw a pile of files lying on a side table where they needed to be returned to the proper filing cabinets—some open cases, others cold.

As she grabbed them up, one of the files slipped from her grasp and a few papers scattered onto the floor. She bent down to pick them up and saw that it was a missing-persons case from four years ago that had gone cold.

Katie remembered the incident and the mass searches that had followed. Eight-year-old Chelsea Compton had been walking back from a friend's house in the middle of a summer afternoon. She had never made it home. It was a heartbreaking case. Many Pine Valley residents had their own ideas about what had happened, but it was nothing more than idle gossip, and no new physical evidence had been found since.

She opened the file and skimmed the notes from the lead investigator, Detective Rory Templeton. As she turned the pages, she stopped on a large eight-by-ten color photograph of Chelsea. It was the smiling, eager face of a little girl with dark hair, bright-green eyes, a missing front tooth, and her entire life ahead of her.

Like a gavel hitting a judge's desk, a memory fell sharply to the front of Katie's mind, of when she was at camp around the same age as the missing girl. It was one of the most memorable times in her childhood and she could still remember all the friends she had made, as well as the fun activities. She had learned archery that year, which later helped with her skill as a sharpshooter. There was swimming, hiking, canoeing, and various crafts. It was a wonderful lifelong memory of fun, friends, and surviving through the growing pains of being an adolescent.

But…

She also had a much darker recollection of that time. It was something that had always haunted her, one of the defining moments of her life: the last conversation she had with her friend Jenny.

"Hi, Katie," said Jenny eagerly, revealing a mouthful of braces. Her enthusiasm sometimes overrode her shyness. She was one of the nicest girls Katie had met at camp and the two of them had immediately struck up a friendship.

"Hi," replied Katie, beaming with joy. "Where were you? I looked for you before we went canoeing. It was so much fun. You would have loved it."

"Oh." Jenny looked down. "I was… well, I was running late and didn't really feel like it."

Katie had noticed that Jenny would disappear at times and not participate in group activities.

"Well, we're going again at three. You want to come?" she asked. "Please come," she insisted.

Jenny's eyes lit up and she replied, "That sounds like fun."

"Good. I'll meet you right here a little bit earlier. Okay?"

"Okay, I'll be there," Jenny answered as she smiled, clearly excited.

But Katie never saw or talked to Jenny again. She waited for her as arranged, but Jenny never showed up. She didn't want to be late for the canoe class, so she left without her friend. When Jenny didn't appear at the canoe dock or later at dinner, counselors realized that she was missing from the campgrounds.

A casual search began, but soon it was established that law enforcement was needed to continue looking for the girl. There was no sign of her.

Two weeks after Katie returned home that summer, she overheard that a body had been found two counties away. It was identified as that of Jenny Daniels. According to the news, her parents had been involved in a nasty custody battle. When they couldn't come to an amicable agreement, things turned deadly, and her dad killed both Jenny and her mom.

Memories of that incident haunted Katie for a long time, and still continued today.

She had known something hadn't seemed right about Jenny's behavior. If only she had pressed her to find out what was wrong at the time.

If only she had stayed with her and not made a plan to meet her later.

If only…

An immense sadness filled her. The only solace was that there was closure in Jenny's case, but there was no comfort in someone's life ending before it ever really began. She remembered that Jenny had told her that she wanted to be a nurse, so that she could help people. She wondered what Chelsea had wanted to be when she grew up. Losing a child and not knowing what had happened to her must be a lifetime of heartbreak for any parent.

She focused her attention on the cold case. The notes and interviews seemed inconclusive. Katie wasn't an investigator—she had only worked minimal investigative cases on patrol—and yet there were things that stood out to her. The witness interviews appeared rushed and incomplete. There were a couple of people the detective hadn't followed up on, though it was possible the notes were filed somewhere else.

When Katie's parents had told her that Jenny had died, she had immediately demanded how and why. At first, she didn't believe it. It was too horrible. Her parents tried to be gentle, not wanting to upset her more than necessary, but Katie knew there was more to the story. She didn't rest until she found a newspaper, searching without her parents' consent, and finally finding a copy in the neighbor's recycling pile. And there it was, the grisly and shocking truth of what had happened. She remembered every word after the startling headline as her hands trembled and she cried for her friend.

Local Pine Valley Girl Caught in Middle of Custody Battle Turned Deadly.

The article went on to describe how Mr. Daniels had shot and killed his ex-wife in their home and then gone to find Jenny at the camp, making up an emergency to lure her to her death just under a mile away.

Jenny's smiling face came to Katie's mind again as she thought about how senseless her murder was. She felt that they would still have been friends today and would have had so much in common. Instead, a wonderful person had been taken from the world. That fact chilled her deeply, and had been one of the reasons she became a police officer.

She made a swift decision. There was a small copy machine in her uncle's office, so she photocopied the entire file, slid the copies into a plain unmarked folder, then returned the official documents to the original file.

"How are you doing?" asked Denise as she poked her head into the sheriff's office.

"Great. I found more files to return." Katie straightened the pile of folders in her hands.

"There're *always* files to return. I have dreams about files coming at me in endless waves," Denise laughed. "I managed to find more data entry for you. I left it at your workstation."

"Thanks, Denise."

As the other woman turned to leave, Katie called after her, trying to sound casual.

"Does Detective Rory Templeton still work here?"

"Yes. He's over in the detective division. Why?"

"Just curious. I've heard from my uncle about some of the interesting cases he's worked."

"If you want to go over there, there's an assistant, Kelli, who buzzes everyone in. Tell her I said it was okay."

"Thanks."

"Let me know if you need anything," Denise said, and was gone.

It was against protocol to remove any information from an investigation, open or closed, but Katie would come clean to her uncle if she found anything useful—if not, she would destroy her copies. She had to make sure there was nothing more that could be done on the case. She hadn't been able to save Jenny, but she might be able to help Chelsea.

CHAPTER 4

The painting hung in the corner, overpowering the entire exhibition with its dark contrast and dramatic hues. The abstract scene wasn't anything in particular at first glance, but it made a lasting impression due to its use of color and shape. The heavy brushstrokes in crimson and deep arctic blue washed across the canvas with great flair, with black lines accentuating the picture both horizontally and vertically.

Katie stood studying the work, searching for the artist's motivation or some kind of story. She wondered what it was they were trying to capture. The simplest answer would be darkness, misunderstanding, or loneliness. The painting was mesmerizing and appeared to change subtly every time she looked at it.

She glanced at her watch. Her uncle was already fifteen minutes late. She decided to slowly peruse the gallery rather than wait any longer, and took several moments at each exhibit before moving on. There were oil paintings, watercolors, bronzes, a sculpture made of recycled items, and photography. Every piece made her relax and enjoy the moment. Ever since she was a little girl, she had loved looking at paintings, photographs, and any type of artistic exhibits. She shared this interest with her uncle, and that was one of their strongest bonds—before the law-enforcement bug hit her too.

She found herself drawn back to a series of black-and-white photographs from 1950 depicting everyday scenes of people interacting with one another in the streets and at home. It gave her pause. It was well before her time, and so many things had changed. She wondered what people from that era thought about the changes in technology, crime, and social identity. Life then had been so simple.

"Makes you think," said a voice behind her.

Katie turned and smiled at her uncle. "Yes, it really does."

The sheriff was dressed casually in jeans and a dark long-sleeved shirt. His eyes had a cool blue stare that could waver between calm and loving and an intensity that made many criminals confess.

"You know, I remember when your favorite types of paintings had ponies, rabbits, and raccoons in them," he laughed.

"I don't know how much I've changed. I still love ponies, rabbits, and raccoons."

A memory caught at her, of her mom when she was teaching Katie how to draw. Memories could be cruel, like a gust of cold wind, but wonderful for the very fact that she had been lucky enough to experience them.

Katie and her uncle wandered around the gallery discussing technique and mood, sharing laughs and friendly debates. It was another forty minutes before they decided to go to one of their favorite diner restaurants, Burger Mania, reputed to serve the best hamburgers west of the Mississippi.

After they'd placed their orders, they settled in at their compact booth, sipping colas. The place was crowded, and the conversations around them rose in volume, but it couldn't spoil Katie's enjoyment of this time spent with her uncle. She realized that since she had been back, she had been struggling with her emotions and feelings of anxiety. Keeping certain feelings in check still caused her some grief. She looked down at the table.

"What's on your mind?" asked Wayne.

She took a breath and answered honestly. "What's not? I don't know. Everything's on my mind. Does that make any sense?"

"Ever since you were a little girl, you were so serious about every-thing. So yes, I believe that you hold a lot in that brain of yours."

"There's no lying to you." She watched the ice cubes in her soda slowly melt.

"Not likely."

"I thought things here would be like they've always been. Slow, laid-back, and keeping that same small-town charm."

"Like before you left?"

"Well, yeah, why not? It hasn't been that long."

"Places change all the time. People change. A way of life changes. You can't freeze time or expect things to stay the same. They never will, no matter how hard you try to hold onto them."

"I'm looking for an easy answer, but there isn't one." Katie ran her fingertips across her paper napkin. "I guess I'm having difficulty making decisions right now."

"Then don't."

"It's just—"

"Katie, you're young. Don't be so hard on yourself. I assume you're talking about going back to Sacramento PD?" He watched her carefully.

"Yes."

"And perhaps some feelings for an old friend?" He smiled.

"No… Well, maybe."

He reached out and squeezed her hand. "Don't push yourself. Let things move the way they should—naturally. You'll know what to do when it's time."

"You're right," she said. "I don't want to make any rash decisions yet about getting back on patrol. Don't tell anyone, but I kind of like working in records. It's quiet, soothing, and keeps my mind busy. No gunfire, no explosives…"

A tall, thin waitress with an extremely long braided ponytail brought their plates, with towering burgers and heaping piles of fries. "You need anything else?" she asked, resting her hands on her hips.

"No, we're fine right now," the sheriff replied.

"I'll freshen up those sodas in a bit," the waitress said, and was gone.

"I think there's more you're not telling me, that you're not wanting to process right now," Wayne said.

Katie nodded and couldn't quite meet her uncle's gaze.

"I've always been one of your biggest supporters in whatever you've decided to do. And you still haven't reached your potential—not even close." He poured catsup onto his plate and immediately dunked several fries into the red sauce.

Katie took a bite of her hamburger, and swallowed before she continued. "I know you want to ask me why I joined the army."

"You wanted to do something bigger than yourself. At least that's what you said at the time."

"True. That's part of it, but…" It was difficult for her to articulate. She took a few moments before continuing. "I wanted to leave here, leave Sacramento; I wanted to get away from my life. Be somewhere else." It seemed strange for her say it aloud after it had been kept compartmentalized in her mind.

Her uncle listened and waited patiently for her to continue.

"I know it sounds crazy."

"No, it doesn't sound crazy. I didn't know how you felt before you left because it was so abrupt. And you stayed an extra tour before coming back home. It was worrisome."

"I'm sorry." She picked at her hamburger bun.

"Don't be. You did what you thought you needed to do at the time."

"Uncle Wayne, are you psychoanalyzing me?" She smiled.

"I never divulge my secrets," he joked.

"I wanted to escape. After Mom and Dad died… that day… how it…" She couldn't finish her sentence. "It was too much for me, but I managed to finish school and the academy, and begin patrol at Sacramento PD with the help of you and Aunt Claire. Nothing felt quite right. I felt like I was supposed to be a certain person and act a certain way." Taking a sip of her soda, she said, "I know no one made me do anything I didn't want to do. I had to find my own peace, I guess."

"We all do at some point in our lives, some sooner than others," he reassured her. "You're doing everything you need to right now. Just recognize it. The more small stuff you accept, the easier it will be with more weighty things."

"I'm working on that," she said. "I just wasn't prepared to lose friends so soon on the battlefield, and it's difficult to get that straight in my mind."

"If you need anything, absolutely anything at any time, just ask."

Katie knew that her uncle was being careful not to push her about her experiences in the army and what she had witnessed. It was the same thing with cops. Many held their feelings close and didn't want anyone to have a sense of their weakness—which in reality was their strength.

"I will," she said.

"I'm not just saying that. I mean anything…"

CHAPTER 5

Katie was putting away case files, both recent and old cases. Her mind kept running over the facts of Chelsea Compton's disappearance and whether to talk to Detective Templeton directly. She didn't know exactly what to expect, but her gut told her that she needed to ask a couple of pertinent questions. At the very least it might give a gentle push to reopen the case again.

In her mind, this was a case that needed to be solved whether it had a happy ending or not. There was one theme that ran throughout her textbooks and true-crime books: cases need closure no matter the outcome. But she wanted to check a few things first.

Denise was busy in a meeting, while most of the data entry and files were already completed. Katie sat at her desk pondering. The more she thought about the case, the more edgy she became. She glanced around the room; there was only one other administrative person and they were involved in a project and not paying any attention to her. With a few clicks of the keyboard, she searched for cases of missing girls broadly matching Chelsea's description over the past four years from the surrounding five county areas. She found three that were roughly similar. Three years ago, Amanda Harris and Megan Lee, best friends, nine years old, got off a bus and were never seen again until their bones were discovered in Arizona a year later. That wasn't going to help the case—two suspects had been arrested and were awaiting trial.

The third girl, Tammie Myers, also nine years old, was last seen three years ago when she walked from her aunt's house to the small local grocery store, Tango's Corner Market, to buy ice cream and a dozen eggs. She was visiting her aunt while her parents worked out some type of marital problems. She wasn't from the area and didn't know anyone. The case quickly became a cold case. One of the investigating detectives suspected that the aunt was involved but could never prove any evidence of her connection.

Katie frowned. Instinct and knowledge told her that Tammie was already dead and would probably never be found. As numerous textbooks had taught her, the likelihood of a missing child still being alive after forty-eight hours was slim.

She twisted her neck and looked around her. The administrative area was completely quiet. No voices were audible and no one approached her desk. She moved her fingertips adeptly across the keyboard and continued a more detailed search until she finally came to a database where she could enter the parameters of what she was looking for in comparable cases. She also wanted to try and find out if there were similar cases of abductions in neighboring counties—if necessary, in the entire state of California.

It took longer than expected, but after about twenty-five minutes she was able to find two other abductions that resembled Chelsea's case. Both incidents had happened more than two hundred miles away. She wasn't getting anywhere, but the searches did show that young girls around the same age as Chelsea were missing.

She took some quick cryptic notes and then cleared the screen and search history and sat staring at the blank monitor. The blinking cursor was like a consistent heartbeat prompting her to do something—anything. She kept staring at it and didn't want to blink because then she would see the smiling face of her long-ago friend, Jenny.

Find her.

Even the few things Katie had checked so far seemed to point in one direction. The evidence still needed to be sifted through, but it appeared to indicate that Chelsea Compton's disappearance wasn't random due to the other girls in the area who were missing without a trace. There was something going on, and she just had to put all the clues together to find out what.

Katie waited patiently for Detective Templeton to finish a phone call. The significance of this missing-persons case still weighed heavy on her—especially because it had to do with a child's welfare. The more she thought about it, the more determined she was to breathe life back into it.

"Ms. Scott." The detective addressed her formally, forcing a stale smile.

"Hi, Detective Templeton, nice to meet you." She shook his hand, instantly noticing his exceptionally calloused palm.

"What can I do for you?" he inquired.

Katie realized that he had either already heard she was the sheriff's niece or guessed some relation due to their same last name. It wasn't clear if that was a bonus or not—at least not yet.

"I have a few questions about an old case of yours. Would you have a moment?"

Templeton hesitated but then gestured to Katie to join him at his cubicle. "Of course."

There was a large container of small chocolate candies at the corner of his desk; the lid was askew, meaning the detective had either just had a handful of sweets or someone else had helped themselves. Taking a chair across the desk from him, Katie noticed the same scribbly, all-capital-letter writing on the notepads and file folders as in the cold-case file.

She estimated the detective was in his mid-forties. He had a receding hairline and was about twenty pounds overweight, and he wasn't wearing a wedding ring. She also noted that he still hadn't mastered a more effective organization process when working on cases.

The little sign on his desk read: *Detective Rory Templeton, Robbery/Homicide.* She wondered why he had been leading the investigation of a missing-persons case, unless the department knew, based on experience, that Chelsea was most likely dead before they began looking for her.

The detective appeared to be annoyed at Katie's presence, but his curiosity seemed to override his initial emotion. "Ms. Scott, what would you like to know?"

"Please call me Katie," she began. "As you may or may not know, I'm helping out in administration while they're short-handed."

"Yes," he said. His eyes narrowed as if he was studying her behavior and judging whether she was telling the truth.

"There's a cold case I came across. Chelsea Compton."

"Yes," he said again, his jaw clenched tightly as he leaned back in his chair. "What about it?" he inquired icily.

Katie had the sinking feeling that she might have overstepped her bounds, but the truth needed to be stated. The case deserved fresh eyes and it needed to be reopened. She pushed a little more. "I noticed that there were things missing from the case."

"Like?"

"Well, the interview with the neighbors of the Comptons—I believe their name was Stanley—was never followed up. And Terrance Price said that he saw Chelsea in the park that day, and there was a truck he had never seen before a little while later… Wasn't he known to do odd jobs in the community as a handyman? Did he ever work for the Comptons?"

"Let me stop you right there," interrupted the detective.

Katie waited patiently, never taking her eyes from him, watching every slight gesture and movement he made. She knew that she had stepped on someone else's turf, but cold cases were there for anyone within the department to revisit. At least her uncle had always said that, and it had been in his office to be re-evaluated. So here she was re-evaluating it.

"As much as we all appreciate what you did for this country, I think we can take care of our cases in the way we see fit," Templeton said. "But I'll humor you. We were able to check the neighbors' statements, and found they were referring to a different day from the disappearance. They were mistaken. As for Terrance, he wouldn't remember if he saw Chelsea today, tomorrow, or ten years ago. He's a drunk, a drug addict, homeless most of the time, and has been diagnosed with a type of paranoid personality disorder."

Katie nodded, keeping eye contact, never changing her poker face. It was something she'd learned in the army—never let them see your feelings. She still had more specific questions, but realized that she wasn't going to get unprejudiced answers, because she was an outsider and only a patrol officer, not a detective.

"I just thought since it was a cold case and—"

Templeton interrupted her again, this time with more emotion, drawing the attention of surrounding detectives and administrative personnel. "You *thought* wrong. It has been four years since the abduction of Chelsea Compton. She is dead. That's the hard fact, Ms. Scott. The only way we are going to find any more information is when someone happens to stumble upon her bones—most likely in another state. Or if the killer walks in here and confesses."

Everyone was staring at Katie.

"I see," she stated calmly.

She stood up but continued to hold her ground. The detective didn't scare her. She had encountered some real tyrants in the army, from sergeants to training officers, so Templeton was like a yapping little dog to her—fierce, but only annoying at best.

"Well, thank you, Detective. I appreciate your time. It's nice to know that every case receives the same attention and investigative doggedness that it should—even the difficult ones."

She left with her head held high in case anyone wanted to challenge her—but no one did. She had a plan, whether Detective Templeton liked it or not.

CHAPTER 6

Katie finished her first week at the sheriff's department without any unforeseen hitches or confrontations; however, gossip persisted around the office and Detective Templeton made several snide accusations about her to anyone who cared to listen.

Most department employees worked four ten-hour days a week, which meant that Katie had a three-day weekend. She wanted to make every moment count.

Her childhood bedroom was the smallest room in the house. She decided to turn it into her personal library and study area. She had purchased a specialized paint to cover one of the walls, so that she would be able to use it like a giant chalkboard with magnetic capabilities. It would be the perfect way to lay out the investigative timeline for Chelsea Compton—everything that was known from the official file.

It was a covert investigation for now—she hadn't told her uncle yet about having a copy of the file—and if her efforts resulted in nothing new, she would just shred the copies and be done with it. But if there *was* something substantial or important he needed to see, she would come clean and tell him what she'd done, showing him the new discoveries. She didn't like keeping secrets from him, but there was something about the case that made her feel it was important to bring it back to life.

She was returning to the kitchen to fix another cup of coffee when a strange creeping sensation welled up inside of her. It began with her lower extremities tingling, followed by the uncomfortable movements shifting up through her torso, and then to her head and eyes.

Anxiety was a stealthy and unpredictable enemy.

"Oh…" she whispered, barely audibly. She bent forward, bracing herself for the dizziness and fuzzy vision that usually followed. Her nemesis was back.

Cisco had a sixth K9 sense and immediately confronted her with soft whines and quick hand licks. He circled her, keeping his trained eyes on her hands and face.

"It's okay," she whispered to him, not recognizing her own tense voice.

Her breathing caught in her throat and a profuse heaviness pressed down hard on her chest, making it difficult to fill her lungs with air. It was as if a ghost was chasing her down and making her submit to its devious will. It was a scary, debilitating sensation unless you fully understood how to ignore it in order to make the symptoms disappear—a delicate balancing act.

The most difficult aspect for Katie was the fact that she couldn't fight the panic attack head on. Relaxing was key at the moment the anxiety struck.

You couldn't fight it.

You couldn't reason with it.

And it wouldn't make you promises that it wouldn't come back.

Anxiety, you're not welcome here anymore.

Katie wanted to run.

But where?

Anywhere.

She wanted to hide from it as the familiar shakes began to rattle her bones and perspiration soaked her entire body.

"No!" she yelled. She'd had enough. "No!" She gasped for breath and tried to steady her breathing.

Cisco barked three times and ran to the window, staring outside to look for anything or anyone that shouldn't be there. They had coped through these attacks together before, and they'd been happening more often. It was one of the reasons she'd decided to come home for good.

She pushed her trembling and adrenalin-ridden body toward the refrigerator, opting not to drink any more caffeine. Opening the door, she stood staring aimlessly inside. The cool air from the fan relieved some of her distress, and she was able to breathe deeply, slowly, in and out.

Cisco returned to her side, seemingly satisfied that there were no bad guys lurking.

"Crap, Cisco, I hate these episodes," Katie blurted out.

She chose a glass of lemonade. The coolness of the drink relieved the rest of the anxiety episode, but she was left re-imagining the smell of spent rounds of ammunition and the dusty heat from the battlefield. It all seemed so real.

It was an odd realization that her mind could conjure up on a whim the smells, tastes, and feelings of being in the desert of Afghanistan.

Would it ever go away?

After these anxiety attacks she generally became exhausted and a little lethargic. This time, however, she had important things to accomplish and she was determined to work despite her personal difficulties. She drank another full glass of lemonade and stood a few more moments until her pulse became slow and steady.

Her welcome-home basket from Aunt Claire still sat on the end of the counter. Claire hadn't been her aunt for very long; she'd married Wayne barely six years ago. It was such a thoughtful idea to leave a basket filled with necessities, including a small leather-bound journal with a delicately etched flower on the cover.

Katie plucked the notebook from the basket and flipped through it. Each page allowed for a personal entry and a reflection on how you were feeling. It made her think. Perhaps her aunt knew more than she'd realized about war and the inevitable post-traumatic stress disorder that came home with most soldiers. Katie had never kept a diary, even when she was a teenager, because she didn't have much to report or reminisce on. But replacing the journal in the basket, she couldn't completely dismiss the possible therapeutic effects it would have for her now.

She padded barefoot back into her study, which was in full investigative mode. She had some ideas that she wanted to work through to see if there was any credibility to them. If so, it would mean that the case warranted more investigation and digging in order to move it forward to a definite conclusion—good or bad.

Cisco followed her into the room and took a seat in the oversized chair in the corner. He kept an eye on Katie for as long as it took him to fall asleep and release subtle doggie snores.

Standing in the middle of the small bedroom with her hands on her hips, Katie perused the bookshelves along three of the walls, trying to recall similar cases involving a kidnapped or missing girl in a comparable community within a seventy-five-mile radius.

She pulled out two thick true-crime books containing various cases of abducted children. Skimming pages quickly to refresh her memory, she found one case where a seven-year-old girl left a birthday party and never made it home to her apartment complex only a half mile away. It turned out that a resident in the same complex had been stalking her and waiting for the right moment. Because she knew him, it was easy for him to get her into his car without raising any suspicion. He drove her to a remote location, raped and murdered her, and then tossed her body down a ravine. It was not until almost ten years later that some hikers discovered her bones.

Katie read through several other kidnapping and murder cases and found a number of similarities. She decided to jot down the obvious ones.

- At least eighty-five percent of cases involving a child abduction and murder were committed by a family member, friend, or acquaintance.
- Most involved the perpetrator making the child feel at ease in order to easily whisk them away to another location. The child didn't initially feel threatened by the perpetrator.
- Many perpetrators had a premeditated location as well as means of sexual assault, murder, and disposal.
- Most of the crimes were committed by a male between the ages of twenty-five and fifty-five.
- There was a distinct modus operandi in a number of the cases.
- Investigators were usually led initially on a wild-goose chase.
- Cases were closed when an unrelated person or persons found the remains of the child.

She decided to pinpoint the county boundaries and work out what areas had been searched for Chelsea. She used her laptop to mark out the search areas, based on news articles and the investigative notes from the file. Some of them were the usual places: home, school, friends' houses, backyards, and parks. Other areas were more rural, including campgrounds, hiking trails, vista points, and historical areas.

She spent an hour blocking out a map grid she took from the Internet with the areas searched, and was stunned at the regions that were left over. There were several places kids frequented to drink beer and hang out, and some more remote areas that according to her notes on similar cases would be more comfortable for the perpetrator.

Why weren't they searched too? she wondered. Shortage of time? Lack of volunteers? Everyone in town knew about these areas, but no one deemed it necessary to search them for the missing girl. Why not?

In addition to these locations, there were two extremely remote regions that would need an avid outdoorsman or survivalist to investigate properly.

Possible.

She jotted a few notes on the chalkboard, then wrote down the names of people who'd been interviewed, using only their initials. Then she transferred the list to her cell phone so that she had something to work from out in the field.

"Well, Cisco," she finally said.

The dog sat up, ears pointed in her direction as he waited patiently for a familiar command.

"We're going on a little trip."

CHAPTER 7

The man used slow, even strokes and a steady hand with the walnut-colored furniture stain. He ran the pristine animal-hair paintbrush across the bare wood carefully, making sure that every pore was saturated as he darkened the custom-cut lumber to his liking. Every movement was done with a gentle touch, and the hand-crafted detail made each piece close to perfection. He strived for extreme fastidiousness; there was nothing that was too good for them. It was the least he could do. If he could have included his actual love in the construction, he would.

An open laptop sat on a sawhorse. It was tuned to a national news station spewing everything ugly going on in the world. The volume was set to high; it was difficult not to hear all the gruesome stories. There were murders, gang shootings, police executions, home invasions, and crooked politicians, each story uglier than the last. The sensationalism and community outrage made for a dangerous cocktail, addictive for some, so that they could not stop listening to the news.

A pretty blonde reporter wearing a bright-blue dress read from her teleprompter with a smug matter-of-fact manner.

"It is not known at this time…"

The man stepped back to stare at his latest project, searching for any imperfections or inconsistencies. He loved every part of the process. It took him more time to build the coffin than it did to find the perfect occupant.

"… whether the father is a person of interest or a suspect."

The four major stages of building the wooden boxes were: finding the right wood, patiently applying numerous layers of stain, stitching each section of fabric perfectly, and finalizing every finishing nail.

"What we do know is that seven-year-old Candy Carter went missing after she got off the school bus."

The rectangular box was more than a work of art to him—it was his communication to the afterlife through his own labors.

"Police have been tight-lipped about other potential suspects and have not responded to allegations of ongoing physical abuse from a family member."

It was the closest thing to hearing the other side, the right side, championing his efforts for his chosen recipients. He loved his little girls and only wanted to protect them from the harm that would eventually circumnavigate their lives, leading to destruction, torment, and grave sadness. That was something he couldn't bear.

"As the hours and days tick by, police are becoming more concerned. If anyone has any information about the whereabouts of this little girl, please contact them immediately."

CHAPTER 8

Highland Center Park was the town's most popular park, and was centrally located in the oldest part of Pine Valley. The town had originally been named Sheraton Basin; it was not until 1905 that it was renamed Pine Valley after a vote.

The history of the town revealed rivalries between families searching for gold at various locations in the hills. Gossip and long-revered beliefs handed down through the generations changed slightly over the years, but there were stories of ghosts, missing buildings, and people disappearing into thin air. Most referred to these accounts as purely fiction, but it made for an interesting tale for tourists.

The area around Highland Center Park, unlike the renovated downtown area, was full of historical landmarks and county meeting buildings. All kinds of people frequented the area, from families with kids to the homeless community and visitors.

Katie wanted to investigate who might have witnessed anything pertinent in the Chelsea Compton abduction. Someone might have seen something without realizing it—it was a matter of seeking them out.

The park was a favorite spot for families and anyone wanting to play team sports. There were three playgrounds, two baseball fields, various picnic areas, a pool only open in the summertime, and several miles of meandering trails for walkers and runners. As well as the various open grassy areas, there were countless trees, mostly California pines and oaks. The county maintenance kept the numerous shrubs and flowers sustained throughout the seasons.

It seemed there was always something blooming, which made the park teem with life year round.

Katie sat in her Jeep studying the area on her iPad. She moved from one section to the next, expanding the details she wanted to see clearly. The geographical locations appeared different at ground level compared to aerial vantages on maps.

She entered the address of the friend Chelsea had been visiting, who had since moved away, and Chelsea's home at 1411 Bakersfield Avenue. The distance between the two was barely three quarters of a mile, if Chelsea had taken the walking route through the park. The only other alternative was weaving through the neighborhood streets as if driving a car, which would take twice as long.

Chelsea had left her friend's house at approximately 3.15 on a Thursday afternoon in August. It would have been hot, in the mid-nineties, and she would have wanted to walk in the shade and get home as quickly as she could.

Only one person claimed to have seen her walking that day: Terrance Price, a fifty-eight-year-old homeless alcoholic, who was known to most people in town to be unreliable and to have a personality disorder. He claimed to have seen Chelsea get into a dark pickup truck, which then drove away. He didn't get a look at the driver—it could have been a man or a woman. Police later disregarded his statement on the grounds that it had too many inconsistencies and inaccurate information.

"Well, Cisco, you want to go for a nice leisurely walk in the park?" suggested Katie.

The dog pushed his nose toward her face in excited agreement.

Katie laughed. "Well, okay then."

She opened the driver's door and immediately Cisco followed her out, letting out a couple of whines of happiness. He stayed obediently at her side and waited for her to snap on the leash. His glossy black coat shone in the sun, contrasting with his amber wolf's eyes.

Katie placed her cell phone, keys, and extra doggie bags into her pocket.

"C'mon, let's go," she urged the dog.

She decided to take the path that wove around the park. It would be a great way for her to see the entire location at a glance before tracing Chelsea's last potential walk. She had been to the area a few times a number of years ago, but it was located on the other side of town from where she lived, so when she was a kid they had usually gone to another park.

A couple of ground squirrels with high-pitched chatters ran down a tree, crossed the path, bounced into the deeper grass, then scrambled up another tree.

Cisco let out two low barks.

"*Aus*," Katie ordered in German, meaning "leave it". She wanted to blend in and not have a loud barking dog drawing attention to them.

A slight breeze cooled the vicinity, making it quite comfortable, unlike when Chelsea had last been here. Walking briskly, with the occasional pause for Cisco to sniff something only interesting to him, Katie realized that the little girl would have entered the park near one of the community buildings. She noticed several cameras on the corners of it.

It couldn't be that easy, because it rarely was. There was nothing in the files about looking through security footage. Nothing much was mentioned about the park in general.

Were there security cameras four years ago? she wondered.

It suddenly struck her momentarily that even though she was investigating, she felt well rested and relaxed in the park setting. She was home. It felt strange, but wonderful. She took a nice slow inhale and concentrated on her beautiful surroundings, decompressing from where she had been.

"Can I pet your dog?" asked a child's voice.

Katie turned to see a little girl about five or six years old with large brown eyes, mesmerized by the sight of Cisco. She smiled. "Sure. If your mom says it's okay."

She made eye contact with a young woman sitting on a bench with another, heavier woman, watching several children play on the slide.

"Okay," Katie said.

The little girl slowly walked up to Cisco. The dog obediently sat and allowed the child to pet him, licking her a couple of times.

Laughing with pure joy, she said, "He's funny and very pretty. What's his name?"

"Cisco," Katie answered.

After a few minutes, Katie decided to walk to where the two women sat. She pulled down her right sleeve to cover the army tattoo on the inside of her arm. She wanted people to think she was just a woman out walking her dog—not someone collecting intelligence on a missing child.

"Hi," she said in a positive, upbeat tone.

"Hello," the women responded.

"I didn't want you to worry. Cisco loves children and doesn't miss any opportunity to get fussed over."

By this time, the other children were surrounding the dog, petting him and kissing him.

"Well, he is gorgeous," said the younger woman.

"I was just wondering... I haven't been to this park in a while, but were there always security cameras over there?" Katie gestured. "I don't remember seeing them."

"Oh, didn't you hear?"

She shook her head.

"It was because of the homeless and loitering problem, which turned into crime issues. The county finally installed cameras on all the buildings, and also near the baseball fields and pool area."

"Oh, I didn't realize they'd done that."

"Yeah, it was about a year and a half, maybe two years ago now."

Her hopes were dashed.

The other woman piped up. "The thefts and vandalism have literally stopped."

"That's good. It's a beautiful place here and they need to keep it safe for everyone."

"Amen," the heavier woman muttered under her breath.

Looking down, Katie said, "Well, let's go, Cisco." To the women she added, "I think he's had more than his daily pets today." She said goodbye and continued on the walking trail.

Now that she was gaining perspective of the layout of the area, she was confident that she knew where Chelsea had walked that day. There were areas of the park blocked by trees and buildings that might make it difficult for people to see anything suspicious. Most people would be busy having fun and wouldn't pay attention to anyone else—especially a little girl getting into a truck that didn't have anything unusual about it.

She retrieved her cell phone and snapped some photos of three places of interest. One well-shaded area had several large trees growing close together and an abstract statue. It was a place with ample shade and several benches to sit down and rest. It was possible Chelsea had sat in this exact spot to cool off. One of the many drinking fountains in the park was barely ten feet away.

Another area was at a sharp left curve in the path, heading north, where there was a generous grove of dense bushes on both sides. Flowers bloomed year round here. In the summertime, there would have been roses, cosmos, and marigolds.

The third possible blind spot was a popular area with the largest trees in the park clustered together in a tight circle. It was almost like a magical outdoor room, with several benches in the middle where people could sit and enjoy the solitude and shade.

Katie thought she had better be thorough—even a bit obsessive. A gut instinct told her to take photos of the three obstructed locations in a panoramic sweeping motion. Cisco sat down in a cool spot, watching her curiously.

As she moved the cell phone screen carefully in a slow circle, she realized that there was only one area where a truck could drive close and where most people wouldn't have seen Chelsea: the shady benches beneath the trees near the statue. She would have walked past the flowers, but would most likely have been seen if she'd been taken there.

Did she make it this far?

Something else troubled her: Detective Templeton's disregard for Terrance Price's account. Although it was true that someone mentally incapacitated and under the influence of drugs or alcohol would have been a problem in a court of law, his statement should at least have been considered.

He had claimed: *I had been sleeping in the corner by the statue and I saw the Compton girl. Then I went to sleep, and when I woke again, I saw the little girl get into a truck and drive away.*

When he was pressured about his account, the statement fragmented each time. What the little girl looked like and what she was wearing differed, while other times he hadn't seen her at all. More troubling was that Price had done some minor repairs to the Comptons' house—fixing rain gutters and painting some trim—a year prior to her abduction.

Katie stood for a moment considering everything as she studied her surroundings. Birds chirped loudly above her in the dense trees; she could hear them clearly, but it was difficult to see them. Laughter filled the playgrounds. A car passed by every couple of minutes to find a parking place. A large group of people were gathering at the baseball field. There were layers of sounds, conflicting to a person who already had a mental disorder.

She walked to the area where the statue stood and moved to where a homeless person might take a nap. It was obvious that the best view of Chelsea and the truck would have been where the benches were located, even if the flowers and bushes were denser then than they were at present.

She believed that Chelsea was taken—lured, perhaps—from the park. And that meant that there was some truth to Price's statement, unless of course he had had something to do with the abduction. Maybe he knew more than what he'd told the police?

But her speculation was just that—a theory. Chelsea could have been snatched a couple of houses away from her friend's place, or just before she arrived home.

Still, everything seemed to direct Katie to the park area as the abduction location. It gave her little to go on, but it would help to support a preliminary profile if the body was recovered.

As she led Cisco back to her car, heaviness filled her, almost weighing down her stride. She kept seeing in her mind's eye Jenny's smiling face the last time she saw her at camp. It was as though her murdered friend rode shotgun, as if she were Katie's steadfast subconscious, making sure she did everything possible to find Chelsea.

CHAPTER 9

An assertive knock sounded on Sheriff Scott's office door.

"Come in," the sheriff called, not looking up from his large pile of paperwork.

The door opened and Detective Templeton stood there awkwardly before entering the office. His body tensed as his stride became stilted and unsure, not knowing whether to sit or remain standing. It was clear he had something weighing heavily on his mind as he kept shifting his bulk from side to side.

"What can I do for you?" asked the sheriff.

"Sir, we've known each other for a long time," began the detective, trying to sound matter-of-fact.

Sheriff Scott stopped writing, set down his special gold pen, and looked directly at the detective. "Of course, it's been quite some time. We were patrol officers together," he reflected.

"Well, I've always been straightforward with you, right?"

"Yes, I suppose that's true."

"I wanted to bring something to your attention that I think is important." Templeton's eyes shifted to the framed photographs on the office credenza. There was a picture of Katie when she'd graduated from the police academy, smiling brightly, eyes fixed and serious, her hair twisted up in a stylish bun.

"I think I know where this is going, Detective," the sheriff interjected. "Let's get this out in the open now, because I'm not one to gather my facts from idle gossip going around the office."

"It's just… it's just that I wanted you to know that your niece, Ms. Scott, has questioned me about my cases."

"What cases?" countered the sheriff. His eyes narrowed, scrutinizing the detective as he waited for an answer.

Detective Templeton chose his words carefully. "She came to me and asked about the Chelsea Compton case."

"And?"

The detective licked his lips nervously. "She questioned my investigation."

"How?"

"Well, she wanted to know why the neighbors weren't followed up on, and why Terrance Price's statement was ruled out—"

"Let me stop you right there." The sheriff held up his hand. "Did Ms. Scott accuse you of anything?"

"Well no, not exactly, but—"

"Did she behave in a way that you would deem unprofessional or unbecoming of an officer or employee?"

"No, that's not what I'm trying—"

"Do you have a real, viable complaint?" the sheriff pushed.

The detective let out a sigh. "I just don't think that a temporary employee should be going through cases."

The sheriff remained quiet for a moment. He appeared to have a heavy load weighing on his mind. "Let me ask you this. What's our department's clearance rate?"

"I don't know the exact number…"

"Ballpark."

"It's about sixty-seven percent. A little higher than the state average."

"Sixty-seven percent. Do you think that's satisfactory?"

"Well…" the detective stammered.

The sheriff leaned forward, pressing his forearms on his desk. "Let me tell you something: sixty-seven percent is unacceptable.

I don't care what the state's average is; that percentage shows we aren't doing everything we can to close cases."

Detective Templeton was about to object, but decided to stay silent.

"This isn't about politics; it's about solving cases, giving closure to families, making sure the community has trust in us. That's why every three months I go through a stack of cold cases. Ms. Scott probably saw the missing girl's file on my desk."

"Why would you pull that case?" asked the detective.

"Why not? It's what we do, Detective. I read over these cold cases, and I reassign them to whoever I want for a fresh perspective and a chance to find new evidence, question witnesses again, and do whatever it takes to close them."

"And Chelsea Compton?"

"Unfortunately there's no reason at this point to reopen the case. It would take a major new development to convince me otherwise."

Templeton nodded his head in agreement.

"Is there anything else, Detective?"

"No, you've answered my questions." Templeton hesitated, as though he was going to say something else, then opened the door and walked out, shutting it quietly behind him.

Sheriff Scott shook his head and glanced at the photo of Katie, then picked up his pen to continue his work.

CHAPTER 10

Katie's second week was mostly similar to the first, but now she had the confidence not to ask as many questions. The department ran smoothly, the work was fairly straightforward, and there seemed to be an enjoyable mundane quality to it. The ten-hour day moved at a brisk pace.

Her heaviest workload seemed to come at the beginning of the shift and then again after lunch. She finished her first half-shift duties quickly, so she decided to use the free time to follow up on her own investigations.

The truck that Terrance Price had allegedly seen Chelsea get into wasn't known to her family or friends, which meant it might have belonged to someone she knew but her family didn't. Katie decided to look up the middle school Chelsea had attended and search for teachers, counselors, coaches, and community-services officers who were employed there four years ago.

Using the government database had become easier for her; she knew how to use shortcuts and move around with ease. Sometimes she went off the database and onto the Internet. She managed to access the Pine Valley Middle School website and looked at the teachers and other employees. She mainly searched for men, based on the fact that most big pickup trucks were driven by men, and statistically the abductor was more likely to be male.

She'd never thought much about it before, but most of the teachers were women. Scrolling through, she studied each male teacher and ran a preliminary background check on them if they were employed at the school at the time Chelsea disappeared. Only one came up with a record: for possessing a controlled substance fifteen years ago. The community police officer assigned to the school four years ago was Deputy Scott Schneider. His file didn't reveal anything unusual or indicate a red flag. There were three teachers who no longer worked there and two substitute teachers who were employed on a semi-regular basis. She made quick notes for her files.

Almost as an afterthought, she decided to run a search for news articles about the previous missing girls. Several local papers had the same brief stories, as if they cut and pasted the articles from one newspaper to the next. There was nothing new to add to her notes. The girls didn't resemble one another. Nothing stood out. There was no information about family, friends, hobbies, medical ailments, problems in school or at home, or anything unusual leading up to the disappearances. It seemed that the abductions were not family-related, but rather carried out by strangers—a strong piece of evidence in itself.

She let out a sigh. None of her quiet investigative work meant anything if there was nothing to compare it with. It would only prove useful once new clues or suspects became available, and especially if Chelsea was found.

She looked at a stack of well-worn file folders waiting to be returned to the vault. It was as good a time as any, so she grabbed them up and headed down the hallway leading to the room where the stored files were housed.

She realized how dark the hallways were and wondered why. Was it to save on rising energy costs? Was the maintenance department overwhelmed and they hadn't had a chance to change the bulbs? As she contemplated the reasons, she picked up her pace until she reached her destination.

The door of the archived file room was closed. When she opened it, the light was on, but the room appeared to be vacant. The musty smell of an old basement accosted her senses instantly.

She headed to the area where the "R" files were located to return a folder. The cheap metal filing cabinet squeaked as it opened. As she thumbed through to find the right place, she heard someone move behind her. A swish and a light bang followed.

Thoughts of someone hiding to scare her plagued her mind, triggered by her experiences of waiting for long periods of time on patrol in the army. A creeping sensation of anxiety assailed her.

"Hello?" she said tentatively, bracing her back against the cabinet.

A man with cropped hair, wearing casual khakis and a long-sleeved shirt, came around the corner, barely looking in her direction. He clearly knew she was there, but didn't have the inclination to engage in pleasantries or idle chit-chat. Katie glanced at his identification badge but couldn't read the name; she assumed he was one of the detectives.

A slight smile crinkled his face as he passed her. "Afternoon," he said, and was gone.

Katie slipped the file into its correct space, closed the drawer, and then peered out the doorway. There was no one in sight. She didn't know what to think of the man in the vault, but dismissed it from her mind. There were more important things to worry about. Things like finding Chelsea.

CHAPTER 11

It was barely seven a.m. on Friday morning, her off day, and Katie was already dressed and showered. She finished her high-protein breakfast, then began to gather everything she needed for the day.

Cisco didn't want to get up as early as Katie did, and stayed on his warm doggie bed, but he perked up when he saw the preparations she was making. He realized she meant business when she unlocked the gun case and retrieved two weapons: a shotgun and her favorite semi-automatic choice—a Glock 19. He followed her around the house in close proximity as she packed.

"Cisco, give me some space. I'll make sure there are some treats with your water supply."

She assembled a day's worth of food—power bars, various nuts and seeds, plain sandwiches with turkey and cheese, and plenty of water—and loaded a small duffle bag with some basic tools, ropes and climbing gear, binoculars, a digital camera, a compass, and her iPad. She knew that her Jeep had everything she needed in case of car trouble or needing to change a tire. She lined it all up at the front door and spent a few moments deciding if she needed anything else.

Hurrying to her bedroom, she quickly selected a change of clothes with extra socks and some warmer layers. The weather looked mild, but she didn't want to be taken by surprise by a cold snap. She rolled up everything tightly, taking her back to the battlefield, where your belongings needed to be compact and carried on your body.

Cisco ran in and out the front door as she packed the car. The breeze picked up and blew leaves across the long driveway.

When she was done, she stood in the front yard and surveyed the property. The trees and low-lying bushes were dense and growing prosperously. Everything looked different after a few years away.

After being in combat conditions, Katie had perfected her gut instincts and honed her powers of observation. It was a matter of paying attention to the smallest details in order to make the biggest impact.

For some reason, today her nerves were heightened, as if someone was watching her and studying her habits.

"Cisco, here," she called.

The dog obediently trotted out the front door and jumped easily into the Jeep, settling himself on the passenger seat.

Katie double-checked the front door, then locked the deadbolt with her key. With her semi-automatic sidearm secured in a holster under her lightweight jacket, she walked toward her car. The search areas that she had mapped were extremely rural, and you never knew who you might run into or what their motivations might be. She wasn't going to be caught without a practical plan of action. She was prepared.

She was just about to climb into the Jeep when a strong instinct kicked her into high gear. She turned and scanned the front yard, then shut the car door and decided to take a quick walk around before she left.

Cisco stood up, peering out the window, and watching every move she made.

She walked casually down the long, slightly curving driveway. Her nerves tingled and her muscles twitched. There was no doubt that her senses had amplified during her time in the army.

She heard Cisco's high-pitched whine from inside the car.

The sides of the paved driveway were exposed soil, which still had visible signs of raking from the gardener's last visit. The bushes and rose bushes had been recently pruned, resulting in exposed branches. As she turned the corner, she spotted fresh impressions of footprints from a common work boot. Glancing at them, she estimated they were at least a size ten or twelve. Out of habit, she photographed the impression with her cell phone.

She continued to walk the property, surveying anything that might prove unusual, and then began her walk back. It was certainly possible that the boot print had been made by her uncle, but he hadn't been here over the past week and a half, and it looked more recent than that.

As she got into her Jeep and started the engine, she decided it didn't warrant any more thought or examination. She eased the car down the driveway, ignoring the doubts she'd previously had.

She set her GPS and began the forty-minute drive to the first area on her search map. As she drove in solitude, she reflected on Chelsea Compton and what was on her mind when she left her friend's house and started her walk home.

Was she thinking about what her mother was making for dinner that night?

Was she excited about some event that she would be going to before school started?

Did she have a school crush?

It was a double-edged sword for Katie that struck her violently in the gut. Every time she thought about Chelsea, it was forever sewn together with her camp friend Jenny.

There were so many other similar victims and cold cases nationwide that it appeared to Katie to be an epidemic for the law-enforcement world. The layers of social depravity were growing like cancer. Everyone needed to keep children safe. No cold case involving a child should ever be relegated to a file full of paperwork, left in a cabinet to be forgotten.

She concentrated on the busy traffic, cars darting in and out. Slowly it became more sparse, with only the occasional vehicle passing. Before long, she was on the back-country roads, almost devoid of any other cars. Houses too became less frequent, and the landscape grew denser and more fierce. In many places, driveways were clear, but the houses themselves were hidden in the deep recesses of the forest.

She had started out with optimism and a sense of doing what was right, but now, as she headed northeast, studying the vast countryside, her mission seemed implausible and foolish.

"Oh Cisco, what am I doing?" she asked the dog.

A couple of times she was tempted to turn around and head back to town. But there was always a reason to continue forward, and she kept to her personal pact. She remembered her drill sergeant at boot camp, who'd hammered at the new recruits never to give up. She pressed the accelerator harder and the car sped up the dusty road.

A sign indicated that Eagle's Ridge was less than a mile ahead.

The road had been the victim of excessive rain from last season, leaving deep chuckholes in the surface. Katie and Cisco bounced, bobbed, and weaved for almost a half-mile. The Jeep was a champion at handling off-road conditions, never hesitating or grinding into a wrong gear, and they inched their way forward.

The GPS made a chiming sound, indicating that Katie had reached her designated area.

Cisco barked.

She pulled the Jeep into a flat area for parking, leaving the engine idling, and studied the map. She wanted to work in two- to three-mile quadrants, making it a strategic search instead of wandering around without any type of blueprint. The region appeared to be accessible—rated three out of five for hiking.

She cut the engine and got out of the Jeep. When she walked to the lookout point, she could see that the trees and rolling hills went on for miles. It was picturesque, but an immense amount of countryside to search. She knew there was a decent cell-phone signal due to the tower about thirty miles away, which gave her some relief in case something were to go wrong.

Cisco followed his team leader, but was more interested in some bushes and relieving himself than the beautiful view.

Katie encouraged herself with positive thoughts. Some fresh air and exercise would be good for her, without having to worry about enemy forces with bombs intruding on her walk. Her mind lingered on the possibility of having a panic attack, but she quickly dismissed that idea and concentrated on the vast forest.

Her cell phone rang.

Seeing the call was from her uncle, she decided to ignore it for now. He would want to know what she was doing and could sense in a second when she was being evasive. He was a great cop who could read people like an open book, and Katie didn't want to be that book at the moment.

She returned to her car and loaded up the essentials in a small backpack. She calculated that each section would take approximately two hours, giving her enough time for three sections.

She retrieved her small field notebook, which had graph-like pages that enabled her to sketch her routes and indicate anything unusual or potentially useful in her investigation. She had used this type of technique in the army when tracking the enemy, and it was now a part of her investigative and deduction skillset.

After engaging the alarm lock on the Jeep and checking her compass, she set out on the first hiking trail, with Cisco walking to heel beside her. She opted to have him off the leash for convenience, but if something were to arise from other hikers or loose animals, she would leash him.

Katie enjoyed the solitude and the meandering walk up and down the trails as the day progressed. The previous year's rain had helped the environment immensely, leaving everything lush and green. It was a clear, cool day, but the sun's rays beamed down on them. She peeled off her hoodie and tied it around her waist, leaving her bare arms exposed in a tank top. It relieved some of the heat, but she had forgotten to apply sunscreen and knew she would be burned by the time she returned home.

The first quadrant of the search area didn't reveal anything that would raise suspicions. Nothing was out of place or unusual. She noted her findings—gauging the possibility of locating anything of importance, which kept her mind alert and thinking forward—and made sketches of the trail as she walked.

Not knowing exactly what she was looking for, she slowed her pace to study the undergrowth to either side of the pathway. It was dense, almost impenetrable, and she decided it would be next to impossible for someone to dispose of a body there.

She kept heading steadily northeast. Glancing at the sky, she spotted several buzzards circling, reminding her that if Chelsea's body had been dumped anywhere in the vicinity, the wildlife would take care of any evidence—even the bones would be scattered.

Unusual cleared brush caught her eye, and she stopped and studied some portions of upper and lower leg bones, femur and tibia, deducing they were from a medium to large animal—most likely a deer or cow. The rural area was brutal to every animal in the food chain. When she stood up, she took a three-hundred-sixty-degree view. Frustration welled up inside. Finding the remains of a body or a gravesite from four years ago was like looking for a needle in a haystack. Doubt clouded her objectivity and made her frustrated as she moved forward along the trail.

She finished two of the grid searches she had mapped out without coming across anything of interest. She stopped for some water, giving Cisco a well-deserved break as well. The breeze shifted direction, bringing a cooler temperature and relief from the heat. After walking for more than four-and-a-half hours, she felt fatigue beginning to set in.

The trail transformed into a steeper walk, much more so than she had imagined from her research. Rocks, loose gravel, and sand made each step unsteady, as if she was part skiing and part riding a skateboard. She had to stop and make Cisco slow down, not wanting him to hurt himself.

Mad at herself for not having realized that a number three trail would turn so quickly into a full stage five, she moved forward with caution, contemplating whether to turn around. She peered ahead down the steep slope, straining her already stiff neck. It was clear that this particular hiking path hadn't been travelled in quite a while; it was heavily overgrown, making it even more difficult to negotiate.

She took one step… two… and on the third step her right leg slipped out from under her body, like walking on ice, followed by her left leg, leaving her to flail her arms in an effort to stop the momentum. She let out a garbled yell as she slid downward, hitting several protruding rocks. Reaching her hands out, she tried to grab anything that would stop her, but it was not until she slammed into a large dead bush that she came to a halt.

She moaned, winded and dazed. For a moment she couldn't breathe; the same feeling as when she'd had the wind knocked out of her after a large bomb blast. At least her backpack had helped to protect her and had eased some of the bumps and scratches on the way down.

Cisco barked incessantly from above. He must have been trying to get to Katie, because fine dirt and gravel sifted downward, covering her body. He continued to bark, deep and rapid.

Taking a breath for the first time in a couple of minutes, Katie was able to yell up to him. "Stay… Cisco, stay…" she told him. "*Bleibe*, Cisco," she repeated in German.

Trying to maintain focus, she concentrated on examining her body, running her fingertips along her arms and legs. She quickly assessed that nothing appeared to be broken, though there were some scrape she was bleeding from her left wrist and the right side of her leg, and she tasted some blood in her mouth.

"Well crap," she muttered, irritated that she hadn't been watching where she was going.

She was lying in a flat spot resembling a nest on the side of the hill. Sitting up, pain radiated from her legs to her lower back. With a few more groans, she managed to stand, wobbly at first before the ground became solid and steady under her feet.

"Cisco," she said, sounding more like herself.

His whines and low, guttural barks continued. Katie estimated from the sound that she had fallen a little more than twenty feet.

"Cisco, good boy. Stay," she ordered again.

She readjusted her pack and her torn clothes then attempted to climb upward, only to slide right back to her original position. There was nothing to grab hold of and no visible footholds. She tried again, several times, but no matter what she did, she ended right back at her starting point. There was one relatively flat area, but she couldn't get to it on her own. She needed a foothold to steady her weight until she could pull herself up.

She contemplated her options, but she was exhausted and beginning to feel a panic attack creeping up. More dirt and sand spilled down the cliff, landing on her. This time Katie heard Cisco's whines and grumbles getting louder, and she realized that he was trying to make his way down to her.

CHAPTER 12

A team of ten- and eleven-year-old kids were engaged in a group run to warm up before the soccer game. The brightly colored orange-and-blue uniforms buzzed across the field in small groups. The Pine Valley Wildcats were preparing to defend their undefeated title on their own turf. Their opponents, wearing burgundy and white, followed their example and raced across the grass.

The bleachers were filled to capacity, more than usual for the co-ed game. The parking lot was jam-packed, some cars even parked precariously on the grassy areas, blocking other vehicles. People of all ages had come to watch the spectacle. A photographer was in attendance, taking photos for the local newspaper and website.

Everyone was excited and focused on the game, which was why no one would notice someone who was more interested in watching children than in the score or which team won.

There she was, and she was perfect.

The man had a specific agenda, unknown to anyone. He wasn't a stranger, but a part of the community. He nodded and smiled to a few people he knew, and no one thought it was strange that he was attending the game. It was a close-knit, supportive community and many of the residents participated in public events and spectator sports.

His hand moved frequently to his pocket, where he had stashed his wallet. The impulse to pull it out was compulsive and hypnotic. It had been a couple of days since he had opened it. With little regard to anyone who might be watching him, he gave in to the urge and flipped it open. Tucked neatly inside was a piece of yellowish newspaper, the crisp corners still folded perfectly. The smiling face of a young girl stared out at him.

Clouds moved frequently across the sky, casting shadows over the field. The game had begun and the ball was in play. The energy of both the spectators and the players was high, every person's focus on the field.

The man stared a moment longer at the face of the girl in the photo, then carefully folded the article before returning it to its hiding place.

He focused on the field, where a dark-haired girl was yelling to her teammates to pass the ball. Her intense facial expression made her look older than her eleven years. Her smooth skin, expressive eyes, and obvious determination made her particularly special.

She had caught the attention of the man more than two weeks ago. His due diligence had forced him to check her background in order to find out if she would indeed be the chosen one to be saved, protected forever from the evils that roamed the world, looking to destroy the innocent. Her name was Dena Matthews, and she lived with her parents and a younger brother, Brady, who would be five years old in four months and six days.

Dena, I have found you.

This girl was distinctive and irreplaceable. The man knew it the moment he began studying her family and found out that her parents were on the brink of divorce and two months behind on their mortgage. It was the precise résumé he wanted.

It was so typical these days—irresponsible, selfish parenting—but that was what made the man's opportunities so readily available. He had followed both of Dena's parents to work and found out that her dad had intentions towards another woman, while her mother had difficulties with several of her co-workers, resulting in loud arguments. They were complacent, unhappy, and didn't realize that their actions had thrust their daughter into a dangerous situation beyond anything they could imagine.

The man continued to blend into the crowd as he studied Dena and how she handled herself on the field. She was a good player; not great, but her assertiveness and ability to push past the insecurities resulting from her home life made her especially interesting to him.

He stayed and watched as the home team kept their undefeated record. Celebrations burst out among the parents and other students. As the players left the field, he waited with particular interest to see Dena up close again. She made her way past him, skipping and clapping, and he had to restrain himself from reaching out and touching her. He knew that it was almost time for the final preparations.

It was almost time.

CHAPTER 13

"Cisco, stay!" Katie yelled. Her mind flashed to all sorts of catastrophes and injuries that the dog could sustain in his eagerness to get to her.

The dirt and sand kept raining down, covering her clothes and sprinkling onto her head and face. She couldn't waste any more time.

She used her hands to dig footholds about hip high, then plunged her feet into the hollows, letting out a sigh when they held her weight. More dirt, now infused with small rocks, tumbled down, slamming against her body. She feared a full-blown dirt avalanche, and being buried alive.

She raised her hands and moved them around above her head to find a solid section to grip onto. Forced to keep her eyes closed against the dirt, she inched her fingertips side to side and slightly up and down, desperately searching for anything that would be stable enough to support her.

"C'mon," she encouraged herself. "C'mon…"

Her heart raced, pounding in her chest. The tendons and muscles in her ankles and knees tensed with a torturous pain, and her fingers were numb, making it difficult to feel the terrain with any accuracy.

She heard Cisco bark again.

"It's okay, buddy," she whispered, more to herself than the dog.

Her phone rang. It seemed surreal under the circumstances, as if she was waiting for the director of the movie to yell, "Cut!"

"Jeez, can't really come to the phone right now…" she mumbled, trying to release some of the anxious tension.

The ringing stopped, and she realized that Cisco had fallen quiet and the crumbling hillside had subsided.

"Cisco?"

There was no indication that he was above her anymore. He was trained to get help, but any first-responder assistance was miles away.

"Cisco?" she said again.

Determined to get out of her predicament, she managed another foothold a couple of feet above the previous one. She kept working until progress was made, but now she was exhausted to the point of collapse.

When she next looked up, she could see a paw a couple of feet above her. Cisco barked and began to climb down to her.

"Stop!"

The dog dug his front paws downward, causing more dirt to rain down on Katie.

Racking her brain trying to figure out the best way to get back to the trail, a thought occurred to her. It was a crazy idea that just might work.

Leaning against the hillside with her cheek pressed to the dirt, she carefully took her right hand away from the cliff and began to untie her hoodie. Once it was free, she grasped the end of a sleeve, arched her arm and swung the sweatshirt upwards. It didn't make it far and slid back down to her.

Breathing heavily, and with dwindling energy, she pitched the hoodie once again. This time it stayed above her.

"C'mon, Cisco, get it, get it," she ordered.

After a few grumbles and whines, the dog managed to lower himself toward the sweatshirt.

More dirt slithered down the hillside.

"C'mon, get it," Katie urged.

Her burning biceps ignited into an inferno that wouldn't subside. She tried to adjust her position to relieve the pain.

That was when she felt it: a tug, light at first, and then harder.

"Pull!" she yelled, sounding like a banshee in the wilderness. "Pull!"

Cisco tugged hard in short bursts, jerking her upward. She managed to find a more stable area where she could use her left arm to pull herself up. At one point she lost her footing, kicking and striking the hillside until she saw Cisco's face. The dog's teeth held firm to the sweatshirt.

Katie let out a sigh that was part moan, realizing that she was almost at the top.

Only a little bit further.

"Pull!"

With one final effort, Cisco pulled Katie onto her belly before letting go. She rolled onto her back and he ran to her, dropping down next to her and licking her face in frantic bursts.

"I'm okay, I'm okay…"

She lay where she was for a few minutes, gathering her energy. She looked at the sky, which had now become overcast, watching the buzzards fly around her in formation. It made her shudder to think about being a carcass for them.

Finally she sat up, aware of every scrape, cut, and bruise plaguing her body. Grabbing a water bottle from her backpack that luckily hadn't burst during her fall, she drank with enthusiasm. It was the best beverage she could ever remember. Turning to Cisco, who was now sitting next to her staring out across the horizon in watch mode, she offered him some of the water. He wasn't as interested in drinking as she'd thought he would be, but she remembered that in Afghanistan he knew how to ration his water intake when they were on a mission.

Rolling slightly to her right, she pushed herself upright and stood up. Although she was wavering a bit, she steadied herself and made her way to the trail, Cisco following. With each small step, there was a new pain radiating in her body, but she pushed past the discomfort and kept walking—something that she had become accustomed to both in the army and at the police department.

The sun had completely disappeared and the air turned cooler with a brisk whipping breeze. Katie realized that she hadn't had anything substantial to eat for hours and was starving. They kept walking, and finally she saw the beginning of the trails and the area where she had parked her Jeep.

Her cell phone rang. She had completely forgotten to check who had called her after her fall.

"Hello?" she said.

"Where have you been?" demanded her uncle with some authority to his voice.

"I'm not one of your suspects in interrogation," she replied smartly.

"Cute."

"I've been hiking with Cisco. Just needed some quiet time on my day off." She tried to sound upbeat.

"What are you doing tonight?" he asked.

Katie just wanted to take a long, hot bath, nurse her wounds, and figure out what to do about the Chelsea case.

"Um, nothing really," she replied.

"Good. Be at my house around 1900 hours; no later than 1930."

"Well…" Katie stammered.

"We'll see you then. Dress nice. Bye."

The call disconnected.

"Great," said Katie as she returned the cell phone to her pocket. She had a few hours to get home, shower, and make herself look presentable.

She opened the driver's door to the Jeep. Cisco obediently jumped in, circling a few times before making himself comfortable in the passenger's seat.

Katie felt defeated as she slung her backpack into the car and took off her holstered gun. She looked around at the vast area one last time and wondered if she would ever find out what had happened to the little girl.

Where are you, Chelsea?

CHAPTER 14

Katie stood in front of her full-length mirror with a white towel wrapped around her body. She carefully dabbed more antibacterial ointment on the scrapes on her arms, sides, and neck, then appraised her appearance. It was as good as it was going to get.

She decided to wear her hair down and around her shoulders, slightly curled, to hide some of the scratches. The evening lighting should help to disguise them further. However, her muscles had seized up as the afternoon progressed, so that even getting up out of a chair made her groan. It would take a couple of days for her body to heal and get back to normal. In the meantime, she kept moving.

It took her another fifteen minutes to choose a simple navy dress and lightweight lace jacket. She had lost some weight while she was away, but the dress still fit. Slipping into low- heeled shoes, she was ready to go.

As she walked to the door, Cisco cut in front of her with eager eyes and a wagging tail.

"Sorry, Cisco, I'm flying solo on this one." She leaned down and gave him a kiss. "I won't be gone long," she reassured him.

As she drove to her uncle's house, her thoughts weren't on the dinner party, but rather on Chelsea—as usual. She couldn't seem to think about anything else. She was aware that she didn't want to become downright obsessed with the case, but it didn't stop her mulling over all the theories of what might have happened and who was responsible.

She knew, though, that her time, thoughts, and searching wouldn't mean anything unless she found a major piece of evidence—or the body.

She rounded a sharp curve on the familiar winding road and drove a ways further until she came to a driveway with an ornate black wrought-iron gate that was conveniently open. A pretty design of twisted vines and flowers adorned the top of the gateway. The beautiful property was situated on ten sprawling acres: a large Tudor-style home with a Californian architecture influence. As she drove slowly up the long, paved driveway, she saw more than a dozen parked cars and realized too late that it was a welcome-home party for her.

She definitely wasn't in the mood, but there was no turning back now.

A huge banner took up most of the front entrance, with red, white, and blue decorations, including balloons and glittery gold stars, softly swinging in the wind. It stated boldly: *Welcome Home Katie*. The evening had all the hallmarks of her Aunt Claire's event-planning skills. She rejoiced in the opportunity to throw parties and make people feel special.

Katie parked in an available space at the side of the property, then took a deep breath and headed to the open front door, trying to keep a relaxed and positive attitude. Breathing deeply and relaxing her aching neck helped temporarily as she crossed the threshold into the beautiful house.

"Hello, Katie dear," said Aunt Claire, taking her arm and squeezing it affectionately. "You look lovely." She was dressed elegantly in a beige dress and spiked strappy sandals.

"Thank you," Katie replied, feeling self-conscious as her aunt proceeded to parade her around the room.

"Everyone, our beautiful guest of honor has arrived," Claire announced.

The other guests proceeded to clap and cheer, and Katie felt her face flush and her pulse race as she greeted them all. Some were people she had never met before; others were old friends or people from the sheriff's office. To her surprise, she saw Chad standing in the corner drinking beer from a bottle. He had a genuine smile on his face as he watched her.

Sheriff Scott entered the grand room and moved toward Katie, giving her a hug. "Glad you could make it," he said in low tone.

"Did I have a choice?" Katie whispered back.

"C'mon, I'll get you some wine and you'll feel better. Then you can tell me why you have scratches on your arms and cheek," he said, steering Katie to the beverage area.

"What?" Katie said with alarm.

"Don't worry, your secret is safe with me. For now." He laughed and moved back into the crowd to mingle with the guests.

Katie had always known she couldn't keep secrets from her uncle. He had been the youngest officer in the county's history to become a detective, and his solve rates were higher than those of any other officer in the department, a record that still held today. But he hadn't been content with that; he'd aspired to become sheriff and he didn't stop until he had achieved that goal.

No one else commented on her scratches, even if they noticed, and that was fine with Katie. It made her evening that much more enjoyable. A few people asked about her experiences in Afghanistan, but it was on a superficial level, and no one tried to dig at her dark secrets or the horrors of the battlefield.

It was fun catching up with friends and meeting new people. Katie usually preferred simple gatherings with just a few guests, but tonight she enjoyed the company of a diverse group of friendly faces. Even so, she found herself having to step outside for a moment to decompress and get some fresh air.

The evening was cool and the temperature relieved the stinging pain from her injuries. The yard was lusher than she had ever seen it before. The ground cover and vines seemed to contain every green on the color wheel, while small white blooms reflected the moonlight, giving the appearance of an enchanted garden.

She closed her eyes and let the gentle breeze caress her face, followed by the wafting scent of jasmine. She heard laughing voices and multiple conversations in the house behind her. The simple act of breathing deeply automatically released relaxation endorphins, making her calm and focused. It was a technique she used quite often when she had down time after a stressful day in the field.

When she opened her eyes again, she saw Chad standing a few feet away from her, gazing out at the garden area. She didn't startle at the sight of him, though she was surprised he had got out there without making any sound. It was as though he had materialized supernaturally.

"So is there a specialized stealth course at the firemen's academy?" she asked with mild sarcasm.

He turned to face her, his gaze admiring. "That's supposed to be a guarded secret."

"Oh." She nodded and turned her attention back to the garden. "I forgot how much I love it here."

"Me too."

"So Uncle Wayne roped you into this celebration?"

"Maybe. But I wanted to see you again anyway," he said.

"To watch over me?"

"Never thought about it that way."

"I know my uncle is a little worried about me making a smooth transition back into civilian life."

Chad took a couple of steps closer to her. "What do you think?"

"I think…"

He waited patiently.

"I think I need a few more days of sleep."

He laughed and took a drink of his beer. "Ah yes, sleep, wonderful sleep. And how has work been?"

"Just ask what you want to ask," Katie said.

"What?"

"It's what everyone has wanted to ask me tonight—my uncle must've put out a memo not to mention it. Am I going back to Sacramento PD?"

"Well, now that you mention it…"

"I don't know," she said. It was the truth: she wasn't sure if she wanted to go back.

"You know what I think?" Chad's smile had a way of melting even the toughest person.

Katie sighed. "What's that?"

"I think you'll know when it's time."

She laughed.

"What?"

"Chad Ferguson, I've missed you."

He raised his beer in agreement. "Welcome home, Katie Scott."

Aunt Claire came out then. "Look at you two, out in the chilly air. The party is inside. Come in and rejoin the others."

"Now who can argue with that?" said Chad.

Katie laughed again and they followed Claire back into the house.

Katie tossed and turned in her bed, accompanied by moans and heavy breathing in a stressful symphony of sleep.

Cisco's head popped up from his cozy dog bed and he stared in Katie's direction, sensing stress that was above the norm. He watched her for a while until he was satisfied that everything was okay, then slowly lowered his head and remained in his restful position until his eyes closed again.

It was rare that Katie didn't have at least one stressful dream every night. They were dreams her subconscious mind had created from previous defining moments, experiences to annoy, taunt, and frighten her, never allowing for a full restful sleep.

Tonight was no different.

In her dream, she ran to catch up to whatever she was chasing. But there was nothing there.

Someone was chasing her.

But no one ever appeared.

Breathless.

Helpless.

Vulnerable.

Most of her dreams had the same theme and had begun to mesh together. The vivid images were fading, but the intent was still alive and graphic.

She stopped and turned to see a little girl with her back to her. She asked repeatedly if she was okay, and if there was anything she could do.

The little girl slowly turned, revealing familiar sad eyes and a mouth full of braces.

"Help me… Please help me… Help her… Katie, please help her…" she said, slowly and deliberately.

Katie woke with a shocking jolt and sat up. Immediately Cisco was next to her on the bed, sniffing and licking her.

Her breathing was fast and heavy until she managed to control it.

Her nightshirt was soaked with sweat.

It haunted her to receive a message from the great beyond, asking for help.

She knew what she had to do; there was no other option.

She reached for the journal her aunt had given her, opened it to the first page, and began to write what was on her mind.

Saturday, 0300 hours

Tough day, but I will make it through. The vivid images and sounds from the battlefield are fading some. I miss my team. I always knew where I stood with them and we worked together.

It was a closeness, a family, a tight-knit group that I never knew could exist. I couldn't have done anything without Cisco at my side. Jenny visited me tonight in my dreams and asked me to find Chelsea... *I cannot say no.*

CHAPTER 15

The sewing needle poked up through the fabric and then arced, piercing it again in an upward motion and repeating the maneuver in a slow, deliberate fashion every quarter of an inch to bind the fabric together. Each stitch was neat and mimicked the last. The steady, calloused hands were extremely nimble and able to complete the delicate work with ease, as they had so many times before.

When the needle ran out of light-blue thread, the man made a securing stitch with the short leftover string. Using tiny sharp scissors, he snipped the thread as close to the fabric as possible without piercing it, then carefully took the remaining cotton from the eye of the needle and discarded it in the trashcan. Pulling a long new thread, he wet it between his lips and carefully inserted it through the eye, securing it with a knot at the end.

Making a dress by hand was not beneath his abilities or his manhood. It enhanced his craftsmanship and kept his hands in expert form for all types of things. It also made him an intimate part of the process. It was a way for him to put his soul, his hard work, and even an occasional drop of perspiration into the fabric's consistency.

Every dress was a work of art—no two were ever alike.

Every dress, in a specially chosen color, was made for a particular girl, who would be saved from the world's debauchery and filth.

Every dress helped to make his process complete.

The delicate short sleeves with a slight pleating gave a modern-day fairy-tale effect. The gentle gathering of thread around the waistline created a skirt with a slight flare, but not too much fabric, to lie smoothly on the body when positioned in its final resting place. The finishing touch was the sash, neatly stitched, expertly ironed, and then perfectly tied around the girl's waist to complete the outfit.

He enjoyed the process, but it was the ultimate goal that excited him. It gave him hope. It made him experience life: someone else's life—an innocent life. Every day there were too many disturbing things that contributed to the loss of innocence. There was nothing that could be done except to protect the pure.

He readjusted his eyes, blinking several times and looking across the room, before continuing with the task.

The bulb in the lamp flickered three times but continued to illuminate. It was almost as if it was a distinct message in Morse code speaking only to him.

One. Two. Three…
Pause.
One. Two. Three…
Pause.
Capture. Protect. Sleep…
One. Two. Three…
Capture. Protect. Sleep…

CHAPTER 16

Katie forced her aching body out of bed, beginning with her legs flopped over the edge of the mattress, followed by her feet pressing against the cool floor. Bones ached and muscles throbbed, each vying for her undivided attention. She had watched from the comfort of her warm bed and fluffy pillow as the day slowly began to brighten outside her bedroom window. It was gradual at first, like a volume dial, and then finally built momentum with an eye-opening illuminating wonder.

Cisco paced around the bedroom, whining his usual early-morning complaint of wanting to go outside.

"Okay, give me a minute," Katie said in a gravelly voice.

Feeling like the hunchback of Notre-Dame, she gently moved through some basic stretches to loosen up her shoulders, back, and hamstrings. She progressed through each exercise three times before there was some relief. Then she slipped on her lightweight robe and shuffled to the sliding doors in the kitchen area, where Cisco waited patiently. She opened the doors just wide enough for the dog to squeeze through, and he shot out into the backyard and made his rounds to find the perfect location to do his business.

A cool breeze blew through the house as Katie waited for the dog. Even though it caused goose bumps to prickle up her arms, it made her feel more energized, more awake, her mind focused.

Cisco padded obediently back into the kitchen to wait for his breakfast.

Katie fixed a pot of coffee and prepared a bowl for the dog. The aroma of the ground coffee percolating filled the house and somehow made it warmer and more inviting.

As she looked around at the calming hominess of the kitchen and the comfortable living room, she realized that the warm light of the morning hours smoothed out any anxious thoughts she had in the middle of the night. Light pushed away darkness. Light would ceaselessly drown the darkness at every opportunity if you knew where to look.

The fierce heat of the coffee helped to soothe Katie's aches and pains as she reflected on last night's party. She couldn't help but smile at the thought of Chad being back in town. He was one of the few people who knew her well. He knew when to ask questions, and when to back away and let her decide whether she needed to talk. She didn't know how deeply she felt about him and what the future would bring, but for now, she didn't want any more complications with a relationship.

"Cisco, you ready for another adventure?"

The jet-black dog made a scrambling dash to the front door, wagging his tail like a helicopter propeller.

"Well, okay."

Katie made herself some eggs and packed sufficient supplies for the road. She wanted to make sure she hadn't overlooked anything, and decided to add some extra tools and her first-aid box. It was difficult to plan for the unknown, but she would rather have too much kit at her disposal than not enough.

As previously, she mapped her areas of search and set her GPS to get her to the correct location. She and Cisco drove down the familiar road, but instead of turning right, she made a left and slowly they began to climb. It had been one of her favorite areas to visit, camp, and hike growing up. The fond memories flooded her mind and kept her company until they arrived at a fork in the road.

She eased the Jeep to the curb and double-checked her directions. Once again there was a strong cell-phone signal and she didn't foresee anything that would prevent them from taking the two main hikes she had mapped out.

She decided to make the extra effort to study the trails more closely on websites chatting about the area, to make sure there weren't any treacherous spots or anything that was under reconditioning from the county parks department.

All areas clear.

She decided that she would drive as far as she could and park. There hadn't been any vehicles for the past five miles, so she shouldn't run into any unsuspecting hikers or campers.

She parked and exited the Jeep, changed into her most appropriate heavy-duty hiking boots, and re-inventoried her backpack.

Cisco's energy had heightened since their previous adventure. He ran circles around the car and then nudged her to hurry up.

"What's up with you, Cisco?"

The dog gave a deep bark.

"Okay, maybe we'll get lucky today."

She didn't think so, but saying it out loud made her feel a bit more optimistic.

Her sore and stiff muscles loosened up the more she moved around, which in turn gave her more energy and momentum to forge ahead. She kept her small field notebook close so that she could update it when necessary with her exact movements.

After checking the compass, she headed out to the first search area.

The day was cooler than the last hike and there were fewer birds circling above, replaced by smaller birds chirping in the trees. The usual flies and other winged bugs seemed to have vanished from the area. The wind gusted slightly and then fell away to a steady stillness.

Katie maintained a moderate pace and kept a subtle watch on her breathing—slow and even. Everything considered, she felt great. She took an additional moment just to enjoy the sights and being able to roam the outdoors.

The denseness of the trees became more intense and darker, blocking out some of the sunlight as she moved down the easy trail. Hills and rocks became the norm and provided interesting interruptions in the landscape. The area would inspire most artists with its beauty and serene surroundings, which seemed to go on forever.

Katie stopped at an open, level area. As she performed a three-hundred-sixty-degree turn, her instincts alerted her with the delicate raised hairs on her neck that something was not right. It didn't happen often, but she had honed her internal skills to never overlook anything.

She glanced down at Cisco; he seemed to have picked up on the fact that something was amiss as well. He had stopped his incessant sniffing and marking, and now stood completely still, tail down, head and ears straight forward. His eyes darted from one side to the other searching the wilderness.

Katie wasn't sure if it was just the place—some type of electromagnetic energy—or whether there were wild animals near. She stood perfectly still and listened. The wind had stopped completely—she wasn't sure when—and silence had taken over. It was pleasant at first, but the more you noticed it, the more a certain kind of sinister feeling swirled around it.

Glancing at her compass, Katie noticed that she was facing southeast. There was about a square mile she wanted to explore, the terrain easily navigated by any moderate-level hiker.

A screech owl cried out. It was an unusual sound early in the day, unless there were predators lurking about. Animal behavior and weather characteristics were the first indications of change, or something being wrong in the natural world.

Katie stood for a few more minutes without anything happening. No noise.

No wild animal slamming through the brush.

Cisco went back to his sniff and search.

She decided to walk the area, on and off the trail, then circle back in the opposite direction until returning to the starting point.

Her first impression was of the clusters of beautiful trees, some dense, while others appeared to grow in circles or perfectly straight lines as a natural barrier. Most were various California pines, including the ponderosa pine trees that proliferated throughout the forest hills, along with a mix of sequoia and oak trees in the lower canyon sections.

She was able to maintain a vigorous pace, keeping a steady eye out for anything that appeared to have been caused by a person rather than nature, such as strange worn pathways, broken or cut branches, or disturbed soil; anything that looked out of place or caught her attention.

She stopped at five different locations. Each time she focused Cisco and had him do a sweeping search. He wasn't trained specifically for cadavers or gravesites, but he could track anything to do with human scents. In addition, German shepherd dogs invariably alerted on features that appeared out of the ordinary.

He initially made a large circle around the designated area, and then honed his sniffing to each section as Katie moved behind him. Every once in a while she would gesture with her hand for him to keep searching, and he would obey. She looked at every area but nothing required a closer inspection.

After a little over an hour, she began to make her way back to her Jeep. She wanted to see if she could access the upper roads near the trails. The trees were more crowded there, nestled together, but designated spots were open along some of the hills.

Her stomach rumbled and her energy was waning, so she decided it was an appropriate time to take a lunch break to refuel.

Within five minutes, she was back at the car. It was still deserted and eerily quiet around them. She brushed her right hand against her sidearm to make sure that it was still in the correct position and ready to use at any given moment. She didn't expect anything to happen, but she reminded herself that she was quite a distance away from any place where there were people around, and she wanted to be prepared if something went sideways.

Deciding to drive the Jeep deeper into the forest before lunch, she jumped behind the wheel, Cisco riding shotgun, ready for anything. They continued for about two miles along the uneven road, the Jeep bouncing and rattling though they were barely going above idling speed.

Parts of the road had been washed out, but there were still sections that were barely wide enough for the vehicle. Slowing down to scarcely five miles per hour, the Jeep did its job and inched forward to start climbing at a steep angle.

"Hang on, Cisco," Katie called.

The dog faced straight ahead, sitting motionless on the seat, even in the bumpiest areas. Katie held her breath and kept a steady pressure on the accelerator.

The road turned to the right, where there was a narrow entrance.

Katie stopped the Jeep and referred to the GPS on her phone, which now wavered in signal strength. She found that the road on the right led to an area she had never noticed before. It looked accessible and an interesting location to search.

She drove the car a little ways up the main road before cutting the engine and jumping out, leaving the driver's door open so that Cisco could join her.

She retrieved a special bag and had the dog's undivided attention. First she unfolded a collapsible water bowl and filled it with water. While Cisco lapped up the refreshment, she opened a Ziploc bag and emptied out organic chicken pieces and rice.

A chicken salad sandwich with mayonnaise, tomatoes, and arugula lettuce was her own lunch choice. She carefully peeled away the deli paper and began eating.

"Yum," she managed to say through a mouthful of food. Hiking and searching had made her ravenous; the cool chicken mixture had just the right amount of seasoning and tasted like the best food in a fancy restaurant.

A loud crash interrupted her enjoyment.

She jumped to attention facing the direction of the noise and instinctively drew her weapon. "Return," she said quietly to Cisco. Once he was safely back in the Jeep, she shut the door until she was able to establish the source of the noise.

Cisco watched her every move as she inched toward where the sound originated, across the dusty road.

Slowly at first, and then gaining momentum, the sights and sounds of approaching enemy territory flashed through her mind. Her mouth turned dry. The normal sounds around her had a funny tinny noise. Her pulse raced, pounding in her chest. She was catapulted from the present moment into an earlier time with her entire team behind her, relying on her skills.

She stopped in her tracks.

Blinking several times, she managed to regroup into the present moment. It frightened her that she could recall with such clarity everything that had been around her back then.

She re-evaluated her current situation and realized that she was in a non-hostile place. Her perspective changed, and she inched stealthily toward where the sound had originated.

A slight breeze blew through the trees, carrying the unmistakable aroma of pine. It was a scent that could conjure up past memories of camping and hiking. The branches and leaves made a musical harmony rivaling most orchestras.

She inched closer, and then even closer. When she was about a foot away, a startled juvenile deer popped his head up and then bounded away into the forest.

Lowering her weapon, Katie sighed. She was angry that she'd almost fired off a round at an innocent and harmless animal.

Her battlefield-induced stress was worse than she had originally thought.

There was something strange, even a little unsettling, about the area she was now preparing to search. It wasn't a feeling that was easily described, but there was an unforeseen force or energy that made her jumpy. Being alone wasn't the issue. Katie had been in all types of situations and found that the solitary ones were usually quite comfortable for her.

She walked back to the Jeep and saw Cisco sitting in the driver's seat, steaming up the window with his heavy panting and escalating apprehension about the situation.

She glanced at her watch: 11.47 a.m., early enough in the day to consider another area of search. She could still see Jenny's ghostly face asking for help in last night's dream; it was almost as if the little girl was shadowing her searches.

The investigation felt like a wild-goose chase, or wishful thinking on her part, but she still didn't want to give up on it too soon. There just had to be something she could do for Chelsea. But she could only do what she could do. Maybe the little girl's body would never be found.

As she stood at the car, she almost gave in and drove home. A gust of wind whooshed by her, scattering leaves and dust along the road. She waited for a few more minutes, fighting with her conscience, then she grabbed her pack, called to Cisco, and secured the vehicle before moving out.

She focused on the path to the right. It was wide enough for the Jeep, but the walk would settle her anxious energy and she loved to hear the whispering pines all around her. The wind continued to blow through the area and press against her face.

There were no trails off the path, and it appeared to be a dead end, narrowing a little before reaching a high ridge. It was a lookout, but it didn't appear to have been used much, with overgrown trees and bushes camouflaging it.

Katie moved closer until she could see the vast area below: mostly treetops, but with sporadic areas of land peeking through. She surveyed ahead and could see rolling hills and valleys. It would be ridiculously impossible to find anything out here. Perhaps it was time to call it a day.

"Well, Cisco," she said, moving carefully through the overgrown brush.

The dog was nowhere to be seen.

"Cisco!"

Nothing.

Her heart skipped a beat as she began to frantically search around for her dog. "Cisco!" she yelled again.

She heard two barks coming from inside a group of trees.

"Cisco?"

He began barking again and burst through the trees, trotting in large circles, tail wagging.

"What's up?"

Katie approached the area from where the dog had appeared. The branches formed a tough natural barrier that couldn't be penetrated. She ran her fingers up and down them, and a broken branch caught her hand. Leaning closer, she saw that there was a small rope that looked as if it marked some type of entrance.

Cisco joined her and whined at her side.

"How did you get in there?" she said, not expecting an answer.

With a little bit of muscle, she pulled a branch up and immediately saw what appeared to be a man-made tunnel. There was no way an animal could have made it—the branches were intricately woven together.

Dropping her backpack to the ground, she searched for her small flashlight. She flipped it on and crept into the tunnel with Cisco close behind. Everything appeared to be sturdy; it wouldn't cave in, leaving her buried alive underneath the massive branches. It surprised her that the tunnel didn't have the same pine aroma as the rest of the forest. It indicated that it had been here for some time and any new growth had been trimmed back.

She kept moving forward until she came to a sharp right turn. Hesitating for a moment to get her bearings, she carried on, going from dark to daylight as she emerged onto a narrow landing with a similar view to the one she had just experienced. Carved steps led downward. Anticipation mixed with an eerie intuition made Katie's legs tremble. Taking the steps one at a time, she descended onto another landing. This one was quite large and stable, and she examined it closely. To the left, there was a small yellow flag affixed to a pole about a foot high.

She gasped, and stopped short.

Part of the landing had clearly been disturbed, the earth fresh as if it had been dug up and laid again. The outline of the area was the perfect shape and size for a grave.

CHAPTER 17

Although military training and police work have made an indelible impact on my life—my own personal defining moments—they still haven't prepared me for the evil that lurks within the mind of a serial killer.

*

Katie ran at full speed to her Jeep as a million scenarios ran through her mind—some terrible, some horrendously grisly. What she had found might be nothing, or it might be an actual buried body. Whether it was Chelsea would be determined at a later time, by the medical examiner.

Out of breath and anxious, her hands shaking slightly, she drove as far up the narrow road to the tree tunnel as she could without catapulting off the ledge. Cisco sat next to her, panting heavily in anticipation of what would happen next in the adventure.

Making sure she parked in an area where the ground was solid and no accidental passerby would see her, she exited the Jeep, lowering the windows four inches and leaving the dog behind. If there were any evidence left behind on the route to the grave, she wanted to make sure it wasn't contaminated. High-pitched whines filled the silence of the forest. Cisco never wanted to be left out of the game.

Opening the Jeep's back door, she retrieved a crowbar, a small shovel, and her cell phone. Her firearm remained snug in the holster on her side. She was taking nothing for granted, especially in an area that a killer might have used as his secret dumping ground.

As she shut the back door, Cisco was still whining in a desperate plea to join her.

"Sorry, Cisco," she apologized.

Walking back through the tree tunnel, she retraced her steps exactly. She knew it was highly unlikely that there was anything worth processing, but she treated the scene as if everything mattered. It was difficult to ascertain whether anyone had visited the area recently, though there were moderately visible boot prints layered on top of each other. The person had walked around several times, making the prints impossible to identify.

Katie took out her cell phone and decided to document the area just as she had found it, taking photos in a sweeping motion. She didn't want to call her uncle until she knew exactly what or who was buried. It might yet be the family dog, or some bizarre garbage ritual.

She took three careful steps and stopped before the outline of the grave. A prickly shudder took hold of her body as she realized that it was possible the killer had prepared his victim exactly where she stood now. She shook it off. Only one thing mattered.

Using her crowbar, she dug down in a small area until she hit something hard; she guessed it was some sort of box—wooden perhaps. The solid mass appeared to be buried eight inches deep. Rather shallow for a body. Her anticipation began to dwindle.

As she gently brushed away some of the dirt, she saw the box clearly. From the type of stain and the well-finished edges, it looked as if it were hand-crafted. She carefully began to pry away the nails that closed it.

One…

Two…

Three…

They were rather small, like the nails for hanging pictures. There was also a seal around the box, and from what she could see, it was airtight.

Strange.

She continued to pry out the nails, trying not to damage the box, making sure that she documented each step with photos. After about fifteen minutes, they were all out. She kneeled close, pressing her shins against the dirt, and paused for a moment, taking a deep breath. Then she gripped the lip area tightly and slowly raised the lid. There was no squeak or resistance. It came easily, smoothly, until it was finally open wide.

A familiar stench permeated the immediate air around her; a stench that could only be described as death.

It wasn't just any box; it was a carefully hand-crafted coffin with a silk lining that looked hand-stitched. The contents mesmerized her, so that she couldn't look at anything else; time slowed down and she forgot that she was sitting on a ledge in a forest. She couldn't take her eyes away from the cute brown teddy bear with yellowish-brown glass eyes, or the bright-green ribbon that was tied perfectly around his neck.

Anywhere but here, the stuffed animal would represent happiness and safety.

Katie's eyes grew wider and her mind began to process what she saw. The little girl was clutching the teddy bear tightly. She wore a pretty blue dress, perfectly ironed, hair brushed and smooth, and most of her dead skin was still attached to the bones. The decomposition was still in its early stages, which didn't make any sense. From Katie's calculations, the child must have been dead for four years, but she looked as if she had died only a few months ago.

Even though the body had decayed to some extent, it was obvious who the little girl was. Eyes closed, expression relaxed, with a slightly downward-turned mouth, she looked peaceful, like she was sleeping.

Katie flopped back on the ground in a sitting position and let out a breath. She couldn't believe what she'd found. Barely able to tear her eyes away from the frozen girl's face, she finally took a photograph to send to her uncle.

As she began to compose a text message, something colorful caught her eye: a piece of yellow ribbon partially buried in the loose dirt next to the casket. She gently picked at the area and realized with horror that there was another box next to the little girl's coffin. Her curiosity urged her on, and she dug faster until she revealed a second coffin.

She sat back, trying to catch her breath, still staring at the graves.

Glancing at her cell phone screen, she saw that she had a weak signal. She pressed a recall button and waited. Tears welled up in her eyes and she wiped them away with the back of her left hand. She was mad at herself for becoming emotional; she felt slightly unhinged. The gravity of what she had found weighed heavy upon her; she felt the raw emotion of loss and grief but mixed with relief. Together with her own painful memories, it left her exposed and vulnerable. She hated that feeling.

"Hello?" Her uncle answered after the third ring.

"Uncle Wayne?" Katie's voice was barely audible.

"Katie, what's wrong?"

"I… I found her. She's right here."

"Who? Who did you find?"

"It's like she's just sleeping."

"Tell me what's going on."

Katie looked back at the face in the open casket. "I found Chelsea Compton," she said.

CHAPTER 18

It took Sheriff Scott two hours to coordinate and dispatch CSI, morgue technicians, deputies, and the medical examiner at the remote crime scene.

Katie waited beside her Jeep, impatiently pacing back and forth. Her mind still spun in circles with how the killer was able to get the coffin into place.

Did he have a partner?

Were there more girls?

Was this just the beginning?

The longer she waited, the more anxious she became; difficulty catching her breath, blurred vision, and an incessant hammering in her chest were just a few of the symptoms that plagued her.

Everything around her was quiet. She was still alone. No birds sang. The wind suddenly dropped. Katie kept remembering the sight of Chelsea's face. She knew she would see it in her nightmares, and that the eyes would open with a questioning expression, asking her, "Why?"

At last she heard several vehicles in the distance, creeping up the road at a snail's pace. She walked down to the main roadway and watched them approach. Heavy dust swirled in the air as the four-wheel-drive vehicles made their way in a procession. From her quick assessment, there were three sheriff SUVs, two patrol cars, a forensics van, and a white van from the morgue.

Two forensic technicians were the first to arrive. Their stone faces were difficult to read as she led them to the area where she had found the girls. Once they had deduced what they would need, they returned to their vehicle.

She calmly watched as they secured various areas in the tunnel as well as the final resting spot. They were preparing to document the coffins, which would later be transported to the morgue. One of the technicians took photographs consisting of an overview of the crime scene, a middle-distance shot with a one-hundred-eighty-degree view, and of course close-up pictures to record all the details.

Katie felt nauseated, exhausted, and in desperate need of sleep to banish the horror. In the deep recesses of her mind, she really hadn't thought she would actually find the body—much less two.

"Katie," greeted her uncle. He approached her quickly and hugged her tight. "You alright?"

She glanced around. The scene unfolding in the forest looked like a rehearsal of a strange stage play. She sighed. "I will be."

He turned and began organizing the area, barking orders. "Only the absolutely necessary personnel are to excavate those coffins. Keep everything as is and don't move or touch anything inside yet." He turned toward Katie, who was at his heels. "Tell me everything you saw when you got here. What made you pick this area?"

"I mapped some of the more remote locations that hadn't been searched four years ago. I hiked over toward the northeastern area yesterday," she explained.

"Okay," said the sheriff. It was difficult to tell if he was slightly annoyed or full-blown angry.

"I wasn't going to even come up here today, but then I just wanted to be thorough."

"How *convenient*," said Detective Templeton as he approached. "Are you sure you didn't receive information from some *other* means?"

Katie's anger rose up; she gritted her teeth, fighting the urge to scream at him. There had been several instances where she had been challenged by those in charge, and it felt to her like someone had just lit that familiar fuse. "Excuse me?" she said. "I actually took the time and read over your report, which was quite frankly unprofessionally incomplete. Unlike you, I didn't dismiss the idea that Chelsea was possibly dumped or buried somewhere in the local area, and what do you know, I found her. Tell me again, what have you done for this case?"

The detective moved close to her as if accepting her challenge. "I don't believe in coincidences, or even luck for that matter. You should be a person of interest in this case and—"

"Enough," barked the sheriff. "They're beginning to exhume the coffins, so why don't you take notes and make sure they don't inadvertently contaminate any evidence."

Templeton hesitated, as though he wanted to say something more, but then turned and followed the police crew to the gravesite.

"Making friends, I see," said Uncle Wayne with a faint smile. "Katie, I know exactly how tenacious and driven you are, but let's just lighten up and get through this. Okay?"

Katie let out a breath, feeling her nerves and ruffled feathers calm down. "Fine. I'm sorry."

"It's going to take a while to get those coffins excavated, so why don't you just take a break," he said, showing his caring uncle side.

"Okay. But…" She hesitated. "I think I know the identity of the other body."

"What makes you say that?" He eyed her closely.

"I did a bit of searching for any missing girls with similarities to Chelsea's disappearance, and I think it's quite possible that it's Tammie Myers."

"Okay. I'm going to need the entire story of how your search got you here. Understand?"

"Of course."

"Go take a break now," he said. It wasn't a request, but an order.

As her uncle followed Templeton to the gravesite, Katie decided to walk Cisco down the road to clear her head and give the dog a break. She opened the driver's door and ordered, "Come, Cisco." He obeyed and trotted alongside her.

The entire area appeared completely different now with all the emergency vehicles parked haphazardly. The familiar static sounds of police radios rose at varying levels, and everyone hustled to their duties. A few of the deputies glanced at Katie with quizzical expressions, as if to say, "How did you find her?" and "What made you pick this exact place?" She assumed that several of them had been involved in the initial search for Chelsea; they must have found it strange that it was an outsider who'd discovered the dumping ground. Hearing Templeton's accusations wouldn't have helped any. She knew there would be idle gossip around the department by tomorrow.

She ignored the looks and instead gazed up at the pine trees, recently so stoic and magnificent but now polluted and disconcerting. They loomed along the roadway like a warning to stay away. The wind, which had been breezy, was now calm.

It was true that in an instant everything could change.

CHAPTER 19

Countless news vans with giant antennae and overzealous reporters from various California areas crowded the parking lot of every police substation in the county. They roamed every possible public area to secure comments from any local resident who would give an opinion, and everyone seemed happy to comply.

The usual media outlets had already posted the breaking story with different slants:

Bodies of Two Missing Girls Found in Specially Constructed Graves.

The Toymaker Fulfills Fantasy by Killing Local Girls and Making Teddy Bears.

The story was in every newspaper and on every news site. Anticipation rattled through the networks whenever there was anything involving dead children and serial killers. Pine Valley had been descended upon and there was no sign of interest in the case easing anytime soon.

The detail about the teddy bears and the coffins had leaked and spread like wildfire, much to the dismay of the sheriff's office and the investigative team.

*

"Everyone please settle down. This is going to be quick and painless. I'm going to make a few in-house announcements before I go outside and make an official statement to the press," stated Sheriff

Scott. His steely stare and ability to use his authority to quiet a room was unprecedented.

Mayor Stan Miller stood quietly behind the sheriff.

Katie sat and watched her uncle prepare to tell his staff about how the Chelsea Compton investigation was going to play out. She had spent hours the previous evening explaining in detail everything leading up to her discovery of Chelsea's body, presenting her lists, notes, maps, and personal field notebook. She explained that she had photocopied Chelsea's file from his office. He was not pleased with her rash decision, but accepted that it was justified by the outcome.

Glancing around the training room, she observed the usual personnel, including Detective Templeton, two other detectives whose names she didn't know, several deputies and forensic personnel, Denise, and some other women from the administrative staff.

Her uncle was dressed in his sheriff's uniform, adorned with more brass emblems than anyone else. He looked serious as he stood firm and spoke directly to his staff.

"I don't have to tell you that this case has reached national status, and that means no talking to *any* news agency, in person or otherwise. No posting of anything remotely related to the case on your social-media accounts. Understood? Unfortunately, it will be a while before the news interest dwindles. In the meantime, there are going to be a few changes."

Some low voices murmured from the crowd.

"The Chelsea Compton case has been officially upgraded to a homicide, along with the as-yet-unidentified girl discovered next to her. Detective Templeton will be running the investigation, reporting to me on a daily basis. I have full confidence that we will find the person who committed these heinous crimes. I will let Detective Templeton update the task force on how he wants to proceed after this meeting."

More noise from the gathered detectives and deputies.

"I have another important announcement before we all adjourn to our duties. I will have Mayor Miller explain the change in personnel."

"Good afternoon, everyone." The mayor cleared his throat and adjusted his wire-rimmed glasses, keeping eye contact with everyone in the room. "I have received an official confirmation that Sheriff Scott is within his sworn rights as sheriff of Sequoia County to deputize Katherine Ann Scott."

A strange awkward silence filled the room.

"Katherine Ann Scott is now a fully sworn police officer for Sequoia County Sheriff's Office, and temporarily acting as a detective with the department to investigate and assist on this case until otherwise noted. You will now refer to her as Detective Scott."

Katie looked toward the detectives. Their frozen stares of disbelief were priceless, except for the fact that she had to work with them. She would need all the strength and courage she could muster to move forward working the case.

"Excuse me, Sheriff Scott," said Templeton.

"Yes?" the sheriff responded. His poker face never gave away what he felt at any given moment.

"With all due respect, Ms. Scott doesn't have the required experience for this role. She was a patrol officer for Sacramento PD for what, two years?" The detective was trying to keep his tone civil and even.

The sheriff bristled and his shoulders stiffened. "Detective, remind me again who found the graves?"

"Yes, but—"

"And remind me why we wouldn't use someone with great skill and doggedness who happens to be a police officer and a military veteran?"

"Well, yes, but—"

"Perhaps you would like to explain to Chelsea Compton's parents why you don't want to use the best resources you have at your disposal to find who murdered their child?"

The room hushed to silence—an uncomfortable quiet. The mayor stood side by side with the sheriff and it was clear there was no changing their minds on the matter.

Katie felt the light hairs on her arms and neck stand up. She kept looking straight ahead, and not to her right, where she knew the other detectives remained suspicious and Detective Templeton was staring daggers at her. Her uncle had told her about deputizing her and she was absolutely delighted, if a bit terrified, and couldn't wait to get started officially on the case. To be a part of the investigation was something that felt right to her.

"One more thing," said Templeton. "We all know about Ms. Scott's amazing skill in hunting down victims…"

Katie could hear the contempt in his voice, but it was clear he wanted everyone else to buy his kind words.

"… but I would suggest that for the sake of this high-profile case, she should have someone overseeing her investigative techniques—just until she has more experience under her belt." He sat down with a smug smile on his face.

"I concur. There are many leads to run down and new evidence to filter through. Plenty of work for everyone," the sheriff said.

What? Katie looked directly at her uncle, not believing what he had just consented to on her behalf. This wasn't what she had agreed to the previous night after several hours of discussion. There had been no mention of a partner—or, more accurately, a babysitter.

"I've already spoken to Deputy McGaven," Sheriff Scott continued, gesturing toward the crowd.

Katie turned her attention to the officer her uncle had indicated. The large red-haired deputy glanced away sheepishly. It was clear from his posture and lack of eye contact that he wasn't happy with his assignment.

"Deputy McGaven will be partnered with Detective Scott during this investigation until I deem otherwise." The sheriff wrapped up the briefing. "No use wasting any more precious time. Let's get to work."

Katie entered the small meeting room as Detective Templeton was setting up at the podium. His crew took their seats, waiting to hear what the detective in charge had to say. She noticed that Deputy McGaven sat at a desk on the far side of the room and never gave her any acknowledgment.

This is going to be fun.

With nothing else to do, she took a seat and waited. She observed that the energy from the officers in the room was upbeat and happy, rather than serious and businesslike. Idle chatter seemed to be the first item on the agenda as the detectives laughed and joked about mundane things and a few senseless stories ensued.

Katie glanced at her watch and noted that it was already eleven a.m. and counting. Her mind raced through all the things she could be investigating and searching. Obviously, speaking with Chelsea's parents, neighbors, forensics, and the medical examiner would be the priority. With all the clues and details from the gravesite indicating a ritualistic type of killer behavior— the carefully placed teddy bears and the premeditation without anger—it would appear they were looking for someone outside family and friends.

"Okay, okay, I'll make this quick," said Templeton as he quieted the room. "First, this case is going to take some real manpower and due diligence at our end if we want to catch the killer. However, I have my suspicions. Murderers usually don't venture too far from the people closest to them. We haven't ruled out the second body being someone who knew the Compton family. Alternatively, the killer could be trying to throw us off the trail with a victim who had nothing to do with Chelsea. We will begin with the family and see where it takes us."

Katie thought at first he was kidding, but no, he seemed to believe that the first order of business was to find evidence that Chelsea's family had killed her. She clenched her fists, trying not to say something rude despite her emotions.

Templeton wrapped up his impromptu pep talk and gave out instructions to every detective, standard protocol for the start of an investigation. Everyone began leaving the room and he still hadn't given Katie her assignment. She waited a bit longer, until she saw he was about to leave himself.

"Excuse me," she said. "What's my assignment?" She moved closer to the detective and waited for an answer.

"Oh, that's right," he said sarcastically. "Ms. Scott."

"Detective."

"Yes, of course, *Detective*. I need you to collate all the incoming daily information and conduct searches for other detectives when necessary. And file anything that needs it." He turned to leave.

"Is that it? Really? That's your big plan? I think my skills could be used—"

He turned to her, his expression sour and his muscles tensed. "You're the rookie, the untrained rookie, definitely not detective level, and that's the assignment you're going to get."

"Huh."

"What's your problem—Detective?"

"I just expected more from you," she said.

"If you have a problem, go cry to your uncle. There are men here who have earned their position as detective. And *not* by a fluke and special circumstances. If I had my way, you wouldn't be here at all. Consider yourself lucky to have an assignment at all."

He left the room.

*

The spokesperson for the sheriff's office, Sergeant Timothy Grant, stood waiting next to the podium for the press conference to commence. The news reporters readied themselves, each wanting to hear the gruesome details and to be the first to report the information about "the Toymaker" to their faithful readers.

Sheriff Scott opened the door and stepped outside toward the onslaught of reporters. He never missed a step or changed his demeanor, and was ready for anything fired at him. Two deputies followed and stood in the background, scanning the people in the audience.

"Ladies and gentlemen, thank you all for coming. At 1620 hours yesterday, the body of Chelsea Lynn Compton, who had been missing for a little over four years, was discovered inside a coffin that had been buried in a rural location. At the present time the cause of death is not known. Another victim, currently unidentified, was also found; cause of death is unknown for this victim too. I have assigned a special task force to work this case and we will update you when information becomes available, as long as it does not impede the ongoing investigation in any way."

"Is it true that there were teddy bears in the coffins?" yelled a reporter.

"I have no comment," stated the sheriff.

"Who discovered the bodies?" asked another reporter.

"I'm not at liberty to disclose that information at this time."

"Sheriff, has the killer contacted you directly?"

"No. We have not knowingly been in contact with the killer." The sheriff was beginning to lose his patience. "That's all the information we have for now. Thank you."

As he left the podium and entered the building, several reporters shouted more questions after him.

CHAPTER 20

Katie sat at the same desk where she had entered data for crime statistics for the past couple of weeks. She stared at the computer monitor as if something of importance would speak to her and guide her through the next few troubled days and weeks. Everything she had fought for—finding the missing girl, ruffling some egos—had come down to this. She'd been sidelined to do routine work. It wasn't her definition of a detective.

She hit the keyboard space bar and the screen came to life. It waited for her to log into the mainframe, where she would enter data from the detectives. Still watching the cursor blinking, she couldn't help but see Templeton's face in her mind—rude, condescending, and hateful. It was highly unlikely to change throughout the investigation.

"Hey, what's weighing so heavy on you?" asked Denise. "Thought you'd be excited about the change in the case because of your efforts." She was impeccably dressed in a smart dark-brown suit and she watched Katie with curiosity.

Katie sighed. "I've been benched."

"What do you mean?"

"I'm supposed to input data from the investigation, which means I'm going to be sitting here twiddling my thumbs while I wait for updates."

Denise eyed the notes on the desk. "Are those about the unknown little girl?"

"Yes. It's believed from my research that it's Tammie Myers. Nothing official yet."

"Oh."

Katie looked at Denise. "Just what I wanted for my first investigation. Maybe I can do some janitorial work while I wait…"

Denise put down a stack of files on her desk. "I'll do it."

"What?"

"I'll do it. Whatever you need. And when info comes in from the case, I'll take care of it."

"I can't ask you to do that," Katie said.

"It's not a big deal. I'm already right here and I can be working on other things until something needs to be updated."

Katie hadn't thought about that and realized that she needed to learn to delegate. "That would be so helpful. Then I can run down some information from interviews. Thank you."

Denise laughed. "It's my pleasure—it's my job. Leave me the notes. Now go. I'll text or call you with anything important."

"Do we need to okay it with superiors?"

"No, I'm the supervisor for records. It's part of my job." She smiled.

Katie jumped up. "You're amazing. Thank you."

Katie sat in her unmarked police vehicle, trying to push away the memory of the conversation she'd had with Detective Templeton, and how unappreciated she felt. She opened her notebook and checked the names and addresses of people she wanted to speak with who Templeton hadn't assigned any detectives to. She needed to clarify events and facts and to re-interview witnesses who might have more information than previously disclosed. Templeton and his crew were going directly to the Comptons' residence and would most likely then wait around for any news from forensics.

She scanned the last known address for Terrance Price. There were some things about his statement that she wanted to elucidate. She also wanted to verify exactly when he had performed work for the Comptons. He had been staying on a local farm in a bunkhouse doing some odd jobs around the property. The homeowners were Leonard and Elsie Haven and the farm was located on the outskirts of town on Apple Road. She estimated it would take her about twenty-five minutes to reach it.

She turned over the engine and the car roared to life. She adjusted her seat and secured the seat belt before she put the car into drive.

A hard triple-knock on the passenger window caught her attention. Deputy McGaven was peering in. He gestured to her to unlock the door.

Katie hesitated. A part of her wanted to hit the accelerator, but she was a professional police detective now and didn't want to fall victim to Templeton's games or stoop to his level.

The deputy stared at her and frowned.

Katie disengaged the lock and he got in.

"I'm sorry that you're stuck with this gig," she said immediately, "but I don't take orders from you."

"Fine," he said, without bothering to look at her. "I have a job to do and I'll do it by the book."

Katie sighed. If she was going to make any friends at the police department she needed to at least try. "I'm Katie," she said, extending her right hand.

He hesitated, but finally shook her hand. "I'm Sean, but everyone calls me McGaven."

"Nice to meet you. I know what most of the deputies think of me—at least at this point. All I ask is that you make up your own mind. Deal?"

Sean cracked a tiny smile. "I suppose." He leaned back, trying to make himself comfortable. "Aren't you supposed to be using the database?"

"The very capable Denise is running the required programs for me. It's ridiculous to have me sitting at a computer watching it search when someone from records can do it," Katie replied. "It's called multi-tasking."

She dropped the gear shift into drive and drove out of the police parking lot.

There was a somewhat uncomfortable silence during the ride, but Katie had her mind on the case. It was possible that Price had been the only one to see what happened to Chelsea, and it was well worth a try to get more information from him.

She remembered from one of her psychology classes that when dealing with people suffering from personality disorders, anxiety or depression, head traumas, or anything else that impaired judgment and logic, it was important to stay calm and let them rattle out what they needed to say. Never pressure them; it would only stress and inhibit them. She had some hope that the fact that she was a woman might make Price less defensive.

The rural landscape sped by the windows. It had been more than ten minutes since they had seen a house. Katie slowed to see if there were any signs, landmarks, or mailboxes directing them to the Haven farm. The name seemed familiar to her, but she couldn't remember why.

"Do you see an address for Haven?" she asked.

"No. It's still a ways up here," the deputy replied with a deadpan expression.

"How do you know?"

"We receive calls out here a couple of times a month."

"For?" Katie asked.

Deputy McGaven didn't immediately answer, as if he wanted her to guess. But then he finally explained, "Mr. and Mrs. Haven are whacked."

"What?"

"They have a different way of thinking; they yell and scream at one another, throw large objects, and they're convinced there is always someone wanting to break into their house."

"Great," Katie replied. She hadn't realized that she was walking into a crackpot's property, wanting to interview another one who lived in the barn. "And you didn't think this was important enough to tell me?"

"It's your investigation. I'm here to make sure that you operate within the duties and laws of the department."

Another mile on and there was a large mailbox with *Haven* marked on it, and an old sign spray-painted with the word *Eggs*.

"This it?" she asked.

"Yep," was the deputy's reply. His irritation was obvious from his tone.

Katie eased the car down the garbage-riddled driveway. The large farmhouse was in desperate need of repair, with peeling paint, a couple of boarded-up windows, and weeds everywhere. It didn't seem that Price was helping with handyman jobs, by the looks of the place.

She parked and stared at the dilapidated surroundings. "Well," she said, unhooking her seat belt, "let's go see what's up." She didn't wait for the deputy to reply or follow her; instead, she made sure her gun was secure under her jacket.

Outside the car, she stopped for a moment and listened, still surveying the area.

Nothing.

No sounds or indication that anyone was around. She half expected to hear power tools, hammering, chickens, or dogs barking, but there was nothing.

She wasn't sure if anyone was home, because there wasn't a car parked anywhere. She walked up to the porch, stepped up the three stairs, and stood at the door. Knocking three times, she called, "Hello? Mr. or Mrs. Haven? Anyone home?" She knocked again.

Deputy McGaven took his trained cover position behind Katie and a few steps to the right. His hand on his service weapon, he waited, looking in all directions.

Two minutes passed without an answer or the sound of anyone moving around inside. Katie peered into a filthy window. The living room was quite neat and orderly. Nothing screamed foul play or that something was wrong.

She decided to walk around the property just in case someone was working and hadn't heard them drive up. There were junked cars, old refrigerators, and miscellaneous tossed items lying around. Most things had clearly been there for quite some time, as the weeds had taken over and intertwined themselves in every crack and crevice.

McGaven followed at a distance, keeping alert, his focus on anything or anyone that could be waiting to ambush them.

An old greenhouse sat in disarray with pieces of plastic flapping in the wind, a neat pile of fresh lumber lying on the ground a few feet away. Next to the greenhouse structure was a wooden shack. The door stood open and Katie could see that there was a cot inside, but no one was around.

The barn was around back. One of the doors swung gently open and closed in the breeze.

"Hello? Anyone here?" she called again.

No one answered.

She decided to go inside the large structure. McGaven waited outside. The barn was old, but there had been an attempt to maintain it with new paint and replacement of some of the siding. She allowed her eyes to adjust to the darkness. Bales of hay were stacked neatly in two corners. Tools hung on the wall in a systematized manner arranged by type.

"Hello?" she said again. "Mr. Price?" She presumed Terrance Price was most likely responsible for the maintenance on the barn and that he would be nearby.

As she walked toward the left-hand side, an unusual hypnotic squeaking sound made her stop. It was consistent with the gentle banging of the barn door. The wind whistled through gaps in the structure and added a quirky harmony to the other noises.

She moved deeper into the barn. Just as she was about to turn right, movement caught her attention at eye level. Startled, she stepped back. A body was hanging by its neck, swaying gently back and forth. It was the rope rubbing against the beam that made the squeaking sound.

She caught her breath, trying to block out memories of dead bodies in combat, and focused on the hanging man before her. It appeared to be Terrance Price, based on his photo and description from the police file. He hadn't been dead for more than a few hours; there were signs of rigor mortis just beginning to set in.

It was his fixed, bulging eyes that spooked Katie the most, as they seemed to follow her no matter where she moved. She looked around but didn't see anything that appeared suspicious. It seemed Price had jumped from the upper level of the barn and had had no time to change his mind. He would have broken his neck and died instantly.

Retracing her steps, Katie returned to the main doors and practically ran into the waiting McGaven.

"Call in a 10-54—actually a 10-56," she ordered. The first code meant that there was a dead body, but then she changed it to a suicide instead. A full investigation would have to corroborate that initial call, but it was sufficient for now to get things moving forward.

The deputy stared at her, his eyes wide.

"Do it!" she exclaimed.

CHAPTER 21

Detective Templeton and another detective named Abrams had just exited the Comptons' home. Templeton was angry that he had only been able to talk with Mrs. Compton—her husband had moved to Idaho less than a year ago. He hadn't had any luck with her either, as she hadn't had anything new to report. She remained committed to the same information she had first given the detective four years ago.

"Check her original statement and see if there are any inconsistencies," he barked to the other detective.

Abrams nodded and took a cell-phone call. "Yes, we'll be there in about half an hour." He ended the call with a look of surprise.

Templeton demanded, "Be where in half an hour?"

"Detective Scott and Deputy McGaven have just found Terrance Price dead," reported Abrams.

"What?" Templeton's voice was barely a whisper as he stood staring at his partner in disbelief.

"Apparent suicide. They found him hanging in the Havens' barn."

Templeton fumed. "What the hell was Scott doing looking for Price?" he snapped.

*

Katie had arranged for the medical examiner and forensics to arrive. Even though it appeared to be a suicide, it was always prudent to have a death scene examined and documented in case the ME was to state a different cause and manner of death.

She knew that Templeton would be contacted as well. It wouldn't be long before he would arrive and demand an explanation for why she was at the Haven farm.

"Thanks, Denise." She ended her cell-phone call. "The Havens are at County General," she told McGaven. "It seems Mr. Haven suffered a stroke and Mrs. Haven will probably end up in an assisted-living home."

The deputy nodded; he seemed to be more interested in the case now that a dead body had showed up.

With her mountain of information to sift through, and witnesses she wanted to re-interview, Katie knew it was important to have someone on her side. She wouldn't give up on the deputy. Especially now that Price's death had raised more questions than answers. True, the man had been unstable, with mental issues, but why commit suicide barely twenty-four hours after Chelsea's body was found?

An unmarked police vehicle raced into the driveway and braked sharply, barely missing a patrol car. Detectives Templeton and Abrams exited, heading directly for Katie. Templeton's face was red, his arms stiff with clenched fists, and he appeared to want to spill blood.

Here we go…

"Scott!" he yelled.

Katie stood her ground. She noticed that McGaven conveniently found somewhere else to go until the lecture was finished.

"What the hell are you doing?" Templeton accused.

"I secured a crime scene so there wouldn't be any… mistakes," Katie replied.

"Your orders were to update the investigation as the information became available, along with any daily data entry."

"It's being done as we speak. There's tons of work to be filtered through. I'm filtering," she said.

CHAPTER 22

With her hair still damp from a long, hot shower, Katie dressed warmly in a thick robe and began to sort through the paperwork spread over her living room. She made notes of all the calls she had made at the police department after leaving the Haven farm. It was difficult at first to pry answers out of people, but with some coaxing they were able to give her what she needed.

It was late, just after eleven p.m., and she was supposed to be at a briefing tomorrow morning at 0700 hours. Her eyes grew heavy as she organized her notes on Terrance Price into chronological order and began to read through everything carefully one more time.

Terrance Price, born September 1st, 1962, in Sacramento, California. Price suffered a severe head injury in 1982 in a motorcycle accident. He was first diagnosed as having paranoid schizophrenia and later, according to another psychologist, he was thought to have a personality disorder. Self-medicating with drugs and alcohol made him a perfect candidate for homelessness. Price was in and out of jail nine times: drunk and disorderly, theft, trespassing, etc. All minor offenses. He took on several handyman jobs and light carpentry work. Recently he worked for the Havens. People who had direct contact with him said that he was doing better than he had in some time.

She thumbed through some of the photographs taken earlier by the crime-scene unit, which had been emailed to her. She was relieved that forensics treated her like any other detective in the department. It would make her job much easier down the road.

In the photographs, the barn and the body were as she remembered. The photographer had abided by the general rules of documenting a crime scene—or a potential one. There were three basic areas: an overview of the scene, close-up, and medium range. Everything in the barn appeared to be in order and nothing seemed suspicious.

There was no suicide note. It was unclear if Terrance Price had ever spoken to anyone about committing suicide. His behavior had seemed more stable in the past year; those who knew him expressed the belief that his medications seemed to be working.

Katie knew that the medical examiner would rule it a suicide and then the case would be closed. It was troublesome that she hadn't got to talk to Price about the day he saw Chelsea get into a truck. Her instincts suggested to her that there was at least some truth to his statement. When he was pressed by Detective Templeton, it agitated and confused him, leading him to claim he didn't remember. It wasn't surprising that he acted like this; many interviewees didn't want to talk with the detective. His moods and tactics made people want to get away from him.

A long snore rumbled from under the coffee table. Cisco's legs twitched, most likely due to a wonderful doggie dream.

Katie leaned back against the couch and closed her eyes. Just as on previous nights, she immediately saw Chelsea's face, sometimes it was her friend Jenny.

Tomorrow was a full day of investigation with many interviews to conduct. She wanted to come at it through the back door, instead of head-on with the parents. She knew Templeton would take care of that interview and obvious things like the autopsy and the preliminary reports from forensics. She was going to talk to the people of Pine Valley first, and would pay a visit to forensics and the ME after Templeton's mad rush had slowed down.

She scrolled through the crime-scene photographs once again as her eyelids became heavy and then closed. She fell into the dark abyss of much-needed sleep.

A loud crash woke Katie. She sat up and looked around in the darkness, trying to decipher her waking world. It wasn't clear if she had been dreaming or if there really had been a crashing noise.

Her eyes acclimatized to the dark and she slowly scanned her living room in the dim light. The furniture, shelves, and rug all appeared unchanged. But she didn't remember turning off the lamp next to her. The house was in complete darkness. She knew she had left the kitchen light on, and a bedroom lamp too.

Where was Cisco?

Instinct told her to keep the lights off and to move around carefully. She stood up, took two steps to a small table, and opened the drawer. There was a stowed Beretta already loaded with one bullet in the chamber. She kept the safety engaged and tucked the gun in her pocket as a precaution.

She glanced at her ornate mantel clock: 1.42 a.m. The sound of the clock seemed to increase in volume.

She moved effortlessly to the front door area and peered outside. Her car was parked in the same position she had left it.

She tried the outside light switch, but nothing happened. She walked quietly back to the couch, bent down, and tried the lamp toggle. Same outcome. Nothing.

She realized that it was most likely a blown fuse or a tripped breaker. It was actually quite common in the old house.

"Cisco? Here…"

Quiet ensued without any sounds to indicate that she wasn't alone. The only sound she heard was her heartbeat hammering in her ears—rapidly becoming faster.

All the doors were shut tight and she couldn't feel any draft wafting inside from an open window or door.

"Cisco?" she whispered.

Her question was answered by a low guttural growl emanating from one of the back bedrooms. She slowly moved in that direction, knowing she didn't need to call for the dog again. Something was wrong, otherwise he would be next to her. It meant that something more urgent had drawn his attention away from her.

She walked down the hallway, stopped, and tried another light switch, confirming that the breaker was off.

Another low rumble floated down the hallway. The skin at the back of her neck and over her scalp prickled, making her shoulders and upper body shudder. She kept moving, now with her weapon drawn, not knowing what she would find.

She stopped at the back bedroom, which had been her parents'. The furniture and artwork had been left the same as Katie remembered it. She had cleared out their personal belongings and clothes, leaving behind two boxes and extra linens in the closet. The bedroom was now a guest room, so she rarely entered it except to look for additional towels or sheets.

As she stood in the doorway, she saw Cisco's dark outline facing the window, perfectly still.

"Cisco, *here*," she whispered.

She saw one of his perked ears move. She knew there was nothing wrong with him. He was standing guard over something.

"Cisco. It's okay. *Here*."

The dog finally moved, and obediently padded next to her, closer than normal.

"Okay, boy. What's over there?" she asked, just to hear her own voice.

She began to approach the window, which had a blind to keep the light out. She tried to recollect the last time she had looked out that particular window and thought it had been years. It faced out toward the large back yard, framing the older trees and perennial flowers.

Her night vision had enhanced, but she decided to grab a flashlight from one of the nightstand drawers. Balancing her weapon in her right hand and dropping the flashlight in the pocket of her robe, she took hold of the blind string with her left hand and tugged hard.

The window covering clattered and drew upward at speed. The blind hung askew as it thumped lightly against the window frame. Katie pulled out the flashlight and targeted it directly at the window. It reflected back her own image. For an instant, she looked more like an apparition with a pale supernatural appearance than a woman holding a gun.

She drew a deep breath, realizing that she hadn't taken one for almost a minute. It made her slightly lightheaded and her vision blurred. Quickly inhaling and exhaling a couple more times, she regained her composure.

Cisco growled and his body remained fixed to her left thigh.

As she focused her attention on the window again, she saw a piece of paper stuck to the outside of the glass, facing inward. In scrawled blood-red handwriting it read:

STAY AWAY.

CHAPTER 23

Katie sat quietly, immersed in her own thoughts, as the morning briefing stirred up the personnel, causing them to fire questions at Sheriff Scott. The topic was the note that had been stuck to her window by someone who had turned off her electricity and left behind a visible shoe print matching the one she had earlier spotted next to her driveway.

Everyone had an opinion and it seemed they thought it had something to do with Terrance Price's suicide. Exactly how it tied to him wasn't immediately clear—it was just pure speculation.

Forensics were working on the letter to try to find any fingerprints or foreign substance that could identify the author. The boot prints were common, but they performed a casting in hopes of identifying tread characteristics if they ever had a shoe to compare it to during the investigation.

Katie grew weary listening to the group drone on about theories; with less than four hours of sleep, she thought it possible she could drift off sitting in her chair. The investigation was difficult enough, but the lack of sleep was going to take its toll on her, and possibly cause her to make mistakes.

"Detective Scott?" said the sheriff.

Katie looked directly at her uncle, observing his usual authoritative demeanor. She had already answered a barrage of questions from him. Now she was going to have to endure it again for the department's benefit.

"Detective Scott have you observed anyone recently who might be following you? Showing up in more than one place? Anything that seemed out of the ordinary?" the sheriff asked. The room became completely quiet waiting for her answer.

"No, I have not seen anything out of the ordinary since I've been home. No sign of anyone following me when I was searching for Chelsea that I was aware of. Believe me, I've been racking my brain trying to figure this out."

The continued silence held the room hostage for another minute.

Finally, Sheriff Scott spoke again. "It's clear that this isn't a childish prank, and it has been directed at one of our own. What it means exactly will take more investigation. For now, I want to make sure that you are all careful and pay close attention as you go about your duties. Understand?" He waited for everyone in the room to nod in agreement. "Dismissed."

The other officers and detectives immediately stood and made a quick departure. Deputy McGaven loitered in the hall with his hands in his pockets, not looking anyone directly in the eye. It wasn't clear whether he was nervous or he just didn't want to discuss his new detail.

Katie focused and concentrated on what she had to do today as she waited for the official identification of the other girl. It would be a long, tedious day interviewing Chelsea's neighbors and others. After four years, it would be interesting to hear what they had to say now that the body had been found.

"Detective Scott, don't forget to have your daily report on my desk." The sheriff addressed Katie in an official manner. "With all things considered, it wouldn't be frowned upon if you took the day off."

Katie smiled. "With all things considered, the longer this investigation takes, the more likely it is that the killer will abduct another little girl—and kill again." Gently squeezing her uncle's arm, she continued, "I appreciate the thought, though."

She left the room carrying her clipboard and notes from the original case and met the deputy in the hallway.

"Everything okay?" he asked.

"Fine," she replied, and headed out toward the exit, McGaven following her.

There was a cluster of police officers near the door, and Katie heard the distinctive sarcastic voice of Detective Templeton. "… and then she skipped back to the department thinking she had solved the case."

The group erupted in laughter.

Here we go again…

Katie and the deputy made their way around the group to get to the exit. She decided to stop and face the detective. "You're quite the funny guy, Templeton. Did you happen to tell them how you didn't do your job four years ago and find Chelsea Compton?"

A lungful of anger exploded from the man. "You're not as tough as you think you are—you better watch yourself," he hissed. He lunged toward her, but two of the officers held him back.

Katie wasn't sure if he would've actually struck her or shoved her to the floor, but she was prepared to handle whatever he had to throw at her. She wasn't intimidated or scared by him.

She didn't know what had possessed her to antagonize the detective in a direct and provoking manner, but she felt he deserved some mocking, just like any other officer. He was going to have to accept her presence sooner or later. It was obvious that he didn't care what she did, as long as she didn't get in his way or solve the case before he did. It gave her some breathing room to conduct her investigation and check in with her uncle at the end of each day.

She did notice that McGaven was instantly at her side and seemed to be prepared to defend her if necessary. Maybe it was a cop thing, but either way, it was encouraging that the deputy was beginning to warm to her.

Neither spoke when they got to the police car, but there seemed to be something a little bit different between them—he wasn't as agitated and tense as before. Katie would have to be patient, though, if she expected him to treat her like other officers who had sworn to protect and serve.

She scanned through her notes. She knew from the daily investigative sheet where Templeton would hover, so she decided to have a chat with the Comptons' neighbors, Sig and Ella Stanley. She had done a little background on them and found they weren't a quiet conservative couple as she had imagined, but had had brushes with the law over trespassing, drunk and disorderly, and restraining orders. Officially, they stated that they had seen Chelsea on the day she disappeared, but then they changed their story and said they were mistaken.

She glanced at the deputy as he worked his cell phone with his thumbs; he kept his solemn stare focused on the tiny screen.

"You do realize that we're working on a case involving the abduction and murder of two little girls?" she said, cutting through the silent treatment and hitting the truth right between the eyes.

The deputy turned to her, eyes narrowed and jaw tightened. "Of course, that's why we're here," he replied.

"Then I would suggest you start acting like it." She realized that she sounded a bit harsh, but her nerves were wearing thin from dealing with Detective Templeton.

"What's your problem?" he asked.

"Okay," she said. "I thought we were past this. I have half a mind to dump you out here and go on by myself." She sensed anger teetering in her body, muscles tensed and growing more agitated.

The deputy leaned in as if to say something unprofessional, then decided against it. A big sigh ensued instead.

Katie took a slow breath. "Look, we've all had jobs or duties we've hated. But get over it." She waited patiently for his response.

"Fine. Let's go," he said finally.

"Not good enough," Katie persisted.

"What do you want from me, Detective Scott?" He stared at her directly, his eyes boring into hers.

"We've got a job to do, so let's do it," she said.

"It's just…" He stopped before he finished his sentence.

"It's just what?" Katie watched him closely.

"Look, I don't have anything against you. But I'm getting more than my fair share of harassment and I'm the butt of every joke."

"I see," she said softly. "A little ribbing from the guys and you fold like a paper bag. Whining and complaining."

"Well, that's not really fair," he said slowly.

"Fair?" she said, raising her voice. "You want to talk to me about *fair*? Is it fair to watch two of your teammates have their limbs ripped from their bodies because they happened to be too close to a bomb when it went off? Is it fair to sit with a friend who was there for you when everyone else wasn't, and watch him die because that's just the way it is?" She caught her breath and curbed her anger. "And tell me, Deputy McGaven, is it fair that two girls were murdered while the killer is still roaming free?"

The deputy looked away, visibly shaken by what she had said. His eyes were wide in astonishment as he fidgeted with his hands. "No, Detective, of course not."

Katie started the car. Her heart pounded and that familiar feeling of panic tried to overpower her, but she pushed it away by concentrating on the case. The conversation was over, and she didn't want to have to explain herself again.

She drove to the Stanleys' house. She knew Mrs. Stanley would be home while her husband was at work—she had called them earlier. After speaking with Mrs. Stanley, it was clear she wasn't enthusiastic about talking to the police again.

Katie slowed the vehicle and pulled into a parking space between the Compton and Stanley homes. It wasn't difficult to imagine children playing on the quiet street filled with trees. The scenario was the same all across Middle America. Neighbors waved and smiled to one another. No one was loitering who didn't belong; no one had any devious acts in mind. It exuded the appearance of a middle-class family neighborhood that would be portrayed in a book or movie; though in reality, no one knew what happened behind closed doors or who might wander through.

Chelsea's house was quiet and there was nothing to set it apart from other homes. The yard had a sad appearance; many plants and flowers were dead, as was the lawn. It had most likely not been tended after Chelsea disappeared.

The Stanleys' house showed the exact opposite, with blooming plants, dozens of vivid shades of green, and the fence recently painted. It was a house that had been maintained and loved. There was a window, presumably the kitchen, facing Chelsea's house, with a clear view of the road and driveway.

Katie slowly exited the car, still observing the area, before shutting the door behind her. McGaven appeared to study the neighborhood as well and followed Katie's example before joining her at the front door of the Stanley house. They appeared to be on the same page in the investigation at last.

Katie rang the doorbell and waited.

The door opened and an attractive middle-aged blonde woman wearing yoga pants and a pink tank top stood there. She studied Katie and the deputy for a moment.

"Mrs. Stanley?" said Katie. "I'm Detective Scott and this is Deputy McGaven. We spoke on the phone."

"Of course, please come in." The woman opened the door wider, allowing them to enter.

Once inside, Katie immediately noted the Chinese theme to the decor, with Asian rugs, several Buddha statues, and a myriad of collectibles signifying good luck in traditional Eastern beliefs. There were also framed family photographs scattered around, and some holiday snaps. Katie noted that there were no children in any of the pictures.

"Please sit down, Detective," Mrs. Stanley invited.

Katie wanted to make the conversation as casual as possible, but for a moment, all three of them sat uncomfortably. She realized she had little experience in interviewing witnesses in an investigation. Most interviews she had done on patrol were immediately after a crime occurred. She began the process by forcing a smile. "Thank you for seeing us at such short notice, but time isn't a luxury we have on this case. I know it has been four years, but I wanted to ask you a few things about that day."

"Of course, though I don't know what I can do to help that I haven't already told the other detective," Mrs. Stanley said.

"Well," Katie began, "I wanted to clarify a few things that were in the original missing-persons case. To begin with, did you see Chelsea the day she disappeared?"

Mrs. Stanley seemed slightly agitated and stood up, picking up one of her knickknacks distractedly. "Chelsea was always going to friends' houses and I would often see her walking down the street."

"Which way would she go?" Katie asked.

"Most days she would head out to the main street," Mrs. Stanley replied.

"Not toward Highland Center Park?" Katie pushed.

"No, I don't think so. Not that I remember."

"How well do you know the Comptons?"

"Oh, Beth and… Chuck." Mrs Stanley's eyes lit up. "Fairly well. They've been our neighbors for more than eight years. Such nice people. Sad that they divorced after… well, you know."

"Did you ever know them to have problems before Chelsea went missing, anything you might think we should know about?"

"Oh no, nothing. They were a wonderful family."

Katie leaned back in more of a relaxed manner; she sensed some deception but wanted to continue in a friendly way. She looked to her right and saw that McGaven was watching Mrs. Stanley closely— her movements, hesitations, and body language when she spoke.

"Did you ever notice anyone in the neighborhood you'd never seen before, perhaps someone watching Chelsea or other children?"

"What do you mean, like a pedophile?"

"It's possible. There are a couple of registered sex offenders in this area."

"Oh my," Mrs. Stanley said with some alarm; obviously the thought had never occurred to her. "No, I've never noticed anyone like that."

Katie watched her mannerisms and hand movements when she talked. Certain words—"pedophile", "divorced", and "Chuck"— made her gestures increase in intensity.

"Was there anyone working for the Comptons, or any of your other neighbors, around that time—service workers, gardeners, contractors?"

"No… Oh, wait, the Crandalls on the other side of the Comptons had some new kitchen cabinets installed."

"When?"

"A couple of weeks before Chelsea went missing."

"Are you sure it was before she disappeared?"

"Yes. When something of that magnitude happens to one of your neighbors, you don't forget anything that happened around that time."

"What type of workers? Local? From one of the superstores or an online company?"

"Oh, from town. The Darren boys, Malcolm and Frederick. They do large remodels as well as small projects. They took over their dad's business after he died. It seems everyone has used them at one time or another."

Katie jotted down their names. "And you're sure they were here a couple of weeks before Chelsea went missing?"

"Yes, I'm sure. They're cute boys too," Mrs. Stanley added, and her eyes lit up again.

"So just to clarify, you never saw Chelsea the day she disappeared?"

"No, I'm sorry, I didn't."

"Did you ever see a truck?"

"A truck?"

"Yes, any truck driving or stopping that day, or possibly a day or so before."

"Everyone around here either has sedans or SUVs. No trucks. Well, except for the Darren boys." The way she said "boys" lingered in the air.

Katie stood. "Just one more thing, if you wouldn't mind. May I see the window in your kitchen?"

"Of course," Mrs. Stanley said, and led the way.

Katie stood at the sink and looked out the window. It was the perfect vantage point to see the street in both directions and had an open view to the Comptons' house. She turned around and moved toward the front door, taking the time to glance at the photographs again.

"Thank you for your time, Mrs. Stanley."

"Good luck, Detective," Mrs. Stanley said, and forced a smile.

Katie and McGaven left the house and went back to the car.

"Interesting, but nothing," said the deputy.

"We learned a lot," Katie said, still thinking about Mrs. Stanley's affection for Mr. Compton and the Darren boys. Her subtle movements and the tone of her voice had given her away. Katie wondered if there was more to the day that Chelsea went missing than the woman was telling them.

CHAPTER 24

The Pine Valley Elementary School let out at three p.m. every day during the week. Kids carrying loaded backpacks hustled to their assigned buses or their moms waiting in the pickup line, or walked home. The high-energy chatter and laughter from the students was unmistakable.

The man watched, studying the behavior and movements of various children. He began to catalogue each child according to their ability to fight or fend for themselves. There were certain traits that distinguished his chosen ones from the average.

Dena, where are you?

It didn't take him long to spot the eleven-year-old girl whom he had watched almost every day for two months. She never wore dresses, but sported jeans and a bright shirt. Her long dark hair was loose around her shoulders now instead of her usual braids.

Every subtle move…

She tore off her blue-and-yellow backpack and swung it into the silver SUV before jumping in after it. She moved her hands to her neck and flipped her hair out of the way. It was obvious she was annoyed she hadn't braided it to keep it off her face. It glistened in the sunshine. Soft. Silky.

She was waiting to be protected. To be saved from all the ugliness in the world. It was coming quickly.

She was perfect.

A smile crept across his face.

He watched as she spoke to her younger brother inside the car, resulting in arms flailing. It was unclear what was said, but her mother turned her head to speak to her, and the flailing stopped.

The man's mind wandered to his picture-perfect gravesite, which he had diligently and doggedly created. He had studied the area with maps, he'd walked countless trails, and then he'd camped out and scoured more of the rural areas. He had done everything he could think of to ensure that the site fit every need—and more.

And now he had learned from the Internet news that an off-duty police officer, Katie Scott, had found the final resting places of his little girls sleeping.

Anger flooded into his body at high velocity, muscles tensed in his arms and legs, his fists clenched, and all happiness disappeared from him. He internally pleaded with himself to stop the hate and anger from festering.

Katie Scott had spoiled everything.

His new search had moved along with great expectation. Nothing else mattered to him. It had to have been a fluke, a lucky stumble, for the woman to have found his most sacred location.

Someone will pay.

In an effort to block out bad thoughts and bad memories, the man blinked his eyes several times. To his surprise, the thoughts perished as quickly as they had consumed him.

He watched the silver SUV merge into traffic and drive away.

It was almost time.

CHAPTER 25

"What are you doing?" asked Katie as she watched McGaven double-check his weapon. They were driving to the Darren residence to interview the two brothers.

"There have been a number of visits there in the past," he replied. "It helps to be prepared for the... unexpected."

"Why didn't you say anything before?"

"You didn't ask," he stated flatly.

"I would appreciate the courtesy of a heads-up if you know something of importance—like the fact that we could be walking into an ambush or a sketchy situation."

She made a detour and sped down one of the main streets.

"Where are you going?" the deputy asked.

"Need some caffeine."

"Great idea." His mood perked up and he actually sounded civil.

Katie pulled up in front of a small coffee bar. McGaven got out of the car and then hesitated, looking back at her.

"I have to make a quick call—I'll be right there," she said.

She watched him until he was inside and in the queue facing away from her before she made a break for it. How long she would have, she didn't know, but she wanted to stay motivated and get some answers from the brothers without any distractions. She clearly wasn't getting through to the deputy. His agitation while checking his gun had made her nervous and unable to focus clearly. She would apologize later. She knew she would receive a reprimand for her behavior, but the priority was still the same—find Chelsea's killer.

While she drove, she pondered what Mrs. Stanley had told her. Why did the woman initially tell Templeton that she had seen Chelsea that day? What was she hiding? Was it something to do with Chelsea, or her own secrets? It was another piece of the puzzle. Katie wasn't sure where it actually fit into the investigation, but she knew that things would begin to fall into place and eventually lead to the killer.

The Darren property wasn't exactly how Katie had pictured it. It appeared to be more of a junkyard than a carpenter's workplace. Cars, refrigerators, air conditioners, small household appliances, and other things that Katie couldn't readily identify littered the front area leading to a huge metal barn.

She took a few moments to search the backgrounds of Malcolm and Frederick Darren. Both brothers had quite a number of drunk and disorderly, petty theft, and disturbing the peace citations. It was clear that Malcolm was more of a troublemaker than his brother.

She noted the highlights in her small field notebook and made a shorthand notation of how she would proceed. Then she exited the car and walked to the back, popping open the trunk and retrieving a stun gun from her police duffle bag. She secured it underneath her suit jacket.

The afternoon was becoming warmer, and under any other circumstances she would have shed her jacket, but she wanted her firearm and Taser to be hidden from immediate view. She felt conspicuous in her dark-gray pant suit, crisp white blouse, and dressy boots. Not her usual army attire, which was not only more comfortable, but practical when working in unknown conditions.

She surveyed the immediate area; it appeared quiet and deserted. Nothing stirred. Not even a dog barked. An oversized pickup truck with hefty tires was parked near the metal building. The large toolbox lid was open and the lift gate was down. Someone had to be around.

A twinge of anxious energy revealed itself. Katie chose to ignore it and walked through the front yard, zigzagging around the junk to make her way to the barn and glancing at each piece of dumpster material to make sure that no one was hiding from view and could get the jump on her.

Muffled voices emanated from the barn. Listening closer, it sounded more like talk radio or a news station than a conversation.

Katie decided to make her presence known.

"Sheriff's office, Detective Scott here," she announced. "Hello? Anyone here?"

She unsnapped her holster just as a precaution.

"Hello, Mr. Darren?" she said. "Frederick, Malcolm? Anyone here?"

Any time a police officer walked into an unknown situation, no matter where it was, nerves and instincts became heightened.

Katie passed the truck, taking notice of the contents inside and along the bed: various tools and small boxes identifying parts for a car. She moved at a slower pace, acutely alert for unusual sound or movement. She realized that maybe she'd been hasty ditching McGaven. It had been more about her feelings than safety. She wouldn't make that mistake again.

"Hello? Anyone here?"

She moved steadily into the entrance of the metal building. She expected to see a carpentry workshop, but was surprised to find it was more of an auto garage, with two vehicles in the middle being repaired. Both had their hoods up, though she didn't see anyone bent over the engine compartment or lying underneath. Deeper inside the workshop, there was an area for cabinetry work and assorted carpenter specialties. She deduced that each brother had a different job; most likely their father was the original carpenter and the sons had turned the business into both types of work.

A tool dropped to the ground, causing a high-pitched metallic sound that echoed inside the structure.

Katie spun around and saw a grayish tiger-striped cat slink underneath a worktable and move away from her as fast as it could to disappear into a dark corner.

Along one wall there were three boxes filled with receipts and file folders. Compared to the disarray of junk scattered at the front of the property, the metal workshop was surprisingly clean and organized. Meticulous care had been taken to make sure tools and supplies were kept in specific areas.

A gunshot blast followed by whooping and hollering interrupted Katie's search. Several more gunshots followed.

She retrieved her semi-automatic sidearm, prepared for trouble, and hurried to the area where the gunshots had originated. When she saw the man responsible, she retreated but still didn't completely relax, not sure yet that there weren't others involved or that things wouldn't turn ugly fast.

The man was in his mid to late forties, dressed in blue jeans and no shirt, with scraggly hair, an unshaven face, and bare feet. He was clearly under the influence of alcohol. He sat on a crate, surrounded by a dozen or so empty beer cans. A .45 revolver was held in his right hand down at his side. The target, which was nothing more than a chunk of plywood and some scattered pieces of recycling, was thirty yards away next to a crumbling fence.

"Mr. Darren, put down the gun," stated Katie. It was an order and not a request. She kept her weapon targeted on the man.

"Well hello there…" he said, swaying from side to side. "What do ya got there?"

"I'm Detective Scott from the sheriff's department. Can I talk to you?"

"A detective? Pretty one too," he mumbled. "I didn't know detectives could be pretty." He laughed, still not relinquishing his weapon.

"Mr. Darren, put down the gun," she ordered again.

"I was just having some fun," he replied, turning in the direction of the targets. He readied himself and took a stance.

"Put down the weapon. Now!" Katie inched closer to him.

He glanced at her, slurring his words. "Well maybe I don't want to."

"Malcolm, put the gun down now or I'll shoot you myself." Another man had appeared, presumably the other brother.

Katie backed up and kept a watch on both of them. The two men were similar-looking, though Frederick was far neater, with cropped hair, clean jeans and shirt, and steel-toed work boots.

"Mal, c'mon, put it down now," he said. He walked directly up to his brother and swiped the gun out of his hand. Immediately he emptied the weapon and put it down on the crate. Turning to Katie, he said, "I'm Rick, and this idiot is my brother Malcolm. What can we do for you?" He was matter-of-fact and had an almost reserved demeanor. To his brother he said, "Go inside and clean up."

Malcolm obeyed and headed to the house without looking at Katie again.

Katie lowered her weapon and returned it to her holster. Gathering her authority, she said, "I'm Detective Scott, from the sheriff's office. I'm working the Chelsea Compton homicide and I have a few questions for you both, since you were working near the Compton residence before Chelsea disappeared."

"Oh, I heard the news that they found her. It's unconscionable what happened." Rick moved closer to her. "What would you like to know?"

"Were you both working for the neighbors at that time?" she asked.

"Yeah, we were remodeling a kitchen. It was a three-week job."

"Did you know the Comptons?"

"No, not really. Saw them on a few occasions."

"Anything seem out of place? Anything you might remember?" Katie stood in the same position so that she could observe him and keep an eye out for the brother coming back.

Rick went to the crate and began picking up the empty beer cans. "What do you mean? Like arguing or abuse or something?"

"Anything," she repeated.

He shook his head. "No, nothing like that. Although their habits were something else."

"What do you mean?"

He looked at her as if sizing her up. It made Katie uncomfortable, but she remained steadfast in her position and her authority for asking questions.

"I'm not one to judge, but they were rather promiscuous, and they weren't afraid to experiment."

"Promiscuous meaning sexual relations with other people outside their marriage? Did one of them have an affair?"

He laughed. "I'm sorry. I meant swingers; you know, wife swapping."

"The Comptons?"

"The Comptons and the Stanleys. I think that was their name," he said.

Katie remembered the way Mrs. Stanley had spoken of Mr. Compton. "And you know this because…" she pushed.

Her cell phone buzzed in her pocket, alerting her that there was a text message waiting.

"Everyone knew. Look, it wasn't a secret. They liked to act out with the curtains open. You can ask any of the neighbors," he suggested.

"What about Chelsea?" asked Katie, still trying to push away the image of the two couples dancing around in the front living room for all the neighbors to witness.

He shrugged. "I only saw her a couple of times, leaving the house and walking somewhere."

"One more thing. Did you ever see anyone hanging around or taking a particular interest in the Compton house or Chelsea?" She waited patiently and studied him as he answered.

"I'm sorry, Detective, I didn't notice anything like that."

"Okay, Mr. Darren. Thank you for your time." She turned to leave the way she'd entered. "Just a friendly reminder. No discharging of weapons in the town's limits. It's best to be at least one hundred and fifty yards from a roadway, building, or large body of water if you don't want deputies dispatched out here."

"Will do," he said with a smile.

Katie nodded at him and walked briskly back to her car, though not before noticing that Rick drove an oversized tan truck.

Once she was behind the wheel, she looked at her phone. The message was from Denise in the records division, and it read: *Good news. Confirmation ID on second body. More information at morgue.*

CHAPTER 26

Katie hated the morgue; a stainless-steel tomb with spotless polished floors. It emitted a specific scent from the cleaning fluid used, and nothing positive could be said about it. It fouled the mood of any detective, but it was a place to find answers.

She shuddered.

She had seen her fair share of dead bodies from her two years on patrol at the Sacramento Police Department, and in Afghanistan. More than one was too many.

She knew from Denise that Detective Templeton had already been to the morgue and left again. The preliminary autopsy report was sent to all the detectives working the case, but Katie wanted to hear the findings direct from the person who'd examined the body: the medical examiner, Dr. Jeffrey Dean. Though she didn't know much about him, and had never been introduced to him, she hoped he wouldn't treat her any differently from any other homicide detective in the department.

As she walked through the main entrance carrying her small notebook, her boots with their two-and-a-half-inch heels clipped the tile flooring. She didn't see anyone at first, and she felt conspicuous with her noisy footsteps echoing. The deserted area oozed an extra creepy vibe, so she tried to keep her mind on what the findings from the bodies might be.

Where was everybody?

As she rounded a hallway corner, she found herself face to face with Deputy McGaven. He towered over her and intentionally blocked her path. It was easy to see that he was angry.

She stopped abruptly in front of him. She knew she had to deal with the consequences of ditching him at the coffee house, but she didn't want to engage in that conversation here.

"Surprised to see me?" he said in a low, serious voice. His eyes bored through her, accompanied by a sour expression that made him appear much older. His slightly freckled skin, clean-shaven face, and red hair generally gave him the appearance of a big kid, but now his demeanor was cold, hard, and intimidating.

"Look," Katie said. "I may not have handled the situation in the best way, but I'm not getting any cooperation from you. I apologize; I let my anger dictate my act."

"Meaning?" he said, gritting his teeth.

"Meaning we're both police officers, and whether you like me or not, or whether you like this detail or not, we're stuck with it for now."

He sighed loudly and cocked his head as if thinking about the situation.

"I won't ask you this again. Do you have my back?" She stood her ground, even though she was a good eight inches shorter than the deputy.

"Of course." He lowered his voice. "What kind of question is that?"

"An important one."

McGaven took a step back, looking down and nodding his head in agreement.

"Do I have your word?" she pushed.

"Yes of course, Detective."

Katie tried to hide a smile. She could see herself getting to like the deputy. "Call me Katie," she said.

"Well now, I'm glad that's settled," said a man at the end of the hall. He wore Bermuda shorts, dark sneakers without socks, and a loose Hawaiian shirt that helped to hide the extra twenty pounds packed on around his midsection. He appeared to be ready for a vacation on a tropical island somewhere.

"Excuse me?" Katie said, taken aback.

"Detective Scott, I presume."

"Yes," she said warily.

"Oh, I'm sorry. I'm Dr. Dean, Jeff to most." He moved toward one of the exam rooms.

Katie tried not to show her surprise at his appearance or his introduction. All she'd known about him prior to this was that he was thorough and dedicated—one of the best.

The doctor stuck his head out the door. "I assume you want to know my findings on the girls?"

"Yes," Katie said and hurried to the room, McGaven following closely behind her.

The exam room was separate from the autopsy rooms. It was familiar to Katie and she immediately acquired a lump in her throat that restricted her breathing. Her pulse quickened as the flashback rushed into her mind—the moment when she'd had to identify her parents' bodies—causing her vision to skew and making everything in the room move strangely in a dizzying instant.

She took a concentrated breath and focused on the two gurneys, each covered by a single sheet. Flipping open her field notebook, she noticed that both of her hands trembled slightly. She dropped them to her sides and waited for the doctor's report, hoping that her unsteadiness would subside.

Dr. Dean moved to the first gurney and peeled back the sheet to expose the frail body of Chelsea Compton. Her face resembled that of a china doll rather than a rambunctious fourth-grader with her entire life ahead of her.

An image of Jenny flashed across Katie's memory.

Sitting cross-legged on the bed at camp, Katie and Jenny both had their journals open and were sharing stories as well as likes and dislikes.

"No way," Jenny said. "What's your favorite color?"

"Blue."

"Favorite cereal?"

Katie had to think a moment. She was torn between plain Os and a fruity cereal. Both were super-delicious. "It depends," she said.

"You have to pick one. I did."

Both girls laughed.

"Okay, the fruity cereal."

"I knew it. You're so like me," said Jenny. "Now, I promise I won't tell anyone." She sat up straight as if it were something of great importance. "What boy do you like here?"

"No," said Katie. "I'm not saying."

"You have to."

"No way."

"I bet it's Travis."

"No."

"Travis."

"No, it isn't."

Jenny laughed and threw herself back on the bed, chanting, "Katie likes Travis. Katie likes Travis."

Katie stared at Chelsea lying on the steel gurney and couldn't help but compare her to her friend. It felt almost as if she had spoken with Jenny barely a week ago. She wondered if Jenny's family had stood where she stood now, staring at the once vital, happy girl.

"Detective Scott, I have to say that I'm impressed you were able to find the bodies with so little to go on. You have single-handedly brought closure to the grieving families. I'm sure they are forever in your debt."

"Have the Comptons been here to identify the body?" Katie managed to say, trying not to sound like a frightened little girl.

"Mrs. Compton has. Mr. Compton is still in Idaho and won't be viewing the body."

"How did she seem to you?" asked Katie.

The doctor turned and picked up a file from the counter. "Nothing out of the ordinary. Genuinely upset, showing all the typical signs of grief, if that's what you mean."

Katie nodded. She noticed that the deputy was staring at the little girl's body as though unable to avert his eyes, almost mesmerized at the sight. It was obvious that he hadn't seen many dead bodies, and children were the most difficult to process.

She leaned toward him and suggested softly, "You don't need to be here. I can fill you in with the details."

"You sure?" he asked, trying to keep some semblance of control. "It's not a problem."

"It shouldn't take too long."

McGaven swiftly left the room.

"Well, now it's just the two of us," said Dean with a hint of sarcasm, "I have to say, you're not at all what I expected. Police officer, army veteran, and rogue investigator. I'm honored to be in your presence."

"Just following some leads and instincts." Katie didn't know what else to say. She quickly changed the topic. "Any signs of sexual assault?"

"No."

"Cause of death?"

"Asphyxia. Generalized hypoxia evident throughout the organs and body. Her eyes show a slight redness and petechial hemorrhage consistent with strangulation and asphyxia."

"Why was there so little decomposition?"

"That bothered me too, at first, until I found distinct traces of formaldehyde and methanol in her system."

"Was she embalmed?"

"No, just injected with the solutions without the standard process of removing the organs."

"That's why she looks so well preserved," Katie mused as she stared at the small body.

"Well, it's part of it. It's my professional opinion that the airtight coffin played a major role in preservation as well, even though there's no real research to support that theory." He walked around the body. "Lack of oxygen stops the bacteria from doing their work; however, the temperature inside the coffin wasn't controlled. It would have become hotter in the summer and of course cooler in the winter. But either way, the body was kept as well preserved as possible."

Katie took a couple of notes and pondered for a moment. "Could she have been kept alive longer, like months, and then murdered?"

"I will be doing more tests, but right now my belief is that she died within a few days or weeks of her abduction." He moved to peel back more of the sheet. "You can see that her torso and legs have quite a bit more decomposition than her face."

Katie grimaced. She was glad the deputy had left the room. "I take it there was no forensic evidence from her fingernails?"

"Nothing. But forensics are still working on the clothing and the teddy bears."

"Have you ever seen anything like this before?" Katie asked.

"Every case is a little bit different. Of course, I've seen bodies buried in the earth, and in boxes. But no, I can't say I've seen anything like this before."

It was the first time since Katie had met the doctor that he seemed to become melancholy, rather than filled with his seemingly usual positive attitude.

"Anything else about the condition of the body that could help with the investigation? Stomach contents? Potential poisons? Anything really."

"Nothing at this point. If I find anything, no matter how small, I will alert you immediately." The doctor began to pull the sheet back over the body. "Do you need to see anything else?"

Katie shook her head. "What about the identification made on the other girl?"

"Preliminary. We're checking dental records before alerting her parents." He sighed. "We want to make doubly sure after an incorrect identification we had about a year ago. Trust me, it wasn't good."

Katie thought how horrifying it would be to come and identify the wrong body.

"Did you receive information about the missing girl from Denise in records? The timeline seemed to match."

"Yes, I did."

"Can you tell me your preliminary ID?" she asked, though her gut already knew the answer.

Dean moved to the next gurney and opened a file folder. "Tammie Elizabeth Myers," he read.

Katie felt a chill as she remembered the gravesite. It was her computer searches and her instincts that had brought the girl to their attention.

Dr. Dean continued, "She was nine years old; went missing after leaving her aunt's house to go to the store." He pulled back the sheet and stepped away.

Katie briefly examined the body and realized immediately that decomposition was far more advanced than with Chelsea.

"How long has she been dead?" she asked.

"Not as long as the Compton girl," the doctor replied.

"But—" Katie began.

"I know what you're thinking," he interrupted. He gestured to the dead girl's limbs. "This is how decomposition looks after being buried for two to three years."

"How can you explain the difference between the two?" she asked.

"Quite simply, I can't."

Katie gave him a questioning look.

He smiled. "You have to understand that the process of decomposition isn't an exact science. Lots of things affect it: the temperature of the environment, the condition of the body when buried, how long the victim was deceased before burying, and so on."

"I see," she replied.

"I like your questions," the doctor said. "I can tell we're going to work well together. Most detectives hear what I have to say and then they're gone. And some don't even set foot in here."

"I admit, I wanted to run away fifteen minutes ago," she said.

"Just hang in there." He smiled. His relaxed and open demeanor made the experience of being in the morgue a little more tolerable.

"So what you're saying is you have to ask plenty of questions and you just might learn something of value."

"Maybe I should have that written on the wall in here. What do you think?"

"I think I shouldn't worry so much at this point about the exact time of death and concentrate on how and why these two girls were murdered."

Dr. Dean covered Tammie Myers' body and turned to look at Katie. "Detective Scott," he said, "I think you're going to make a first-rate detective. You've got a fantastic career ahead of you."

"You tell fortunes too?"

"Sometimes. A word of advice?"

"And what would that be?" Katie smiled.

"Don't let bullying detectives affect your mind, your drive, or your natural ability to find the killer. I have confidence in you and I know you'll figure out this case."

Katie was taken aback for a moment. Her mind spun in confusion and gratitude. Not many people had been nice or even cordial to her after she returned to town. Her suspicious nature thought that maybe the doctor wanted something from her—perhaps to cover up a mistake or procedural improprieties when the time called for it. She stared at him trying to get a handle on his motivation. Nothing came to mind.

He returned the file to the work counter and turned to Katie one more time. "I've been known to have a nice bedside manner in my job, but I've also been known to tell it exactly how it is." He paused. "Have a good day, Detective."

He walked out of the room, leaving her alone to ponder everything she had just heard and seen. It seemed to indicate the killer was more adept than she had previously thought.

CHAPTER 27

The early-morning air and lack of traffic made the run that much more satisfying. It was more than a feeling. It was an emotion so strong that it filled Katie's entire body with positivity and hope. She vowed that every morning when her schedule permitted she would run.

The two homicides filtered through her mind, backwards and forwards. She had memorized every detail from the interviews and the information she had received on the case.

Since she didn't have an office at the department, she continued to use her spare room at home. It was actually quite effective, with no interruptions or employee interaction. Just a quiet space to consider the investigation. It suited her needs perfectly.

The case continued to run its course in her mind.

Hand-made caskets. Woodworkers? Artisans? Locals?

The sun rose higher on the horizon and peeked through the trees; weak rays cascaded between leaves and branches. It was a shame the fog was closing in and would soon smother the sunlight.

Lonely rural places ending up as well-researched gravesites.

Crisp morning air nipped at her face.

Frustration. Hunting for the perfect prey. Abduction. Murder.

Her fingertips became numb as her arms pumped harder, increasing her speed.

Final resting places.
Cold cases.

Her feet pounded the ground and her pace quickened with strength and determination. Her footfall was a steady beat on the roadway and dirt paths.

Mrs. Stanley: subtle sexuality and her relationship with the Comptons. Improprieties. Perversions?

Her heart rate increased.

Brothers Malcolm and Rick Darren. Malcolm: lack of impulse control. Rick: stoic, steady, calculating, and strong. Protecting his brother—but at what cost?

Her lungs filled fully with oxygen and then exhaled out all the air. The cool outdoors stung her throat as she watched her breath swirl directly out in front of her.

She ran down a trail that would eventually lead her out onto the road again. Her legs never tired from carrying her to the next level.

The faces of everyone Katie had spoken to and interacted with sped through her mind in a logical stream. There were subtle details she hadn't noticed at the time, but now she reflected on them. Everything played a part in the investigation, no matter how small and insignificant.

The case was an intricate, living, breathing puzzle. It was not the usual kind of puzzle where you knew that every piece would eventually fit somewhere. In a homicide, it was up to the detective to figure out which pieces were not of importance and which pieces meant everything, eventually solving the mystery.

The sound of a revving engine stalled her repetitive thoughts about the case. A car was approaching from behind. She adjusted her position on the roadway, veering closer to the side to allow the driver to see her in the foggy atmosphere and drive around her if necessary.

But instead of slowing, the car increased its speed and continued to approach.

Katie turned and looked behind her, but she still couldn't see the vehicle. It didn't have any headlights ignited and it was difficult to make out its shape through the haze.

She slowed her pace and jogged in place.

The heavy fog, which had come in much quicker than she had anticipated, seemed to suffocate the morning light. Her view became muddled. Then a shapeless vehicle burst through the murk and revealed itself to be a dark truck accelerating at high speed. It was headed directly for her.

"Hey!" she yelled, trying to get the driver's attention. She assumed they couldn't see her. "Hey!" she yelled again, waving her arms.

The dark truck, which she now saw had no front license plate, jumped the side of the road, driving with one wheel on the pavement and the other in the soft dirt. It didn't swerve, but continued its course heading straight for Katie.

She glanced to her right, but there was nothing there but low-lying shrubs and trees. No paths or open areas to allow her to easily get out of the way. In any case, she guessed the vehicle would follow her if she tried to avoid it. There was only one option, and she hoped it would work.

She took a fighter's stance and stood her ground as the one-ton truck barreled directly at her. She couldn't see who was driving. There was no way of knowing if it was a man or a woman, or even a teenager, behind the wheel. It wasn't out of control; it appeared to be navigated by someone intent on one thing—running Katie down. She prayed she had made the correct decision.

Three seconds…

Her body trembled, but she stood her ground.

Two seconds…

She sucked in her breath and fought the fight-or-flight response.

One second…

She mustered every ounce of strength along with the determination of an army soldier and catapulted herself to the side of the road just before the truck reached her. She smashed through the low-lying brush, sharp branches scratching her body, and fell down a hillside studded with protruding rocks. Pain radiated up and down her body, compounding her previous scrapes with fierce discomfort. With a few moans and groans, she hit the bottom.

She waited, listening.

The truck hadn't slowed down, and now it was gone.

Silence kept her company. She sat for a few minutes to catch her breath and run through everything that had happened so she could relay it back at the police station.

Then she stood up, wobbly at first, and made the easy climb back up to the road.

One thing she knew for sure: someone didn't like her digging up new information on Chelsea Compton—or any of the missing girls' cases.

CHAPTER 28

Katie sat in the back of an ambulance while the attending paramedic checked her cuts and abrasions and took her vital signs. The more she thought about the incident, the more infuriated she became. Not because she'd been the target, but because she couldn't give any decent information about the truck.

No license plate. No identifying characteristics. No description of the driver. No video cameras in the vicinity to show the incident. Nothing to help identify this person who was intent on harming her—or at the very least, trying to scare her.

The only thing she could think of was obtaining evidence from the tire marks. There were several feet of precise and perfectly preserved indentations. It would help facilitate the investigation only when there were other tire marks to compare, but Katie thought it was best to have crime-scene technicians photograph them and create impressions.

"Hey," said Deputy McGaven, coming up to the back of the ambulance. "You okay?" He sounded concerned.

Katie smiled. "Yeah, just some bumps and bruises."

"Did you see the driver, or a license plate?"

She shook her head. "Unfortunately, no. And believe me, it's going to haunt me."

He gestured to the forensic technicians hovering over the evidence. "Great instincts to get the tire-mark impressions."

"McGaven?" she said.

"Yeah."

"You feeling okay this morning?"

"Yeah, why?"

Katie smiled. "Never mind."

The paramedic took the Velcro blood-pressure armband off her right bicep area and continued to wrap bandages around her forearms, which had seemed to take the brunt of her fall.

Katie began to feel the pulsating pain now, as her adrenalin had had plenty of time to cool off.

"That about does it," said the paramedic. "You should get checked out at the hospital."

"I'm fine, really," Katie stressed. "I've taken worse, that's for sure." She stood up. "McGaven, can you drive me to my house so that I can change?" she asked. Her legs felt fatigued and strangely rubbery. As she walked toward the crime-scene area, it was as if she was trudging through drying cement.

"You're not coming to work today," said the sheriff as he walked up behind her and the deputy.

He had heard about the truck incident from the police scanner. Most of the department had probably heard about it.

"I'm fine," Katie repeated.

"Take the day off, that's a direct order," he said. His voice softened a bit. "Just go home and rest. Forensics haven't completed their examinations of the caskets and clothing. And there might be more to come from Dr. Dean."

"Maybe I will rest for a couple of hours," she conceded. "I'll have my report to you as soon as—"

"The entire day," Sheriff Scott reminded her. Then, to McGaven, "Please take her home and make sure she stays there... and doesn't ditch you this time." He smiled, but the authority in his voice and posture was more like a warning to the deputy.

"Fine," stated Katie. The more she argued, the more tired she became. "Let's go," she ordered McGaven.

This was exactly what the killer wanted: for Katie to be out of the game. She knew this meant she was getting closer to solving the case.

CHAPTER 29

Once Deputy McGaven was sure Katie wouldn't pull a runner on him, and he'd played some high-energy ball with Cisco, he finally left her house. Katie studied the investigation notes on her wall one more time, trying to connect the leads. She decided to add the truck incident to the mix and see if it meant anything or pointed to someone—the Darren brothers, Mrs. Stanley, or even Detective Templeton. It was another puzzle piece that might prove to be helpful, a missing clue, or it might be one more thing for the trash. What was the motive? Was there a connection to Chelsea? Tammie Myers?

Cisco was stretched out on the kitchen floor, cooling off after his morning of fetching ball with the deputy. Within minutes, he was softly snoring and recharging his battery.

Katie had changed into warmer sweats and sipped some water with lemon. She'd thought she would be edgy and anxious after getting home, but to her surprise, she was tired and relaxed. She stretched out on the couch, and before she could run through the investigation in her mind, she fell asleep.

Cisco's barking and a loud knocking rattled her awake. She sat up and saw Chad standing at her door peering through the small upper window, while Cisco ran in circles demanding to meet the visitor.

Crap.

Katie knew that she looked like hell after her run and then taking another fall down a hillside.

"Quiet," she said to Cisco. The dog backed away and went to his down position.

She opened the door slowly.

"Hi," Chad said, holding up two bags. "I'm sorry, I realize now that I should have called you first."

"No, don't worry about it." She opened the door wider. "Please come in."

"How are you?" he asked.

"Oh, just the usual first official week as a detective. You know, taking insults from colleagues, interviewing lying witnesses, and having a truck try and run me down."

Chad laughed showing his appealing charm. "So you're saying I caught you on a good day?"

"You want some coffee?" she asked, walking toward the kitchen.

Chad took a step to follow and Cisco gave a low grumble. "Uh, maybe I should meet him first?"

"Cisco, here," Katie ordered.

The dog obediently circled around her and sat at her left side. She rubbed his head and scratched his ears, then made a gesture with her left hand in Chad's direction. Cisco made a circle around the visitor and caught an intriguing scent from one of the bags.

"Go ahead and pet him. You're fine."

Chad set the bags on the coffee table and slowly moved toward the dog. "Wow, you're a handsome boy with an intense look. Such a shiny black coat." He kneeled down in front of him. "I bet you have some stories to tell, Cisco."

"Unfortunately, he does," interjected Katie. "He likes you a lot."

Chad looked up. "Oh yeah?"

Katie fumbled around in the kitchen until she had the coffee maker perking away. "So what brings you here? Oh, wait. Did the sheriff call you?"

"Maybe."

Katie sighed. "He still treats me like a little girl."

Chad moved to the counter and took a seat. "Is that so bad?"

"Depends on how you look at it."

"And how do you look at it?"

"Well, for one, I'm all grown up. I've been a cop and I've been in the army. And I'm now working a homicide case."

"He'll always see you as a little girl."

Cisco had followed Chad into the kitchen. He really did seem to be taken with him.

Chad looked around. "You know, being here brings back such memories."

It made Katie a bit sad, but she agreed.

"I remember the barbecues you guys used to have. Your dad at the grill. And that party here when we were in junior high school."

"Yeah," she said. "I love this house. Even though there are both good and bad memories." She moved to the coffee pot and poured two cups. "Two sugars and cream?" she asked.

"Just cream. Trying to stay healthy."

Katie passed Chad a mug. "What's in the bags?"

"Ah, I was wondering if you'd noticed, you being a detective and all."

She smiled in spite of herself, and even though her arms throbbed in pain. "Nothing gets past me."

"I thought you might want to get out of the house and go on a picnic."

She stared at him, and some of the old feelings of connection came flooding back. She felt her face turn to a heated flush. Turning away, she said, "Depends on what's in the bag." She moved to a cupboard and took down a bottle of aspirin. Popping off the top, she swallowed two tablets.

Chad put both bags on the counter and began to empty them for Katie to see. "We have two sandwiches, one with turkey, bacon, and avocado. You used to love that."

"Still do."

"One meat-lover's sandwich: turkey, ham, and salami with provolone and white Cheddar cheese. Two cups of mixed greens and various nuts and seeds. Two servings of mixed seasonal fruits. And some of those wonderful home-made chips from Frazer's on Main Street."

"Wow, sounds like a food-channel advertisement." She laughed.

"Oh, and iced tea, my secret blend, plus two bottles of water."

"Anything else?" Katie raised her eyebrows and tried to see into the bags.

Chad quickly began to put the food away. "Nope, not going to tell you what's for dessert."

"So?" she said.

"So? So what do you think?"

"Are you inviting me?"

"I think I already did," he said, watching her closely.

Katie looked down and sipped her coffee. She wasn't sure if she wanted this thing to begin again between the two of them.

"Maybe I should have called first," he said with a little less enthusiasm.

"No, not at all. It's nice that…"

"That what?"

"I admit it would be nice to have some time off, even if it's only for an hour or two."

"Good," he said, and slapped his hand on the counter.

Cisco jumped up and barked.

"See." Chad gestured. "Even Cisco agrees."

"Fine, give me fifteen minutes to get changed." She hurried to her bedroom.

Katie rode in the passenger seat of Chad's Jeep, gazing out the window at the countryside. The model was much roomier that her own car and had more horsepower. Relieved that her aches and pains had subsided, she tried to ignore the anxious energy simmering in the background. It was usual when she entered into unknown areas for her response to be geared to fight or flight, but she made a pact with herself that it would change with time.

She saw a truck parked on the side of the road with the hood up.

"Hey, isn't that Mr. Rey?" asked Chad.

"I'm not sure," Katie replied, craning her neck to get a better vantage.

As Chad slowed his speed, a man wearing work overalls came around from the front of the truck.

"It is him," he said. He pulled the Jeep to the side of the road and parked. "He's had some tough times after his wife passed."

"Oh, I didn't realize that," Katie said. "I ran into him at the grocery store. Remember that fort he helped us build?"

"Yeah, I remember that fort, and then working with him building fences. I saved for my first car from that job."

"I think it's a flat tire," Katie suggested.

"Wait here, I'll go see if he needs some help." Chad unhooked his seat belt and jumped out of the car.

Katie and Cisco watched.

Within a few minutes, Chad returned and opened the back of the Jeep. Cisco bounced in his face, tail wagging. "Take it easy, buddy," Chad said.

"What's up?" Katie asked.

"He has a flat and his jack doesn't seem to be cooperating. I'm going to help him. It should take about ten minutes." He took his jack and headed back to the truck.

Katie waited patiently and recalled her childhood. It was something that made her happy, especially when she thought about her parents. Chad had been a good friend as far back as she could remember. It was difficult to think of a memory without him being a part of it.

He returned to the Jeep and replaced the jack, then climbed back into the driver's seat. "Okay, we're on the road again." He pulled away from the side of the road, giving a quick beep and a wave to Mr. Rey.

They drove in silence for a while. It wasn't an uncomfortable type of silence, but rather both of them seemed to be lost in their own thoughts.

"You're suddenly very quiet," said Chad. "Should I be worried?" He smiled.

"Just a lot on my mind," Katie replied.

Cisco moved back and forth behind them, unable to decide on the perfect seating position.

Chad watched Katie, and it was clear from his solemn expression that he was trying to sympathize with her. "Can I ask you a question?"

"I think so," she said.

"You don't have to answer."

"Go ahead. You obviously have something on your mind."

He made a sharp right turn and continued up a dirt track and then a gravel roadway away from the usual thoroughfares.

Katie recognized her surroundings. "I know where you're going."

"Thought you might."

"I haven't been here since high school."

"Well then you're in for a treat."

Katie remembered the area well. Many great times had been had there, including her first kiss. There were wonderful hiking trails and nice picnic areas with a valley view. She rubbed her hands together and let the happy memories flood her mind—at least for a short period. Sometimes it was difficult for her to let the positive things into her life. Her experiences had skewed her perception so that everything seemed on the verge of catastrophe. It was as if she had blocked out anything good in her life.

Finally she said, "You want to ask me about what it was like."

"Only if you feel comfortable."

"There's not much to tell. Every day was basically the same. The same duties. The same orders. Just different locations. The only thing that wasn't the same was whether you were going to die that day."

Her words hung in the air like static. She spoke with simple clarity, but the reality of what she said had a huge impact not only on Chad but on herself as well.

"Don't let anyone misinform you about why the military is still over there and why we need more personnel. If you have personal opinions on this war, it's fifty times worse than what you believe. I fear for this country."

Chad pulled into a parking area as Cisco jumped around behind him. "Wow," was all he could say.

"I'm sorry. Please forgive me. I haven't said anything like that out loud before." Katie looked fixedly at her hands.

"Hey," Chad said touching her arm. "You never have to apologize around me. Okay?"

She nodded, slightly embarrassed. "I don't want to get political or fatalistic on you."

"I hope you have someone to talk to about your experiences—a professional or even just a friend. Promise me that you'll always reach out, no matter what. Don't hold this kind of stuff inside."

"Okay." She nodded, taking in the scenery. She knew all too well what he was referring to.

"Remember all those stories when we were kids?" said Chad, trying to change the mood.

"What stories?"

"You know, about those Gold Rush towns that cropped up all over the area then mysteriously disappeared without a trace."

"Oh yeah, some people said that a great earthquake swallowed them up."

"If I had to guess," said Chad, "I would go with a meteor, then an earthquake—or both."

Katie laughed. "There's a lot of history here and up in the mountains; a lot of untold stories. Maybe one of those towns just up and moved." She breathed deeply, beginning to feel herself relax.

"I'm starving. Let's eat." Chad climbed out of the car, followed closely by Cisco.

Katie opened her door and stepped out too. It would be good to sit in the warmth of the sunshine and soak up some of her hometown. She laughed as she watched Cisco trying to get to the two bags with their lunch inside.

"He's not going to leave you alone," she said.

Chad ran around jokingly in circles with Cisco in tow, then made his way to a picnic table with a view of the valley. "What do you think?"

Katie looked around. It was peaceful as well as beautiful. They were the only ones in the picnic area. Two other cars were parked, but their owners were most likely on one of the hiking trails.

Chad began to unload the bags, laying out a tablecloth, plastic plates, utensils, and napkins.

"You're very organized," Katie said.

"Ha! Only when I want to be."

"It's beautiful here. It's just what I needed after the week I've had." She took a seat at the picnic table and watched Chad unpacking the food. She hadn't been hungry, but now, looking at the spread, her stomach grumbled.

Chad pulled out a small roll of tin foil.

"What's that? Some kind of special sandwich spread?" Katie asked.

"Nope. I came prepared." He unrolled the foil. "It's a little bit of leftover prime rib with gravy for Cisco." He leaned down and put the feast on the ground. "Here you go, buddy."

"You do realize you're never going to get rid of him now." Katie smiled and watched Cisco lap up the meat mixture.

"I love animals, especially dogs. I'd like to get one again."

"That's right, you had huskies when we were kids," she remembered.

"I love big dogs that like to be outdoors and that I can take anywhere." He sat down, raised a thermos and announced, "Here's to friendship and all the great adventures ahead."

Katie took a sip from her own thermos, and then another. "Wow, this is fantastic. I think it's the best iced tea I've ever had." The weight she had been carrying around ever since she returned home had been lifted—not completely, but enough to give her pause and allow her to relax. She couldn't help but smile as she took another bite of sandwich.

"Ms. Scott, you're thinking about something pleasant. Want to let me in on it?" Chad said.

"I was just thinking how nice it is to be home, in all the places I love. Thanks for bringing me here today."

"My pleasure," he replied. "I can imagine how difficult these homicides are."

"Yeah, it's really tough. But what's more difficult is the detective in charge."

Chad stuffed another piece of sandwich in his mouth. "Templeton, right?"

"Yeah," she said quietly. "He just doesn't get that we need to work together, but we don't see eye to eye."

"Wait until everything shakes out. I'm sure he'll calm down."

Katie turned around to face the incredible valley of trees that extended as far as the eye could see. She took a deep breath. Cisco huddled to the side of her leg and looked out as well, alert and ears pitched forward.

Chad got up from his position and joined her on the bench. "I haven't been up here in a while. I've been too busy trying to get on full-time at the fire department. It is truly beautiful here."

Katie turned to him. "What's the situation?"

He took a deep, somewhat disappointed breath. "It all comes down to budget."

Katie nodded; she understood all about budget restrictions at the police department, and it even affected the army too.

"So I've been working a few hours as an ambulance driver and some shifts up at the fire department. The sheriff's K9 unit asked me if I wanted to help out with training." He leaned in and said in a comical tone, "That generally means they need another decoy for the dogs to chase."

She laughed. "No wonder Cisco likes you."

"Oh, I forgot. The morgue also needs someone to fill in as a body guy."

"A what?"

"That's what they call the guy who picks up dead bodies and brings them to the morgue. And that would about round out my week as I wait on budget and politics to get a full-time position."

"You'll never get bored—just mauled, burned, and acquainted with a lot of dead people."

"Go ahead, laugh it up. You're living your dream job."

"I don't know what will happen after this case is closed. I'm still on leave from Sacramento PD and I just don't know…"

Chad shrugged. "I'm sure your uncle isn't going to let someone like you get away—he has something planned, I'm sure."

"I don't know. Even he still has someone to answer to."

That evening, Katie decompressed, trying to empty her busy mind. She had a long, hot bath, and went to bed at a reasonable hour. Just before she turned off the light, she took out her journal and opened it. She reread her first entry. Then she picked up her pen and slowly began to write.

Wednesday, 2230 hours
It was a surprising day of rest for me today. I went on a picnic with Chad. I had so many memories (mostly good)

and familiar feelings flying around in my mind, but in the end I was able to relax without any anxiety issues or panic attacks. I lowered my guard and opened up to Chad. I'd never have done that before. I don't expect anything from him, but I do care about him. I don't feel like I'm ready for a serious relationship, though I'm not sure if Chad would be that special person anyway. I'm taking my uncle's advice to let time take its course.

Am I healing? I hope I can live up to what I've been through and accomplished so far. My thoughts are still constantly with my army teammates: my sergeant, and Billy and Chris. I hope they're doing okay—I touched base with them in an email but haven't heard from them in a while. We are all broken. Forever changed. We are survivors.

CHAPTER 30

The temperature outside had dropped several degrees overnight, but that didn't stop the kids from Pine Valley Elementary School walking or riding their bikes to school. It was Thursday and the last day of the week for them; Friday was a parent-and-teachers' conference. All the kids were extra hyper and looking forward to a fun outing. There was supposed to be an assembly too, and that would mean fewer classes.

Dena Matthews was particularly excited because she would be going to the amusement park in Sacramento this weekend. She could almost taste the food: cotton candy, chocolate-dipped cones, and anything on a stick she desired.

She'd begged her mom endlessly to let her meet her friends at the park near the pond and cycle to school. The last few times there had been a bike-to-school day she wasn't allowed to participate, but she finally pleaded hard enough that her mom permitted her to go.

She put on her backpack, jumped eagerly onto her light-blue bicycle and rode down the driveway. The cool morning air chilled her face, but she didn't care. Dressed in dark jeans, a blue sweatshirt, and her favorite sneakers, she pedaled as fast as she could. She was going to be early, and knew she would have to wait for her friends, Carrie and Jessica. But that was okay, because she wanted to check out the fountain and the pond. It was her favorite place whenever she visited the park.

She coasted down her street and cut across a neighboring one, which then took her in a roundabout way to the park. She took that route because it was mostly downhill and she could cycle with comfort.

A couple of cars passed her slowly.

She noticed the neatest yards and others that were in need of a gardener. Some houses were blue, some light gray, and others yellow. She couldn't make up her mind which ones were the prettiest.

An older woman with a red scarf walking a small shaggy white dog made her way around the corner. Dena followed on her bike, gently pressing the brakes, and said loudly, "Cute dog." She rode on until she made a sharp left turn into the park next to a large community building. From there, she dismounted and pushed her bicycle along the walking trail. It was fairly deserted; quieter than she had ever seen it, in fact. It didn't matter, though. She would wait patiently for her friends.

She looked at her watch. It read 7.35 a.m.; her friends had said they would be there by 7.45. She rolled her bicycle to the side of the path and flipped down the kickstand. The pond had fish and the gentle waterfall was working. It was beautiful.

She heard a car pull into the parking lot but didn't turn her head. She expected her friends to arrive any moment. She leaned over a bit further, closer to the water. Several koi fish swam back and forth. They were beautiful and she couldn't take her eyes off them. She wanted a fish tank, but her mom said it was too much trouble. Maybe when she got older, she'd told her.

Dena smiled and leaned against the rocky outline of the pond. She didn't have a care in the world; she was always happy, except when her little brother annoyed her. But that wasn't too often. She dipped her hand into the water, dangling her fingers with glee. Immediately the fish were alerted and came up trying to feed off the tips. She laughed. It tickled. The fish opened their mouths wide. She continued to run her fingers through the cool water.

In a brief instant, like the turning of a page, a man had rapidly approached Dena with a rag in his left hand. His weathered work boots were silent against the path. In four long strides he was standing over her. She was unaware of his presence as she concentrated on the fish in the pond.

In a perfected move, he grabbed her with his right arm, pressing the fabric against her face.

She uttered no sound.

He swung her up, holding her close to him as if he was hugging his own child after a long day in the park. He spoke quietly into her ear in case someone happened to glance at him.

No one saw the man approach Dena.

No one saw the man put Dena into his truck.

And no one saw the truck drive away and blend into traffic.

The light-blue bicycle remained behind.

Dena was gone.

CHAPTER 31

Katie arrived early at the forensics division. It was cold and she had dressed in her dark gray suit, still sporting the boots that had clicked loudly at the morgue. She had organized her questions in an official-looking notebook, and made sure her detective's badge was securely clipped to her waistband next to her gun. She wanted to speak with the forensic supervisor, John Blackburn, about the emails she had received early that morning clarifying some interesting details.

She didn't know what to expect from John; she'd received both positive and negative reactions from those involved in the investigation, and it felt like she was riding a roller coaster. McGaven was going to be late that morning and said he would meet up with her later.

Walking down the long windowless hallway, Katie reached the door to the forensics area. A small camera was fixed above the doorway, aimed at a forty-five-degree angle toward anyone standing in her exact position. She wondered if she appeared distorted due to the tiny size of the camera, and the fact that she was looking awkwardly up at it.

She pressed the button and waited. She expected to hear it ring like a doorbell or alarm buzzer, but no sound emanated that she could hear. She pressed it again with the same response. Nothing. She stepped backward two paces and continued to wait.

The lock disengaged and the door popped open—a faint sound of air discharged.

Katie pushed open the door and stepped inside. She didn't see anyone; just another long hallway.

Click.

The door shut automatically behind her. She expected to see one of the technicians: Jamie or Don, whom she knew from her run-in with the truck. She walked down the hallway, past several closed doors, and eventually ended up in a large open space—the central forensic hub.

No one was around.

She felt the air recirculating and blowing gently above her, and there was an extremely faint hum that she figured was the air-conditioning system at work.

She decided to say something, "Hello?"

Again there was no answer. Someone had to have buzzed her inside and know she was there. She wondered if it was a kind of initiation to test her reactions, and smiled in spite of herself.

"Hello?" she called out again.

There were two open doors. One room was obviously an examination area, where there were many computers humming away. The other had several desks and resembled a doctor's office. She leaned in to see if anyone was inside, but it was empty.

She was going to grab a seat in the main area and wait when she heard footsteps approaching. Around the corner came a muscular man with colorful tattoos on both arms, dressed casually in jeans, a loose black T-shirt, and work boots. His dark hair was cropped and he was clean-shaven. She immediately recognized him as the man she had run into in the file room.

He saw her standing there but didn't immediately greet her. There was something about his intensely blue eyes and his manner that intrigued her. For his part, he seemed to have assessed her in a few quick moments, taking care to observe her face and demeanor.

"Hi, I'm Detective Scott," she said at last, in an effort to break the weird silence.

"John Blackburn," was his response.

"Is this a good time to talk about the Compton and Myers cases?" she asked, noticing that her voice was higher than usual.

"Of course, Detective," he replied, walking to a closed door. "I take it you've never been to the forensic division before?"

"I'm that transparent?" she said, trying to lighten the stilted mood.

For the first time, he cracked a small smile. "This way," he directed, and opened the door, which led into a large examination room with four white tables. Two of them held the coffins; each had been meticulously taken apart and inventoried. The other two contained the girls' clothes, the teddy bears, and some miscellaneous pieces of fabric.

The room was dim except for the overhead lights, and large magnifying glasses were attached to each table. A strange hum buzzed from the light sources, giving Katie a dull headache.

She was mesmerized by the organization of the evidence, perfectly set in viewing order.

"This really is your first visit," Blackburn said, watching her reaction.

"Yes, the only official area I've been to previously has been the morgue."

"Well, you're in for an education." He walked to the first table. "But from what I've heard, it wouldn't surprise me if you excel in this area as well."

Katie thought that was a strange comment coming from the forensics supervisor. It made her a little bit nervous and slightly self-conscious as she realized what a rookie she really was.

She put down her notebook and quickly pulled out her notes.

"Here, let me take a look at those," he said and took the pages from her. He quickly read over them, nodding a few times. "Well, I can see you actually paid attention to my reports."

"Of course," she asked. "Why does everyone keep saying that?"

"Detective Templeton doesn't seem too interested in them. But that's been his usual M.O. when working cases. Not the easiest guy to chat with."

Katie laughed, even though she knew it was unprofessional. "I'm sorry."

"No need to apologize. I've been dealing with him for a while now. It's just a shame that his arrogance and ingrained insecurities are now directed at you."

"You know about that?" she asked.

John Blackburn smiled. It was genuine, making his entire face light up. "Of course. Everyone knows about how you put him in his place. Don't be so surprised, Detective. You were the one who found the bodies, remember. An amazing feat. And that must really frost his balls."

"To say the least. I don't think I have many friends around here," she said quietly.

"Don't sell yourself short. You have more than you think."

Katie smiled and retrieved a pen to make notes. "Okay, take me through the coffins."

She moved to the first table, standing to the right of the supervisor, and waited patiently for him to give her the overview.

"Well, there is the obvious," he began. "These coffins were specially made—hand-crafted by someone who took great care in constructing them. You won't find anything like these through the usual means. Each one was made for a specific girl."

"How so?" she asked.

"They aren't exactly the same dimensions; the one for the Myers girl was three and three-quarter inches longer and one quarter inch wider."

"Was the wood from the same source?"

"Yes. From what we can tell from the grain and consistency, it was from the same oak tree." He moved to a computer behind them. "Take a look." He navigated to a page that showed the wood from the two coffins magnified two hundred times. "You can see they have varied characteristics, making them unique."

"Is it a match?"

"It's never a one-hundred-percent match, but the individual characteristics are similar enough that the likelihood of them being from the same tree is a solid ninety, ninety-five percent in my opinion. You can't get any better than that."

Katie thought about it for a moment as she gazed at the magnification showing the intricate grains like the veins of a living tree. "Would you be able to make a comparison if we found wood at a potential suspect's place?"

"Absolutely."

"Did you find anything on the wood, like fingerprints, fibers, or fluids?"

He moved to the tables as he explained, "There was nothing detectable on it; just a standard stain with four or five layers. We found a couple of brush hairs, but they're too common to compare to anything specific."

"What about the fabric used to line the coffins?"

"Nothing that could be compared, I'm afraid. But the type of silk combination used isn't a common type of fabric you can buy at chain stores. It would have to be specially ordered online or through other means."

"I see," said Katie. "Both coffins had the same fabric?"

"Yes. It's been dyed pink from natural organic sources." He watched with interest as she jotted down some note.

"Is there anything unusual about the coffins, or anything else that could be used as a comparison if we had something to compare it to?"

"I'm sorry, we searched every inch with several different light sources and there was nothing."

Katie sighed in disappointment.

"We're still testing for certain organic and non-organic qualities." He moved to the other examining tables. "I may have something for you later. We took our time searching the graves and the dirt around them, and if we do find anything, we can be pretty sure it's from the perpetrator."

"How long did you search?"

"As long as it took. You can't rush a crime scene. And these particular circumstances are very unusual."

"Is that the usual protocol?" she asked, surprised and impressed.

"No. But with the weather conditions and the unstable nature of the hillside, anything could have happened. I wanted to make sure we were able to find whatever was there. We sifted a lot of dirt and searched for any other potential secret areas nearby."

Katie raised her eyebrows in admiration. "Wow."

"What would you have done in my position?"

She nodded in silent agreement and then surveyed the clothes. "Anything to report about the girls' dresses or the teddy bears?"

"The dresses were made from lower-end fabric that can be purchased anywhere. They were hand-sewn."

"The bears?"

"Interesting. They weren't manufactured by a company but made individually by someone who's not a professional. We're trying to track down how many locations sell this type of fabric. It isn't faux fur; more of an all-purpose material that would be used for towels or lightweight blankets."

Katie looked at the work. The seams of the dresses had been sewn by hand with a needle and thread. She saw where the end of the thread had been knotted. The stitches were all the same length.

"Anything foreign on them?" she asked, hoping for something to go on.

"We found three hairs, but they were all from the girls. There are no fibers, bodily fluids, or anything we can determine to be foreign."

Katie was becoming more disappointed by the minute. She needed more to go on; something—anything—that would move the investigation forward.

"There is something," Blackburn said.

She looked up from the evidence.

"We found organic matter: nitrogen, phosphorus, potassium, calcium, magnesium, zinc, sulfur, chlorine, boron, and iron mixed with iodide, damascenone, and rose oxide." He watched her reaction.

Katie thought about what he had told her. "Plants, flowers… oh wait, are you saying roses?"

"Yes. Red roses to be specific. How did you know that?"

"I read about a case that involved roses at the crime scene. Were there any roses in the coffins?"

"No."

"So that means the clothes or teddy bears came in contact with them. Outdoor roses or from a florist shop?"

"That is a mystery for you, Detective. Like I said, we're still running tests on some sediment and other organic materials, but don't hold your breath."

Katie wrote a few more notes. "I won't take up any more of your time Mr. Blackburn."

"Please, Detective, everyone calls me John."

"Everyone calls me Katie," she replied. "Though I'm sure my colleagues have more colorful names for me."

John laughed.

"So I guess I'm looking for an interesting pile of wood, rare silk fabric, and someone who makes custom teddy bears—and of course, all that has been in contact with red roses." Katie let out a sigh.

"If you have any questions, at any time, day or night, please feel free to call or text." He handed her a business card.

"Thank you, John." She took the card and slipped it into her pocket.

*

Katie left the forensics division with plenty of information, but nothing that she could run with. She was supposed to meet Deputy McGaven in the parking area, and was surprised to see him waiting patiently for her.

"Learned a few things," she said.

"Good. Update me."

"Ready?" she asked, and unlocked the vehicle.

"Yep," he replied. "So what did you think?"

"About what?"

"C'mon, you don't know?" He was clearly amused.

"I'm not going to play guessing games. I'm still trying to digest everything I've just learned."

McGaven laughed.

Katie hadn't seen him in such a chipper mood before. She stared at him.

"Okay, I thought, you being a detective and all, you would figure it out."

"What are you talking about?" she asked again.

"I thought you soldiers could all sniff each other out."

"What are you saying, that Blackburn was a soldier?"

"Not just any soldier; he was special forces for twelve years—you know, Navy SEALs? He can kill someone before they even take a breath." McGaven was obviously incredibly impressed by the forensic supervisor's abilities.

Katie thought back to her immediate sense of Blackburn when she first met him; his attention and self-discipline had been clearly evident. In her mind he was a perfect person to run the forensic division.

CHAPTER 32

"Why are we here?" asked McGaven as they walked up to the Haven barn. "He committed suicide. The way I hear it, Detective Templeton is saying it's possible Price killed those girls. But he has a fixation on the Comptons for some reason—trying to make a connection to the Myers girl."

"If that's his opinion, then every victim's family had better worry," muttered Katie. She thought Templeton was flying all over the map and not making sound investigative moves based on evidence.

The deputy walked around the barn, going through the motions, but his mind wasn't really there because as far as he was concerned, everything was already done. He stood and stared at a large broken spider web.

The barn doors gently opened and shut with the breeze. When they were open, light spilled inside, cutting off when they closed, giving a strobe-light effect.

"So you don't think Price had anything to do with Chelsea Compton's disappearance and murder?" the deputy asked almost as an afterthought, still looking at the broken web.

"I didn't say that," Katie said.

Cracks in the roof and gaps in the beams sifted sunlight throughout the barn. The far corners also oozed light.

"So what made him kill himself less than twenty-four hours after the bodies were found?" he insisted, not looking directly at her.

Katie climbed up to the loft area; she moved carefully and made sure she didn't miss anything. "There are several possible reasons."

"Like?"

"The obvious one would be that he was the killer and didn't want to get caught, which is the easiest to conclude—as long as you don't mind having no corroborating evidence. Another would be that his mental illness finally took its toll on him. And…" She stopped.

McGaven turned and looked upward. "And what?"

Katie had noticed unusual scrape marks on the wooden boards—short, disconnected—and then deep indentations. She took out her cell phone and documented them to the best of her ability. Returning the phone to her pocket, she said, "There's something odd up here. These marks in the wood seem recent."

"What kind of marks?" he asked.

"Like drag marks. It's impossible to tell if they're from something like tools, or if they're from a human."

Her words hung in the air. There was something about Terrance Price's death that bothered her—tugged at her intuition. It was too convenient. Too opportune. There was something more than the obvious suicide. It felt staged, as if it was something everyone was *supposed* to see.

She stood up and followed the trail. "They lead over here."

McGaven stood underneath Katie, next to the broken cobweb. "Anything else?" he asked, now completely attentive.

"I think it's possible—I mean very possible—that Price was murdered because he was…" Katie's voice trailed off. She'd realized the significance of the barn suicide.

Could it be that simple? Was it possible?

"What? What do you think?" probed the deputy.

She explained slowly. "Price was possibly an accomplice, and although he didn't witness Chelsea being taken, he knew it was going to happen. It's just a theory—don't hold me to it."

McGaven stepped back as if the idea was plausible. "So you think, based on your…" He couldn't finish the sentence, because a loud noise rattled the barn with excessive force.

Katie's first thought was that it was a thunder storm crashing down on top of the building. She immediately climbed down and ran for the entrance, followed closely by McGaven. But when she got there, she found the doors were secured. Both of them tried to open them, but they still wouldn't budge.

McGaven took out his service revolver to shoot the hinges.

"No," ordered Katie. "No," she repeated. She cocked her head to one side and smelled a familiar odor.

McGaven gave her a quizzical look.

Katie didn't waste any time explaining; she grabbed hold of the deputy's jacket and pulled him with her across the barn.

Before they had even reached the far side, a loud explosion rocked the ground and deafened them. They both dropped down and covered their heads, waiting for the next assault. For a moment Katie was back on the battlefield. Vivid memories assailed her mind. Smells that she would never forget. Then she snapped back to reality.

Smoke filtered into the barn, followed by an intense crackling noise.

McGaven peered up. "What the…?"

"A bomb."

"A what?" he yelled. Clearly his hearing had been temporarily impaired.

"Nothing too catastrophic; most likely a pipe bomb," she surmised. "C'mon, we have to get out of here now."

Katie stood, wavering slightly, dizzy, head pounding, and began to look for an escape route. The smoke was building, making it difficult to breathe. She coughed several times. "Cover your nose and mouth," she ordered.

McGaven did as she instructed, pulling his shirt over the lower part of his face, and they moved back toward the front, where flames were already licking into the barn.

"There's only one way out!" Katie yelled, choking and coughing.

She climbed back up the wooden ladder to the loft with McGaven at her heels and headed to the window area, but she struggled to open the access.

"Get back!" McGaven yelled. He fired several rounds into the hinges holding the opening closed. At first the shots had no effect, then the hinges buckled before finally giving way. There had been small reinforcement-steel pieces and miscellaneous hardware forged into place.

Katie glanced down to the main area and saw that the flames were approaching fast—in minutes they would be completely engulfed. Frantically they pried, scraped, and battled to get access through the opening. But she began to feel her vision fade due to her incessant coughing, and her legs and arms weakened like jelly.

Finally McGaven managed to clear their escape route. As Katie peered through the opening at the drop, her stomach seized up and she closed her eyes. The deputy shook her hard, rattling her teeth. "Stay awake!" he yelled. His strong grip and bulky build made him seem like a Goliath.

The flames were touching the floor of the loft and inching their way towards them like angry tentacles.

McGaven shook Katie again. "Look," he rasped. "There are a couple of bales of hay next to the lumber that haven't caught fire yet. We can reach them."

Katie nodded. She couldn't speak. Her throat was dry, tightening her vocal cords.

McGaven held her by her waist and gently moved her toward the extreme edge of the loft before turning her body in the direction of the hay below.

Katie struggled to keep her eyes open. She wanted to lie down and sleep—push everything out of her mind.

"Katie!" he yelled. "Feet first, tuck and roll. You can do this—it's easy for you."

She focused intently on the spot where she was going to land. She remembered a time when her squad had to escape a building before a rocket was launched. The sound when it hit the structure was unlike anything she had ever heard in her life.

She snapped back to the present, hearing McGaven yelling instructions and encouragement in the same breath. Intense heat crept up behind her along with huge puffs of black smoke.

"Go!" he yelled.

The free-falling sensation was briefly calming, like being protected under the wing of a bird. The wind smacked Katie's face and revitalized her just before she hit the stack of hay. Instinctively she tucked and rolled several times before stopping. The impact wasn't as bad as she'd initially feared.

Within seconds, her peripheral vision caught the blur of McGaven following her down, but as she watched in horror, he hit the edge of the bale and crashed to the ground, where he lay in a crumpled heap.

No.

The battlefield of horrors gripped her soul. The flames and smoke were closing in on them. She crawled toward the unconscious deputy and grabbed hold of his jacket, then slowly dragged him, inch by painful inch, away from the blazing barn.

When they were a safe distance away, she retrieved her firearm, which was still secured in her holster, and took cover. It occurred to her that whoever had tried to kill them inside the barn was probably somewhere nearby. If they had gone to this much trouble already, it could be assumed that they would finish the job.

McGaven muttered. Katie looked down at him. He was coming round.

"C'mon, we need to get to that shed over there," she instructed. It was the best place under the circumstances to shield them from potential harm and keep watch for the enemy.

Once they'd moved to the storage shed, Katie's senses began to return to normal. Despite the fatigue, adrenalin kept her body rigid and alert enough to make conscious decisions.

The barn continued to burn; flames engulfed the structure, and beams fell like dominoes.

For the first time, Katie realized that the bomb that had exploded was their car. Questions flooded her mind.

When was the bomb set?

Before they'd arrived at the Haven farm? While they were in the barn? When?

She took out her cell phone and dialed. "This is Detective Katherine Scott, badge number 3692. Explosion. Barn on fire. Two officers down at the Haven farm, Rio and Apple Road. Send fire, ambulance, and police. Unknown assailant could still be at location. Repeat, unknown assailant could still be at property."

She ended the call.

McGaven sat next to her, leaning up against the shed wall and surveying the yard outside.

Katie gently squeezed his arm. "Backup is on its way. We can hold our position until they get here."

CHAPTER 33

He stomped his work boots on a dilapidated rubber mat before entering the back door of his house. Smelling of smoke, he hurried inside the sanctuary of his home. Dirt and debris scattered along the wooden floors with his footsteps. He was still angry at what she had made him do. Many people despised her but were afraid to say anything because she had fought in Afghanistan. She was a soldier, a veteran. And now she was a detective in the sheriff's office.

Who cares?

It was the ones who respected her—even liked her—who provoked him to violence, who had him fuming. He would burn down the entire town to get those lost souls to listen to reason or face the consequences.

After quickly changing his clothes for clean ones from the laundry basket sitting on the sofa, the man returned to the kitchen and paused, unsure what to do next.

He was alone.

He only had a few minutes before he needed to get back to work so that someone wouldn't notice he was gone. Grabbing a drinking glass from the cupboard, he watched as his hand shook with anger slowly turning to rage.

Trying not to participate in the emotional baggage that most people struggled with, he filled the glass with tap water. As he concentrated on the swirling of the liquid and the tiny bubbles vying for the surface and then dissipating into the clear, perfect drink, he felt his pulse return to normal. He drank the entire ten ounces in one breath.

He couldn't stop thinking about the search—it was what fed him physically and mentally.

It was what he loved.

He knew he needed to maintain his focus and keep his emotions in check to sustain his work—not his autopilot day job, but his calling. If he wasn't careful, someone would find out his secret; someone would know.

Breathing in deeply, he exhaled the frustrations of the day. With each inhale and exhale, the triumphant soldier resurfaced again.

He carefully rinsed the glass and set it in the drying rack.

Glancing to a small table, he opened a drawer where a photograph of a smiling thirteen-year-old girl lay in a special silver frame. Memories flooded back to him. Sometimes those memories were followed by the exact feelings he had had when he received the phone call. It was nearly fifteen years ago now, but it still felt like yesterday. There had been no warning, and no doubt of the horror. His baby girl had simply been in the wrong place at the wrong time.

He would never forget her lying in the morgue, brutally beaten, stabbed, and raped. The image would never leave his memory.

No one knew about his daughter. She was gone. He would make sure that no little girl would ever have to suffer the horrors his daughter had.

Never.

It was time to complete the next step; to perform his special check.

He walked to a narrow door in the kitchen, gripped the handle, and turned the knob, looking at the wooden stairs leading down into the basement. It was often used as a fruit cellar to store things that required a stable temperature between fifty-five and sixty-five degrees. It was a place hidden from most. Sounds didn't carry. Most of all, it made him feel good being there.

Descending the stairs, he heard the third step make the familiar creak, and then down, down to the bottom. The cool temperature leveled his rage and steadied his pulse. The familiar musty odor caught his senses, and forced him to remember one of the cold nights his father had made him stay in the basement until he was sorry for what he had done. He had said he was sorry, but he wasn't. He was never sorry for anything he did.

As he stood in the darkness, he knew that nothing and no one could ever again make him say he was sorry.

Focus.

He walked to the end of the cellar and turned to his right. He hesitated. A single, unidentified door greeted him. There was no handle and no indication how to open it. To most, it would seem like a closet or another area for storage; perhaps a place where the electrical breakers were located.

He retrieved a key from a Mason jar in the corner. He kept it away from his crowded key ring to make sure no one could accidentally find it. Inserting it into the camouflaged lock—higher than the usual key insert and merely resembling a gouge in the door—he turned it.

The locking mechanism clicked and the man pushed the door inward and flipped a light switch. A low motorized noise engaged and set off a well-tuned reaction.

One…

Two…

Three…

Four specialized fluorescent lights ignited overhead and brightened the room's low ceiling. Every corner was illuminated, casting away all shadows to reveal an organized, compartmentalized room.

One area appeared to be a primitive workshop where large rectangular wooden boxes and bolts of fabric waited. Several small plastic containers containing thread, needles, and ribbon were stacked in the corner.

Along one wall, various clear and dark glass bottles adorned with skull-and-crossbones warnings cluttered a work table. Bags of saline and several different types of pain medications, paralyzing solutions, and sedatives sat neatly at the end. Stainless-steel instruments from a doctor's office neatly filled a black satchel, sterilized and ready to be used. It was an ideal playground for a mad scientist in training.

Next to the surgeon's tools, there was a laptop computer.

A rolling garment rack was pushed into the corner, a few small dresses hanging from it.

As the man slowly sauntered through his workshop filled with ominous items, he ran his hand along the meticulously clean countertops. It surprised him every time he performed this routine gesture that he felt an electric shock through his fingers and up his arm. It was more than a static reaction. It was life given over to him.

He stroked his fingers across a custom table carefully crafted from assorted leftover lumber found at various locations, complete with shelves and drawers underneath. The flat surface measured three feet by five. The beautifully stained and varnished top was one of his most prized accomplishments.

The deep vastness of color.

The brilliant sheen that glowed from every angle.

The amazing depth and density still caused his heart to flutter. It was more than a suitable location for his work; it was his center of creation.

Lying on top of the table, secured with heavy straps generally used to move furniture, was his latest victim. Her long brown braids lay next to her shoulders; her pretty, blue cotton top was smooth and clean.

Dena Mathews would never know what had happened, or the identity of the man who had snatched her at the park.

He leaned closer to her. Her flawless skin accentuated her petite features. Her eyes remained closed. Her chest moved subtly up and down.

"Little girl sleeping," whispered the man as if he was reciting a nursery rhyme. It was his favorite moment. He hummed and then whispered personal encouragements into her ear—he knew she could hear him.

He lifted her eyelid and saw that she was in a deep medicated sleep. Letting his hand linger against her face, he remained a little while longer just to admire her.

"Sleep, sleep…" he said in a loving tone. "I will be back later to complete the task." He smiled slowly as he allowed his lips to gently touch her cheek. "Sleep for now…"

CHAPTER 34

With her eyes closed and taking deep steady breaths of oxygen, Katie began to feel alert and stronger. She could still hear the sound of the explosion in her mind. It was something that changed you, skewed your understanding of the world, but strangely made you feel more alive. Not because you'd barely survived but because you lived another day.

She opened her eyes to see several people standing close. Her uncle and two police officers stared at her with solemn expressions.

She removed the oxygen mask and said, "I'm fine, really." Her voice was strangely hoarse and anxious.

She could see firefighters battling the blaze, which had jumped to other structures on the property but had luckily left the Havens' house untouched.

Voices yelled out. Water drenched what was left of the barn.

"I want her taken to the hospital to be checked out," ordered Sheriff Scott.

Katie shook her head adamantly. "No, I'm fine. I don't need to waste their time."

"I don't think that's wise," the sheriff countered.

Katie stood up and looked around until she spotted McGaven receiving attention from another ambulance. His face was pale, due to shock, but he was awake and talking with the paramedics as they tended to the various cuts on his arms and face.

Katie began to walk toward him. Immediately, she stumbled. One of her boot heels had snapped off. "Shit," she said.

"You alright?" the two officers said in unison.

She pulled her boot off and laughed. "I hated these boots anyway."

She continued to limp toward McGaven. When he saw her, he just stared, and then he smiled, his entire face lighting up.

"Hey, you okay?" she asked.

He nodded and looked at her foot. "Guess the boot didn't make it."

They both laughed, causing a few people to look curiously in their direction.

Katie stepped closer to him. "Thank you," she said. "I don't know what would have happened if you weren't here."

"You know what they say."

Katie wasn't sure what he meant.

"You never leave a partner behind."

She was overwhelmed with emotion. She wasn't going to break down and cry, but she had promised herself that whenever something of this magnitude happened, she would make sure she told the person how much they mattered.

She hugged McGaven tight for a few seconds. "Thank you," she said again, more quietly.

Sheriff Scott had followed Katie over. "If you feel up to it, we need your account of what happened, while it's fresh in your minds."

"Absolutely," Katie replied. "Where's Detective Templeton?"

"He had some personal business and will join us later."

The sheriff moved around the crime-scene area as he talked on his cell phone. Katie couldn't quite hear what he said, but she assumed it had to do with ATF and Homeland Security.

She saw the crime-scene van approach the property and park a short distance away. She wondered if John Blackburn would be attending the scene. It didn't take long to get her answer as he jumped out of the van and gave orders to his two technicians.

A deputy with *Sanders* on his nametag walked up to Katie with a notebook. "You ready?" he asked.

"Give me a few minutes, please," she answered distractedly, and walked away.

He nodded and settled down to wait for her.

She hurried to the CSI van, where John was organizing metal suitcases and inventorying canisters to collect the pieces of bomb fragments.

He turned toward her, not overly surprised to see her but calm despite the high-stakes conditions. "Glad to see that you're okay," he said with genuine concern. He pointed at her foot, "A fatality during the fire?" He quickly pulled on a white hazmat-type suit.

"Yes, but nothing was left behind," she said, holding up her broken boot. "I just wanted to let you know that when we heard the explosion, it seemed to come from the barn doors. I realize now, of course, that it was the car, but the intense heat in the beginning was most likely at the doors."

"Thanks, we'll make sure we search that area thoroughly once the fire is out."

"Okay," Katie said, and turned to walk away.

"Katie," he called after her.

"Yes?" She turned.

"I mean it. I'm glad you're okay." He turned away to meet up with his team.

Katie approached Deputy Sanders. "Okay," she said. "I'll take you through everything after we got out of the car."

CHAPTER 35

"I want to talk to everyone about what's been happening," began Sheriff Scott. He looked solemn as he addressed the department staff. "Not only do we have a potential serial killer on the loose, but we, as police officers, have been targeted. It's nothing new, but now it has finally hit home."

"It seems to be one person in particular being targeted," said Templeton.

The sheriff glanced at the detective. "Ask Deputy McGaven about that." He turned back to the group. "Let me make this crystal clear in case some of you don't understand. When one officer is targeted, it means we are all targets." He paused and looked around the room, catching every eye.

Katie sat quietly next to McGaven. She wanted to stand up and yell at Templeton, but she kept her opinions to herself. She was concerned not only for her own safety, but for that of the entire department. There was someone out there willing to kill police officers because of this case. The suspect pool was still too large to focus on anyone yet. It was overwhelming on so many levels.

"I want every officer, whether on patrol or on an investigation, to be extra cautious and stay in frequent contact with dispatch. I've decided to double up deputies on patrol for certain beat areas that are more isolated than others. Be sure to check with your sergeants to find out your arrangements. I will also have one or two K9 units on each shift," the sheriff explained.

One of the deputies asked, "What's the status of the car bomb?"

"We were able to gather a significant amount of evidence that gives the perpetrator's signature. The sheriff's office is working with ATF and Homeland Security. There is no evidence at this point that the bombing is connected to the Compton and Myers homicides. However, that status may change at any time."

Katie thought differently, but it was true that there was no evidence connecting the two crimes yet. She glanced at McGaven, who appeared to have the same opinion. He looked away from the sheriff and shifted his body uncomfortably.

The watch commander entered the briefing room and walked up to Sheriff Scott, leaning in and whispering something to him that the rest of the room wasn't privy to.

"Everyone get out on patrol except Templeton, Scott and McGaven," the sheriff ordered.

The staff hurried to their duties. Low voices chattered as they left the building.

Katie waited for whatever her uncle was going to share, but she knew it wasn't good news.

The sheriff spoke in a quieter tone than he had been, "A little girl went missing yesterday. Dena Matthews; she was on her way to school. No one saw anything."

Katie's blood ran cold as her breath caught in her throat.

He continued, "I've just received word that they've found a young girl's body on Back County Road. There hasn't been an official identification yet and there's no other information at this time. Just that the girl was on top of the ground in a grove area. I would suggest that you get out there to assist immediately."

Katie and McGaven turned to leave.

"Report back to me," the sheriff ordered.

Everyone nodded their understanding and left the building.

*

There wasn't another available unmarked police car, so Katie was forced to use a black SUV that had been confiscated from a drug operation. It would be going up for auction, so she would only be borrowing it temporarily. It wasn't furnished with the usual police equipment; her cell phone would have to suffice for now. With McGaven in the passenger seat next to her, she drove away from the sheriff's department as fast as she could, hoping to arrive ahead of Templeton and his team.

"What are you thinking?" asked McGaven, looking at Katie pointedly. "Do you think this little girl is connected to the others?"

She frowned. "Don't know yet. But my gut tells me there's possible linkage."

She pressed the accelerator harder and the big engine responded. She was surprised by the vehicle's easy handling. There was barely twenty thousand miles on the odometer, and she caught a hint of new-car smell from the interior.

McGaven remained quiet, eyes fixed on the road. His attitude had done a one-eighty since the first time he and Katie had rolled out together. He was definitely on track with the investigation and he had Katie's back no matter what they found themselves in the middle of.

The SUV sped down a long road that seemed to split from the freeway. Katie slowed the vehicle and looked for an indication that they were going the right way. They crossed a one-lane country bridge, tires hitting the boards with a strumming sound, and straight away she saw the sign indicating that they were on Back Country Road.

"Here we go," she said.

First-responder vehicles were parked precariously along the roadway with a set of rolling police lights. Traffic was minimal on the road. Katie decided to drive by first and select the best place to park. As she did so, she saw the crew gathered around what appeared to be a body. It was as if it were a silent vigil rather than a homicide.

She didn't realize that she had sucked in a breath until she exhaled loudly. Even though the scene was drastically different from the previous gravesite, she still suspected that the same person had committed all three crimes. She hated jumping to conclusions, but her intuition told her that the body was the missing girl. It was now looking as if a serial killer was stalking the town's children.

Giving the emergency vehicles some space, she parked a little ways from the crime scene, noting that the CSI van was already at the location. Then she and McGaven exited the SUV and headed to the area of interest.

The air was extremely cool in the shroud of dense trees. It was a place where the sun rarely penetrated, leaving the surrounding area smelling of moss and wet earth. Katie couldn't detect any unusual sounds, or even the familiar birds that usually nested in the area.

She stepped to the side to allow the CSI technicians space to perform documentation. Jamie and Don worked seamlessly, as one located the evidence and the other photographed it. For now, the evidence and the body were to remain undisturbed until the investigating detectives had a chance to view everything in place. Generally, one detective identified what they saw and another wrote it down, then they would change roles. Katie knew that Templeton wasn't going to involve her, but that was okay. She would train McGaven in the procedure.

The CSI team retreated, allowing the detectives to move in with the least amount of cross-contamination possible.

McGaven moved forward, but Katie caught his sleeve. "Let them investigate first," she whispered. She meant Templeton's team. "It's okay. Once they're gone, it'll be easier for us without it getting combative and disruptive."

McGaven nodded, but he was restless, having difficulty standing still.

Katie decided to take a longer-range view of the crime scene as she waited. She moved deeper into the forest, followed by a curious

McGaven. She wanted to evaluate the scene with her senses first. It was a technique she had used in the field during her searches with Cisco. Honing her hearing and sense of smell gave her valuable survival skills, and made her more in tune with the surroundings.

She closed her eyes. At first she heard the conversations from the CSI team, and Templeton's distinctive voice. Taking deep, even breaths, she began to relax and become intertwined in the moment, and the voices grew distant, becoming a nonsensical buzz.

When they'd arrived, she had thought there was no wind, but now she could hear a slight breeze moving through the trees, cooling the area a degree or two. It was a place of almost complete solitude.

Interesting choice of location.

It occurred to Katie that the location had been picked by someone who knew the area well—just as with the gravesite. The perpetrator wouldn't be easily seen, but the body would be found quickly. It confirmed the reason for this exact location.

Why on top of the ground instead of buried in a coffin?

"Do you think the killer needed to dispose of the body quickly and didn't have time to make a coffin?" asked McGaven, as if he had heard Katie's thoughts.

"No," she said. "He's toying with us. Letting us know that he's in charge by changing up his M.O. He's trying to run us around."

"How do you know?"

"By the location and timing. He wants to keep us concentrating on the latest murder and not the previous ones," she explained.

McGaven didn't say anything, but it was clear that he was pondering everything she told him, and perhaps adding a few opinions of his own.

As Katie walked a little distance into the trees, she discovered a small dirt-and-gravel parking lot for hikers. It wasn't large, but it would accommodate three to four cars. She turned and walked slowly back toward the crime scene, careful to notice anything out of the ordinary that the killer might have dropped.

"Wait," she announced, looking down. She put out her right arm to stop McGaven from going any further. "Hey, I've found something over here!" she yelled.

Everyone looked in her direction.

Katie saw Blackburn approaching carrying official evidence bags, both plastic and paper.

"Over there," she said. "It looks like a kitchen towel, and I don't think it's been there long."

Blackburn quickly took a photograph of the location, and then a close-up, before gathering the evidence. Turning back to his team, he ordered, "Jamie, search this area. Let's give it an extra circumference, double it up." He smiled and nodded at Katie.

Katie returned to where the body was.

"So what do you think, Detective Scott?" asked Templeton. There was a hiss in his words.

"Specifically?" she countered.

"What do you see?" he inquired with mild interest.

Katie kneeled down and took her first proper look at the body. She had been purposely avoiding it because she wanted her objectivity to be untainted and to have a clear initial impression.

The little girl was lying on her back, clothed in a green-and-blue spring dress, perfectly washed and ironed. There was no immediate indication of trauma to the body. No blood, bruising, or visible injuries. Her long chestnut-colored hair was braided and lay evenly past her shoulders, tied with a yellow ribbon. The bow loops were almost identical in length. Her arms were wrapped around a brown teddy bear with a thicker yellow ribbon tied neatly around its neck. It was difficult to tell at first glance that the child was indeed dead—she could've been sleeping.

"Well?" asked Templeton.

"The posing, taking great care with appearance and clothes, appears to be the signature of the killer."

"Anything else?"

"He also took meticulous care to pose her at this precise location. He knew she would be found quickly. He's toying with us. Showing us that he's the one in charge, and that we shouldn't try to profile him because he can change his behavior and signature at any time." Katie paused. "Also... did you notice..."

"What?" replied the detective.

"This little girl isn't Dena Matthews. Wrong hair color, and this girl is a couple of years older."

The detective raised his eyebrows and nodded. For once, he had shut his mouth and listened to what Katie was saying. "We won't know how she died without an autopsy or unless there's any trace evidence," he said.

"Most likely she was smothered." Katie leaned in close to the child's face and breathed deeply. "There's a light, sweet stench, and saliva dried around her mouth. That dish rag back there probably held some type of chloroform to render her unconscious. The killer then placed her the way he wanted and carefully smothered her by pinching her nose and mouth closed. It would leave the least amount of evidence behind," she explained, and stood up.

No one spoke. The only sound was the wind whipping through the pine trees.

Katie began to walk away. McGaven hesitated and then prepared to follow her back to the car.

"Detective Scott," Templeton said.

Katie turned to face him, ready for some type of attack or insult.

"I'm not completely convinced this is the work of the same killer," he said.

"That's your opinion," she replied. "It's really down to what the evidence tell us."

"Why do you think he didn't have her in a coffin?"

"He's pissed off we found his private graveyard. He's going to do whatever it takes to fulfill his fantasy of his perfect little girls... and to make us pay."

"He's not going to stop, is he?"

Katie looked at the detective for a couple of moments. Something was different about him; his demeanor appeared defeated. His shoulders were rounded and it looked as if he had aged since they had arrived at the crime scene.

The van from the morgue arrived and parked.

She took a breath. "No, this killer, the *Toymaker*, isn't going to stop until we find him," she said softly.

Her words hung in the air.

She continued to walk to the black SUV.

"Is that it?" asked McGaven. He sounded disappointed.

"For now. There's nothing more we can do here until everything is transported to the morgue and forensics." She looked at the deputy. "I think it's time to go over everything we have so far."

He nodded. He seemed to still be processing the crime scene in his mind.

"I have everything organized at my house," she said. "Some things are beginning to make more sense."

CHAPTER 36

Katie eased the borrowed black SUV into her driveway and cut the engine. It was twilight and the sun was almost hidden behind the trees, giving a Halloween glow.

"I'm fine," she insisted. "I know my uncle wants me watched at all times, but there's nothing to worry about. Really," she stressed.

"I know," said McGaven. "I just wanted to visit with Cisco." He smiled. "Oh, and take a look at your secret office."

"You like him?" she said.

"Of course. I assume you're talking about Cisco." He hesitated. "I've put in for K9. I heard that one of the guys is going to retire soon, and I've always wanted to work with the unit."

"Really?" she said, smiling. "Didn't see that one coming."

"And you call yourself a detective?" McGaven laughed. The slight creasing around his eyes showed his sincerity.

Katie opened the driver's door and jumped out of the vehicle. McGaven followed, and they both walked toward the house and climbed the steps to the porch.

At the front door, Katie stopped suddenly and froze.

"What? What's wrong?" McGaven asked, his posture stiffened.

She took a step away from the door, pressing her back against the siding of the house. She didn't say anything, just nodded toward the handle.

McGaven immediately saw what she meant: the lock and doorknob were broken and the door was slightly ajar.

Katie's heart dropped. "Cisco," she whispered. The dog should have been barking or at the window to greet her. Instead there was just a deafening silence she couldn't let her mind run away with. She fought back the tears and prepared for the worst as she retrieved her weapon.

McGaven followed suit. "We need to call for backup," he urged in a quiet voice.

Katie shook her head adamantly. "I'm going in now." Something was terribly wrong and she wasn't going to hang around for police cars and wailing sirens. If Cisco needed help, she wouldn't wait another second.

McGaven gave her the stare—it was a police officer gaze that meant "I have your back, no matter what."

Katie nodded and took the point position. She decided not to go in yelling with guns blazing. Instead, she gently pushed the door. It opened slowly without a sound.

The living room had been turned upside down. Sofa cushions were torn open, with stuffing scattered around the room. Two lamps and some of her knickknacks were shattered into pieces on the floor. Black spray paint marred the walls, covering some of her artwork in long sweeps.

Katie's first thought was vandals or kids, but there was a more devious element to the trashing of her house. It wasn't by chance; the term *coincidence* wasn't in any soldier's or police officer's vocabulary. Everything had a reason and nothing was happenstance.

They moved cautiously through the living room and into the kitchen in a two-man formation. Katie led, gun targeted in front of her as she cleared areas to the right and McGaven cleared areas to the left just a couple of steps behind her.

She stopped for a moment, straining to hear anything unusual—anything at all. An unnerving quiet greeted her, but she knew it could turn chaotic in an instant. Both of them waited another few seconds before moving on.

Two of the kitchen's cabinet doors were open, but nothing was tossed or broken. Everything on the counter, including the dishes in the sink, had been left untouched.

Katie eased into the hallway. McGaven worked the rooms on the left and she took the right. Everything was as she had left it. When she came to her old bedroom—her investigation room—she stopped. Her head became light, hands clammy, and she couldn't speak.

McGaven must have sensed the change, because he quickly moved next to her and stopped.

The warning read: *YOU WILL NEVER FIND ME*, in the same black spray paint as in the living room. The words were scrawled across parts of her organized investigation but didn't completely obliterate the lists. The large angular lettering suggested a disturbed individual rather than kids or vandalism. It was personal. It was definite. And it was going to change everything.

"Let's clear the rest of the property," ordered McGaven. He pulled at Katie's arm, making her avert her eyes from the threat. "Now!" he insisted.

Katie managed to blink and direct her attention back to the search. McGaven turned to check on her as he made his way to the sliding doors leading outside.

Cautiously he slid them open. Katie moved through after him and stepped into the backyard, where the large dog run was located. She looked for Cisco but didn't see him anywhere. Her mind settled into the unthinkable, but she struggled to move forward, to convince herself that she would find him safe.

McGaven kept his back close to the house and continued to clear areas, alert and ready for anything.

Katie did the same on the other side. There was no sign of anyone—or Cisco. Overwhelming grief began to take hold of her. After everything she and Cisco had been through, now a killer was stalking her wanting to take revenge on her dog. This couldn't be happening.

She returned to the back exit of the house and, leaning against the siding, slid down to the ground. She was done. All her energy rushed out of her.

McGaven joined her at the doors. He was in the middle of a cell-phone call requesting police and backup.

Katie sat on the ground with her head in her hands.

McGaven finished his call. "We don't know. There's no evidence that something went bad here."

She looked up at him. He had no idea what she had been through, and probably wouldn't understand even if he knew.

She sat for another five minutes.

A dog barked in the distance.

Katie looked at McGaven with hope.

The barking became louder, and there was no doubt now that it was the deep bark of a German shepherd.

Katie stood up. "Cisco!"

Within twenty seconds, the large black dog crashed through the bushes, running as fast as he could to get to Katie. He knocked her to the ground with licks and whines. "Cisco," she whispered, unable to stop the tears from falling down her cheeks.

"Is he okay?" asked McGaven.

Katie checked all over the dog's body but couldn't see any visible injuries. "I think he's alright." She continued to kiss and hug him.

"I wonder if he bit the intruder?" The deputy gestured to the saliva around the dog's mouth.

She pondered on the likelihood. "Can we take a swab of his mouth for DNA?"

McGaven kneeled down to pet the dog. "I don't know."

"It's worth a try. I'll text John and ask him." She began composing her text.

McGaven smiled at her.

"What?" she said.

"John, huh?"

She made a face at him. "He said to call him that. What's the big deal?"

"Nothing. He's not married, you know…" He continued to smile.

Katie hugged Cisco close to her, relieved that nothing had happened to him. There were many questions that needed answers: Who was the intruder? Why was Cisco outside? And what was the primary motive for the break-in? Unfortunately, she knew the answer to that one.

Sirens approached in the distance.

CHAPTER 37

Katie was instructed to hold the swab stick firm and keep it in Cisco's mouth for forty-five seconds, petting him the entire time. She made sure that she moved the stick around the dog's cheeks and gums to pick up anything of significance.

"You're such a good boy, Cisco," she praised.

She put the swab stick into a tube and sealed the top. It was headed to the forensic lab for testing for blood or anything foreign that might identify the intruder. It was a long shot, but no clue was overlooked.

"Wow, a real military hero," said Jamie as he took the tube and put it into the chain of custody with the rest of the evidence from Katie's house.

"He definitely saved my life on several occasions," said Katie, petting the dog energetically.

She stayed out of the way as the team of professionals went to work. Someone had been inside her home, her sanctuary—her parent's house, where she was raised. It angered her as much as it chilled her. He'd torn things up, touched her personal belongings, and spent time looking around.

The CSI team had completed their search of the property. Nothing tangible had come to light, but it was obvious that the front door had been pried open with a special type of tool—not an ordinary screwdriver or crowbar.

Katie waited patiently with Cisco in the one area of the living room that hadn't been trashed. Cisco's ears were poised and alert, waiting for anything out of the ordinary. He seemed to be more protective of Katie than usual.

She watched her uncle checking that everyone did their job correctly. He moved with purpose and gave orders to the patrol officer to make sure they didn't miss anything in the surrounding properties' searches.

McGaven assisted John, pointing out their route and the evidence discovered.

Several patrol officers kept watch at the front of the house, while others searched the back couple of acres and spoke with neighbors to find out whether they had seen or heard anything.

The daylight had dwindled and it had turned dark outside, making Katie feel vulnerable. She swallowed more than necessary, trying to keep the familiar creeping anxiety at bay while not showing to others that something was terribly wrong. An overwhelming sense of vertigo reared its ugly head, causing her vision to distort and the hush of conversations all around her to appear jumbled. She hated that sensation more than anything else.

She pulled her legs up onto the sofa as Cisco made himself comfortable next to her. Vivid thoughts and images held her mind hostage. The broken lock on the front door. The message sprayed on the wall in her private room. Knowing that someone had spent time inside her house, destroying her things and leaving such an evil message, socked her in the gut.

"Katie?" John stood in front of her holding several evidence bags. His expression was solemn; it was clear that he was extremely concerned. "You okay?" he asked.

"Yes, fine." She tried to smile.

"I think we're done here. I wanted to apologize…"

"Apologize? For what?" she asked.

"I had Jamie and Don dust for prints all around your office, since that was where the perpetrator spent a lot of the time. There's black dusting powder left behind. We don't have time to clean it up right now."

"Oh," said Katie. She figured she would have to clean the walls anyway and repaint. "Don't worry about it."

"There wasn't a lot of evidence left behind; we'll see what we can come up with at the lab. I'll let you know anything we find that might help."

"Thank you," she managed to say.

The forensic supervisor hesitated, and then said, "I couldn't help but read your flow charts and profiling for the investigation. Pretty impressive work, Detective Scott."

"I guess the person who broke in here doesn't share your opinion," she said.

He chuckled. "I guess you're right. Take care of yourself, and I hope you're staying somewhere else tonight."

Katie smiled as she watched him leave through the open front door and walk to the forensics van. He looked back once toward the house.

"He's right," said Sheriff Scott.

"About?"

"Your presentation of the investigation details was quite impressive."

Katie remained quiet, thinking about how she was going to proceed now. Her concentration was shattered, and she would have to watch her back until the killer was apprehended. This new burden was almost too much for her to manage.

"You're not staying here tonight," her uncle said.

"I'll be fine. Nobody is coming back tonight. Not after this big show of cops." She tried to make it sound like it was not a big deal, when in fact it was terrifying. The house felt like a haunted shell.

"I've already talked to Claire and she's made up the spare room for you and Cisco," he said adamantly. "A couple of days of rest should be in order as well."

"There's no way I can take time off. I have work to do. Dena Matthews is still missing."

The sheriff sighed, but surprisingly didn't argue with her.

"He's ratcheted up his anger," Katie said. "Especially after I found his special place. See how quickly he left another body. I'm more worried about Dena than about my safety." She watched her uncle's reaction. She knew he wanted to drag her out of the house, but that he also respected her opinion.

"Okay," he said. "This is how it's going down. If you stay here tonight, I want an officer staying with you, just until we have a security system installed tomorrow."

"But—"

"*And* a new heavier front door with a solid lock. Not this quaint farmhouse door."

"Don't you think—" she began.

"That's how it's going to go, no objections." He stood his ground.

"Okay, fine," she sighed. "I'm too tired to argue."

After the team from the sheriff's department had left, Katie began to clean up the worst of the mess. She would save the rest for the next day. Exhaustion had set in, her physical and mental capabilities suffering from the overload of the case, which had now crept into her home life.

The silence wasn't a comforting friend; rather, it became a questionable and unnerving reminder that there was someone out there who wanted to scare her—and possibly harm her.

"I finally got the door lock to work," said McGaven.

His voice startled Katie and she responded quickly. "Thank you. I guess someone will be fitting the alarm and a new door tomorrow."

"I'm sorry," he said.

"Sorry? For what?"

"That you're going through this along with everything else." His voice faded a bit.

"You know, you don't have to stay here. I'll be just fine. There will be people coming tomorrow morning, probably early, to install everything."

"Nope. I have my orders," he said adamantly.

"Did you call your wife?" she asked.

"Girlfriend," he corrected. "Don't worry, she knows what's been going on. Her dad and brother are cops, so she's very understanding." He smiled.

Katie couldn't help but notice the way his eyes lit up when he spoke of his girlfriend.

"I can take the couch," he said.

"Nope, there's a guest room for you—it has a private bath, too. It looks like the intruder didn't bother to deface that room," Katie said sourly.

McGaven followed her to the room that had been her parents' bedroom.

"I'll make the last rounds with Cisco," he announced.

"Okay," she said. "I'm beat. I'm going to try to get some sleep. Goodnight."

"Night," he said as he went to check the doors for the umpteenth time, and most likely make a loop around her backyard for good measure.

Katie fell asleep immediately, but her slumber was erratic as she tossed and turned, waking frequently. Each time, she listened intently for any sound that seemed out of place.

A soft creak.

A hurried footstep.

A door slowly opening.

It was always the same. Quiet. The only sound she heard was Cisco snoring at the corner of her bed. She listened to his steady breathing for a few minutes, and the sound relaxed her enough to fall back to sleep.

Suddenly she heard a low, menacing voice: "You will never find me."

Jolted awake, she sat up expecting there to be someone at the foot of her bed. Of course, there was no one. She waited another minute, but no sound interrupted the silence.

Letting out a long sigh, she leaned back against her headboard. It was still dark outside, and too early to get up. Sleep was a necessity, but she wouldn't waste moments of wakefulness because she never knew how long her days were going to be.

She reached over to her nightstand and retrieved her journal from the small drawer. She was relieved that it had been tucked in a safe place. Switching on the lamp and opening the book to a clean page, she began to write.

Friday, 0430 hours

Today was a bad day—worse than any I've had since being home. The thought of losing Cisco makes my heart break. It's one of my biggest fears. It turned out okay, but it still doesn't take away from the high stakes I've been presented with. My biggest task is finding the killer in time before he kills Dena.

My emotions are running riot. Anxiety. Loss. Rekindled friendship. New and chance meetings. However, it eases my mind that my partner has my back, at least for now. The way it should be. Always. I miss my old team. Please God, watch over them and protect the weary soldiers. I continue to survive one day at a time...

CHAPTER 38

The high-pitched squeal of an electric screwdriver followed by banging noises woke Katie. She had been in a deep sleep, fighting unforeseen demons, which made it difficult for her to fully wake up. The sounds reverberating around her room and in her head made her ready for combat.

It was the usual shortness of breath.

Heaviness pressing against her chest.

The unending tenseness of the muscles running down her legs.

She readied herself for the worst and leaped out of bed. As she gazed at the window, the sun shone through the sheer curtains and her bad dream melted away. Then she remembered the night before, and it all tumbled back with a vengeance.

Her home had a new history—it was no longer a place of safety. Now fully awake, she took a deep breath, grabbed a sweatshirt and walked out of her bedroom. Even Cisco didn't greet her as usual; there was so much going on, the dog was more interested in hanging out with the guys working.

She quietly walked down the hallway and peered into the living room. There were two men at the entrance trying to hang the new front door properly, while McGaven was in the kitchen, cooking.

"Wow," she said. "I have no idea how I could sleep during this." She saw John Blackburn working on a keypad that he was installing near the front door. Quickly she ran her fingers through her tousled hair.

"Hey," said McGaven. He was stirring up some scrambled eggs in a skillet. "I wasn't sure what you liked, but you had eggs. And it's one of the few things I can make that actually tastes good."

Still looking around, Katie said, "Thank you. All of you." To McGaven, "You don't have to do that."

"Too late," he replied, smiling.

"Coffee?" she managed to say.

McGaven motioned to the coffee maker behind him.

Her feelings of embarrassment dissipated because she was in the company of friends; people who had her best interests at heart. It meant so much to her. It also made her miss her army team that much more.

She wrapped her fingers around a hot cup of coffee. Cisco gave her his usual good-morning licks and nudges against her arm. His tail wagged uncontrollably. She realized that he too needed the support of people who were friends.

She took a seat at one of the bar stools that was still intact.

"Oh," said McGaven. "The boss said you're not allowed to come to work today. His strict orders."

"That's fine," she said.

"Really?"

"I've got everything I need here. As soon as I figure out how to clean some of that paint off my walls, I'm going to get started." She smiled at McGaven and took another sip of coffee. He scraped eggs onto two plates, and put one in front of her.

"I've been thinking about that," said John.

"What?" replied Katie. She was a little bit self-conscious about how she appeared after a terrible night's sleep.

The forensic supervisor walked toward the kitchen. Katie couldn't help but notice that he looked rested and relaxed, as if nothing fazed him.

He explained, "I have a mixture that should take most of the spray paint off the walls. It won't be pretty until you repaint the room, but you can at least work for now."

"Sounds great," she said.

McGaven shoveled a large forkful of eggs into his mouth. "That is precisely why you want a forensic person as your friend."

"That and so you know how to make a murder scene look like an accident," said one of the men hanging the front door.

John smiled. "I have a couple of cameras to install outside first."

"No problem," Katie said. "How'd you get roped in to work on my security system?"

"Why not?" he said as he went outside.

McGaven shrugged. "A man of few words."

Cisco barked, wanting his share of the eggs. Katie tossed him a small morsel and then began to eat her breakfast.

After several cups of coffee, Katie changed into work clothes and systematically cleaned her office from top to bottom. To her surprise, the intruder hadn't rummaged through her drawers, so all her office supplies, computer components, and personal items remained untouched, though pieces of paper and notes had been strewn over the floor.

She knew forensics had completely documented the scene, but she wanted to take a few photos herself to attach to the wall. She snapped several, creating a panoramic view of *YOU WILL NEVER FIND ME.*

The words pummeled at her like projectiles. They made the investigation that much more urgent. It was a race for her life and the life of another innocent child.

She moved a ladder closer to the main investigative notes on the wall and climbed up. Studying the scrawled letters within the scattered black fingerprint dust, she fought back the creeping anxiety of hopelessness. It was like facing the devil, eye to eye, toe to toe, and knowing you didn't have the power to overcome the madness.

Holding a bottle full of John's unidentified cleaning potion, Katie squeezed the trigger with her right forefinger and sprayed a small portion onto the wall, watching the tiny bubbles roll over the black paint. As instructed, she dabbed the area with a clean rag. It actually began to work. The paint slowly lightened, leaving a dull, ghostly remnant behind. She continued to carefully pat the solution around her notes, spending more than a half-hour continuing the effective repetitive technique.

"How's it going?" asked McGaven, followed closely by Cisco. The dog had been following him around since early morning—his canine shadow.

"Better than expected," she replied.

McGaven stood in the doorway, his height making the opening appear smaller than it actually was. He studied the points that Katie had highlighted. "You still think Terrance Price had something to do with it?" he asked.

Katie stepped down from the ladder. She wasn't sure she wanted to discuss her thoughts about the case until there was solid corroborating evidence to support her theory. "Too many things point to his involvement."

"Such as?"

"He claimed to have seen Chelsea the day she disappeared—he described in detail what she wore that day. Changed his statement only when he was pressed. Conveniently killed himself less than twenty-four hours after Chelsea was found. There were pieces of lumber on the property that could've been used to make those coffins."

"When you put it like that, I would say there's a definite possibility that he could've been the killer."

"I don't think he was the killer—just the helper," she said. "The third victim was killed and dumped after Price's death, according to the autopsy report."

"So now the killer is lost without his partner? Is that why he was so quick to leave another body?"

"As I said, there are many things that raise questions." Katie folded the ladder and leaned it against the wall. "I believe Templeton closed the case on Price too early in the first investigation. He wrote him off as mentally ill, which may be true, but he seemed to be getting his life together out at the Haven farm."

"And," put in McGaven, "we can't forget what happened when we went back to the barn."

"Any potential evidence there is now gone forever." Katie frowned and thought about all the things they could've searched for and sent to the lab to test and compare.

"Okay, what if we took Price completely out of the scenario? What would we have?" McGaven suggested.

Katie smiled. "I like the way you think." She stepped back into the middle of the room to study her lists. It was a good question, so she deliberated carefully. "Okay, there are still some unanswered questions for the Darren boys."

"I assume you're talking about Malcolm."

"Actually, there were some red flags over Rick," she said. "He's calculating. That calmness you see is a cover. His arms were tensed the entire time I spoke with him, and he kept making fists. A sign of deep agitation—maybe unresolved issues and possibly violence. My first impression is that he's disciplined, highly intelligent, and knows how to manipulate."

"But he's the sane one."

"I realize you know them from disturbance calls, but what do you really know about them? I would love to have a search warrant for their place, but to search for what is the question. Tools to make a coffin, some fabric, photos of young girls, anything." She sighed. "There's nothing solid to go on except theories. It's so frustrating."

McGaven seemed to be thinking back to interactions the police had had with the brothers.

Katie continued. "Neither one of them has a solid alibi for the day Chelsea disappeared, and they definitely know their way around construction activities, like building a coffin."

She fetched her laptop and turned it on. She waited a moment before pulling up photographs from the forensic division.

McGaven made himself comfortable in a chair in the corner. "So how do we move forward? How do we link the murders? Especially since most cases like this point to those closest to the child."

"More than eighty percent of the time," she said matter-of-factly. "That's true, but there are always exceptions to the general investigative rule. To be a good investigator, you must remain objective and not get tunnel vision on one suspect." She sighed. "And you're right, we have to find linkage between the victims."

McGaven raised his eyebrows, most likely wondering how they would do that.

Reading some notes that had been sent over from Templeton's camp, she said, "The next-door neighbors, the Stanleys, were deceitful, but they were both ruled out. I believe that's most likely correct. My gut tells me that Detective Templeton is building some type of circumstantial case to clear these homicides."

"Also known as indirect evidence, used to infer something based on a series of facts separate from the fact the argument is trying to prove," said McGaven, almost as if he was reading from the textbook.

"Wow, someone retained information from their criminal-justice classes."

"It's a curse. Most of the time I remember useless things—that's what people say."

"Who cares what those kind of people think."

"She's absolutely correct," said Blackburn, standing at the doorway holding a remote control in his hand.

Katie was startled at first. She had forgotten that the forensic supervisor was still at the house. She had noticed that he had a certain look about him when he was in new or unusual situations, quickly scouring his surroundings and making sure that he was in a position where he could observe everything around him with ease.

"From what I see," he said, "you're going to need more than interviews and circumstantial evidence."

"We need forensic evidence that points to the killer," said Katie. She turned her attention to what was in Blackburn's hand. "What's that?" she asked curiously.

"This," he held it up for them both to see, "is the remote for your security system. You'll have the same access on your cell phone once you download the app."

"Fantastic. Are you going to give me a tour?"

"Of course."

McGaven got to his feet and headed eagerly to the doorway. "Let's check it out."

Cisco leapt up too; he didn't want to be left out. He trotted behind McGaven, keeping his ears and senses alert.

Katie smiled and followed the men to the front door.

"Okay," began Blackburn. He pointed to a small panel on the wall. "It's pretty self-explanatory. When you want to set the alarm, punch in a hashtag and your four-digit code. You do the same when you enter the house to turn it off or reset it."

"Sounds easy enough," said Katie. She had used security systems like that before and found them straightforward.

"Okay, now here's the cool part," he said.

Katie and McGaven waited.

He punched in a couple of numbers on the remote and he was able to show the views from two cameras on the property from a small viewer. The footage was in black and white, but it was clear in resolution.

Katie retrieved her phone and began to download the relevant app. After a few minutes, she had it loaded up.

"Now you need to pick four numbers for your code," Blackburn said.

She thought about it; she didn't want it to be easy for someone else to figure out. It came to her quickly: 0319, the month and day of her deployment.

"Looks like you're all set," the forensic supervisor said.

"Thank you so much."

"It's been my pleasure."

McGaven glanced at his watch. "I need to go home and get some things done before shift."

"Go, everyone, go. I'm not a princess in my castle here, you know," Katie laughed. "Now I have a security system, like Cisco wasn't already enough."

The dog barked.

"There should be something back at the lab for your case," Blackburn said. "You can drop by tomorrow afternoon and I'll make sure I have it all ready for you."

"Okay," she said.

She watched as the men left; both of them seemed reluctant to go. She assumed her uncle had made them swear to make sure the house was as safe as any high-security prison.

After waving goodbye, she decided to set the alarm. It was just her and Cisco again. And as much as the dog loved the two men, he seemed content to be with just Katie.

Sitting down on the couch with a notebook on her lap, she decided to run the case from the beginning. It would be too easy to assume that the information she needed hadn't materialized yet. Too high-minded. In fact, she thought there were too many clues, too much information, and too many statements, which made a muddled mess. She couldn't see through it clearly. Her cop instincts fired a warning shot over her head, urging her to figure out what she was missing.

Cisco grumbled and scooted himself closer to her, putting his head on her lap.

"Cisco, I can't write when your head is in the way."

The dog sighed and moved a couple of inches.

She listed everything that had happened from the first day she began searching for Chelsea. As with the battlefield, her memories of defining moments came alive with distinct smells and visions. This time it was the gravesite.

The hand-made coffins.
The positioning of the girls, perfectly posed.
The teddy bears.
The professionally tied bows.
No trace evidence.
Behavioral evidence?

There was a lack of viable evidence for a roadmap to the killer. In the way an obsessive-compulsive personality type would approach the case, she ran the investigation backwards to the beginning—and vice versa. She saw the faces of the three little girls in their final resting positions, the hanging body of Terrance Price, her patrol car blown up, the barn inferno, the warning messages—and still nothing clicked.

Why was the killer making it personal?

Why would he direct the messages just at her and not Detective Templeton as well?

She ran through the evidence from the forensic lab and double-checked her emails and Templeton's reports. She formulated some questions for John Blackburn tomorrow, but wasn't hopeful that they would render anything substantial.

Combing through interviews and reports, she concluded the physical evidence that stood out most was the coffin and the teddy bears. The behavioral evidence was the method and motivation.

She kept pushing the evidence and re-reading the notes.

Soon her focus crashed as her vision faded, and she fell asleep.

CHAPTER 39

Katie watched the image on the computer monitor as it was magnified four hundred times. The pictures of interest looked like nothing more than burned-away timber pieces with spiky features. The results from the scanning electron microscope revealed that the impression evidence from her front door couldn't help identify the tool used. The frame and lock were too badly damaged, as if someone had intentionally made a mess so that it couldn't be traced.

She sighed and realized that the evidence from her house wasn't going to lead to any type of breakthrough.

"I know I could have just told you in a report, but I wanted you to see the actual results in case you have any questions," said Blackburn as he studied her.

She frowned and felt her stomach drop in disappointment, not because the evidence was unusable, but because the entire case weighed even heavier on her conscience. She dreaded the eventual news that there was another body posed somewhere for the police to discover. The Matthews girl still hadn't been found and the third girl hadn't been identified yet.

"Katie?" said Blackburn. He had been talking, but she was lost in her own thoughts.

"Oh," she said. "I'm sorry. It's just this case has hit me hard. Excuse my momentary lapse." She forced a smile.

Blackburn moved closer to her. "I've been doing this job for about eight years. I've worked with many detectives, both in-house and from various jurisdictions."

"Your point?" she said.

"My point is that I can tell the difference between competent detectives and detectives just going through the motions not clear about what they're looking for, much less what direction they should take." He took an additional moment to look Katie in the eye in order to make his point.

Katie knew he was telling the truth, but the intensity between them was almost too much to bear. She felt her face ignite with heat. "Thank you, I appreciate that." She moved away from him.

"Hi, sorry I'm late," announced McGaven breathlessly. It seemed he might have run all the way to the lab.

"Good morning," Katie managed to say.

"Did I miss anything?" he asked eagerly.

"Unfortunately, no," said Katie, feeling the warmth dissipate from her face.

Blackburn moved to the other side of the room. "There were no fingerprints apart from those belonging to Katie and her uncle. Sheriff Scott's fingerprints were around the door frame and at a high level. And many areas were completely clean of any prints."

"Well, he did quite a bit of work with the water leakage. That's probably why some areas were clear," she said.

"I suppose," Blackburn replied. "That dish towel you found at the crime scene was indeed soaked in chloroform. It was from an old sample."

"Meaning?"

"Chloroform is not available to the average consumer; in fact, it's been banned since the seventies because it eventually turns into a carcinogen, especially when it's exposed to oxygen. I believe it's available in small doses to the pharmaceutical industry, and it is used as a solvent in pesticides and dyes."

"So are you saying that the killer had it stored for a long time?" she asked.

"It would appear so." Blackburn went on, "The two footprints at your house and the ones at the gravesites are all a man's size twelve. It's not an average size, but most men who are six feet tall or more wear a twelve."

"Anything else?" she said. "What about the message on my wall? Anything interesting or potentially usable?"

"I sent a photo of it to a friend of mine who is a handwriting-analysis expert, to see if she could shed any light on it. She has worked some high-profile cases with interesting results."

"Could she tell if it was a psychopath?" asked McGaven, his eyes wide with intense interest.

"Not exactly," began Blackburn. It was difficult to read his expression because of his intense demeanor. "I forwarded the report to you, but I can sum it up. The message was written by a man, thirties to possibly fifties in age, and he always writes in block letters. From the square lettering she could tell that he was trained in some type of technical school, like as an electrician, or in auto repair, carpentry, perhaps even computer-programming work."

"That doesn't really narrow it down," Katie said.

"Fifty percent minus anyone who doesn't wear a size twelve," added McGaven, trying to lighten the mood.

"One interesting thing is that the author had difficulty forming his block letters in the words 'you' and 'never'. I don't know if that will mean anything to you."

There was a momentary silence.

"It doesn't right now, but who knows, it may help when we have a solid suspect," said Katie.

"What about Cisco's saliva?" McGaven asked.

"It's inconclusive right now due to the dilution, but I'm expanding the testing. There's still the chance of finding something significant, but then again, it won't help until we have something or someone to compare it to."

"Thank you for rushing these tests. I was just hoping for something more," Katie said. She turned to leave.

Blackburn stopped her. "I have your cell number and I'll text you anything new as soon as it becomes available."

She nodded and left the room with McGaven.

As they climbed into the SUV, Katie thought about her house and the two messages. At this point, she couldn't definitively connect the person who'd committed the homicides with the person at her house. It was a threat towards her only and it would be circumstantial evidence at best.

"You should be flattered," said McGaven.

"What?"

He laughed. "For all of your smarts, you're certainly dense."

"If you're trying to cheer me up…"

"No, Detective Scott. If you couldn't see that John Blackburn seems to fancy you, there's no hope for you at all," he chuckled.

Katie stared at the deputy. She tried hard not to let her personal feelings show, not wanting more gossip about her to filter through the department.

"C'mon, when I walked in, I thought I was on a soap-opera set."

"You're a riot, McGaven," she said.

"You see, guys do these subtle little things when they like someone."

"Like?" She was interested in hearing a man's perspective.

"Like wanting to get closer. Maybe to smell her hair or see if she gently touches them in passing. C'mon, Detective, don't play dumb. Women have all the power and you know it." He smiled, watching Katie's restrained reaction.

Katie ignored him and began looking through her notes. "We have several places to hit today and I want to have another chat with the Darren brothers. Are you ready? Can you behave?"

McGaven let out a loud sigh. "Bring it on…"

CHAPTER 40

Katie's head pounded with a familiar pain that always appeared when she was faced with increasing stress—and these cases would definitely qualify as stressful. A tightness in her chest promised an encroaching anxiety attack, but she stayed focused and in the moment. It helped to have McGaven with her to take her mind off unnecessary things. He had lightened up and she had proved to him that she was worthy of being a cop. His personality and intelligence surprised her the more she got to know him.

She had wanted to pay a visit to the Darren brothers, but they weren't at home and had left a handwritten note in block capitals telling people that they were closed for the day. She quickly retrieved her cell phone and took a photo of the sign, then sent it to Blackburn with a message that read: *Could this be the author of the message on my wall?*

Denise had put together a list of fabric warehouses that might prove helpful with the silk and teddy-bear material. Katie had also had suggestions about local people she could visit about the construction of the coffins. But first she wanted to talk with Dr. Dean at the morgue.

She pulled into a parking place back at the sheriff's department.

"If you don't want to come in with me, that's okay," she told McGaven.

"Nope, I'm not going to wimp out every time there's a dead body involved," he said. "I will have to do this eventually."

Within minutes, she was standing in an exam room with Dr. Dean, staring at the body of the unknown girl. Her identity was still pending for dental-record recognition. It never got any easier when a child was involved. Katie glanced at McGaven. He stood stoic and professional, his gaze fixed on the wall.

"I received your preliminary report, but I wanted to talk to you in person again. I appreciate your time," said Katie. "As I learn the ropes, I won't be bothering you so much."

"Not a problem, Detective." Dr. Dean sounded genuine. "Shoot," he said.

"Well," Katie began. "She died of asphyxia?"

"Correct."

"I wanted to clarify that she died due to her airway being blocked off—for lack of a better definition. You stated that she had oxygen poisoning. What does that mean? How can you die from lack of oxygen *and* have been poisoned by it?"

"Good question. Yes, she died of lack of oxygen—technically."

Katie raised her eyebrows and remained quiet as the doctor explained further.

"There was such a huge amount of chloroform in her system that her nose and mouth have slight burns from the contact. It's possible that she fell into a coma due to acute inhalation of chloroform, and then it would have been easy to obstruct her nose and mouth to suffocate her. When such a large amount of contaminated chloroform is ingested into the system, it begins to have detrimental effects on the body, from nausea and vomiting to renal and hepatic damage."

"How would the chloroform have been contaminated?" she asked.

"If it's been stored improperly or is old, it will begin to oxidize in combination with air or light and become lethal. It can show up in the body as a type of oxygen poisoning."

Katie took in all the information and began to create a picture in her mind of the signature behavior of the killer.

"Were her kidneys damaged?" she asked.

"Yes, they showed signs of heavy toxins; not what you would expect to see from an otherwise healthy eleven-year-old girl."

"Are there any other signs of abuse or anything that's not accounted for?"

"She had some older minor bruises that would be consistent with playing sports."

"Could she have been given any other chemical intravenously?" Katie wanted to completely understand everything she could about the drugs.

"There are no tiny punctures where a needle would have been; it would be more convenient to administer it with a rag over the nose and mouth.

"To keep her sedated." Katie nodded. "Given the precise planning, it would make sense that the killer would keep administering the chloroform until he was ready for her to die."

The room fell quiet for a moment.

Katie asked, "Would a large amount of chloroform help to preserve the body, like formaldehyde?"

The medical examiner pulled more of the plain sheet away from the frail body of the girl. "See how the skin on her chest and legs looks translucent, more than normal. Her internal organs show a slight hardening. All of that is caused by the large amounts of chloroform. But to answer your question, no, it's not a formula for preservation."

Katie nodded. "Okay."

"Chloroform is a heckuva signature for a killer," said McGaven.

Katie had almost forgotten about the deputy standing in the room. She was intensely aware of her headache, making it difficult to concentrate.

"Thank you, Dr. Dean. We won't take up any more of your time," she said.

"Jeff."

"What?"

"Please call me Jeff," the doctor said.

"Of course. Thank you, Jeff."

She turned to leave, this time following McGaven out of the examination room. An uncontainable shudder went down her spine. There was something about the morgue and about these cases that unnerved her.

Katie had just spoken to two carpenters who specialized in miniatures and wooden toys, but hadn't learned anything new about the coffin construction. Both men had confirmed that the work had been done painstakingly. She wasn't going to give up yet, though—there was more to learn.

Her phone buzzed with a message, and she pulled to the side of the road to read it. Denise had sent her the details of other carpenters who might be able to help. "Here's someone I know," she said. "Charles Rey. Let's go see what he has to say about the construction." She nosed the SUV back into traffic. She knew the address where they were headed and didn't need a GPS to guide her.

With a possible serial killer on the loose, local people were uncomfortable, distrustful, and scared, but Katie was determined to find and bring that killer to justice. Sifting through her notes, she had seen from many of the comments that the general theme of the town was fear, though it was difficult to decipher and read between the lines.

McGaven broke into her thoughts. "You thinking about the Toymaker?"

"Don't call him that," she said flatly.

"I forgot. Sorry," he said.

She rolled her shoulders a couple of times and tried to shake off her unease from the morgue. She decided to explain further. "When the media gives a killer a clever name, it makes them seem important, when in fact it's the victims we need to be talking about. Plain and simple."

McGaven turned his attention back to the road. It wasn't clear if he agreed with her or not, but he didn't argue.

Katie navigated onto a narrow gravel track, the big SUV taking the bumpy and uneven terrain with ease. Charles lived at the end of a long road that opened into a farm. From what Katie remembered, his family had owned the twenty acres through three generations.

"It's been a while since I've been out here," said McGaven.

"I think I was a kid the last time I was here. He helped us build a tree house and fixed our bicycles."

"I was here about five years ago."

"What do you mean?" Katie asked.

"When his wife passed away. So sad…" McGaven's voice drifted off.

"There's no other family?"

"I think he has a son and a couple of grandkids who visit about once a year, but they live in New York."

The narrow drive opened into a large area in front of the farmhouse. It was a spacious and well-kept yellow house with two stories of balconies. There were two barns further away on the property.

Katie parked to one side of the area and turned off the engine. She sat for a moment, then grabbed a file folder before exiting the vehicle.

Charles walked out of the house and hurried to greet them. "Hello," he said. He shook McGaven's hand—"It's nice to see you, Deputy."—then turned and smiled at Katie. It reminded her of the many times she'd seen him when she was a teenager; he still appeared warm and friendly. "Katie, it's always a pleasure."

"Thank you for seeing us," she said.

"Anything I can do," he replied. "C'mon in."

Katie and McGaven followed him toward the house.

"Mr. Rey…" She corrected herself. "Charles, we have some photos that we need your opinion on."

"Oh?" he said.

"It's about evidence from a couple of cases we're working," she explained.

"You've got my interest. Well, why don't we go to the barn?"

"Sure. That would probably be best."

Charles changed direction and followed a well-maintained path along to the workshop. There were all types of equipment stored neatly to one side, everything from small tools to pickers and backhoes. The path was lined with carefully tended flowers.

When they reached the large barn, he opened the big doors, the hinges squeaking. Immediately Katie thought about the barn at the Haven farm. She glanced at McGaven and noticed he had a frown on his face; most likely he was thinking the same thing.

Inside was a typical farm barn with bales of hay, tools, and a large workstation.

"So what do you have for me?" asked Charles.

"What I'm going to show you needs to be in confidence because of the ongoing case," Katie said. "Please don't share with anyone what you're about to see."

"Of course," he replied.

In the file folder there were several eight-by-ten photographs of the coffins from various angles, close-up pictures as well as overall depictions. Katie took each photo and laid them out on the flat surface.

Charles put on his reading glasses and examined them. One in particular seemed to catch his interest.

"Is there anything that stands out to you?" said Katie. "Anything unusual?"

"These are coffins?" he said with a tightness to his voice.

Katie nodded. "I'm sorry, is this too much for you?"

"Uh, no, it's okay. Anything to help."

"Please take a look."

"Why in the world would anyone… Those poor girls." He picked up the photo showing the end pieces. "Whoever made this is a master craftsman. See here." He indicated the detail. "This is dovetailing, and it's some of the best I've seen. This isn't just a carpenter, but an artisan."

"So someone who built houses wouldn't be this skilled?"

"Not in my experience. This person deals with specialty items, custom-made would be my guess."

Katie thought about it for a moment. In her mind, she skimmed through all the people she had spoken with. None of them had seemed especially gifted in woodworking specialties.

"What are you thinking?" asked McGaven.

"It never occurred to me that someone might have ordered the coffins from an experienced business. They could have bought them online or from a company or individual in any other state."

Charles pointed at another photo. "If you look closely here, the grain matches up perfectly. So I doubt this was made on an assembly line, but rather, from a special section of wood."

Katie looked at him. "Would you know of anyone who could do this type of woodworking with such precision or attention to detail?" She watched his response and body language as he appeared to be searching his recollection.

"Of course, there are many people in town who could make a coffin, but that extra care and craftsmanship is something else." He looked at the photograph again. "There's this wood workshop and store just west as you go toward the town of Stewart."

McGaven nodded. "I know it."

"It's a place where people who might create something like this congregate," said Charles.

"We'll take that under advisement," said Katie. "Is there anything else you can tell us from these photographs?"

He paused, and then shook his head. "I'm sorry, nothing else comes to mind."

"Thank you, Charles, it's appreciated," Katie said.

As Katie and McGaven sat in the SUV, Katie's phone alerted with a text. It was from the forensic supervisor, with some information about the fabric from inside the coffins: *The silk is specially dyed that shade of pink and three textiles companies carry it: Colors Fabrics, Chinese Silk Company, and Fabric by the Yard. Hope this helps.*

McGaven read the message over her shoulder. "Are we going to visit those warehouses?"

"Two are in Sacramento and the other is located in San Jose. Let's see if we can get some information from them about anyone ordering that fabric. I'll ask Denise to call them and then take it from there," Katie said. She was completely exhausted and thought she would cut out of work early. She wanted to pick apart everything the investigation had yielded to date.

She quickly replied to the text with a thank you.

"That's it?" said McGaven.

"What?"

"You should say something a little bit nicer. You know… make it sound like you're approachable and not this hard-ass ex-military homicide detective."

"Is that how you see me?"

"Well, you are a bit difficult to get to know. I would say, guarded."

Katie turned the key and the SUV roared to life. She backed up and then made a three-point turn heading back down the long driveway. "I'll keep that in mind."

The deputy stared at her, trying not to smile.

She laughed. "I promise. I'm just not one of those soft, cuddly kitten girls."

"Wow, now I can't get that image out of my mind," said McGaven. "Hey, you know you look tired."

"Thanks. Is that another compliment? That makes how many today?" she said, good- humoredly.

"See, that wasn't so hard, breaking down those boot-camp walls."

"How much do I owe you, Doc?"

"I'm hungry. Buy me lunch," he said.

"You got it."

"And then you need a nap," he added.

Katie drove to a local diner, where they ate together, comparing notes and theories about the case. Afterwards, she dropped him back at the sheriff's department on her way home.

CHAPTER 41

Detective Rory Templeton left Judge Wade Jeffries' chambers after a long and interesting conversation in the early hours. Dressed in casual clothes—jeans, flannel shirt, and work boots—he hurried to his truck.

The morning sun peeked through the tall trees and made an appearance just above the surrounding rooftops. The energizing yellow-orange sky helped to lift Templeton's mood, especially now that he had received the green light to move forward.

A perfect plan.

As he jumped into the driver's seat, the detective couldn't wipe the smug expression off his face. The Chelsea Compton case would soon be closed once and for all. No one, absolutely no one, was going to make him look bad. The final outcome would be up to a jury, and frankly, he didn't care about the conclusion because he'd done his job and closed the case.

He started his truck, giving it extra gas, and hastily backed out of the county building's parking lot, tools rattling in the back. He knew that no one would see him; he wasn't as recognizable in his casual clothes and he'd made sure to take one of his other vehicles.

His recollection of the conversation with Judge Jeffries kept him company as he drove home to get ready for work. He had a knack for finding out anything unethical or dirty where county employees were concerned. The bonus this time was the explicit photographs he'd managed to obtain of the judge and several sexual partners who didn't include his wife. It didn't take much after he had explained that he needed a search warrant based on circumstantial evidence because it was necessary to close the cases and to make the community, as well as the police department, content.

Everything was falling into place.

As Templeton thought about Katie Scott, he clenched his jaw. Soon she would fall off her high horse and everyone would see who she really was—a fraud, a poser, and a wannabe in the law-enforcement world. He would make sure her career at the department ended as soon as an arrest was made in the Compton and Myers cases. She had no business being promoted to detective over much more qualified officers and given a high-profile serial case.

He flipped on the radio and cranked the music loud. The beat infused his body as he thought about finally bringing this case to an end. He sped down the main road and took a sharp right, merging onto a country road. There were a few things he needed to do before arriving at the sheriff's office.

CHAPTER 42

The ringing of Katie's cell phone ousted her from a pleasant dream at 7.15 a.m. She blindly reached for the phone on her nightstand and looked at the incoming number—it was Chad.

"Hel-lo," she said, managing to pick up in the moment before her phone went to voicemail.

"Did I wake you?" he asked.

"Yeah." She sat up, trying to focus her eyes. Cisco was lying on the other side of her bed.

"I'm surprised."

"About what?" she said, trying to clear the grogginess from her voice.

"I thought you'd be working hard on the case. Hammering out more details."

"I was up until two a.m. doing just that."

"That's why I'm calling. What are you doing this morning?" he asked.

"Working," she said.

"At home or in the office?"

"The crime scene."

"What?"

"I'm heading back up to the graveyard crime scene."

There was a pause, and Katie could hear Chad breathing evenly into the phone. Finally he said, "Want some company? Is the site signed off?"

Katie thought for a moment. She knew McGaven had other duties and was meeting with the supervisor of the K9 unit. "Yeah, company would be nice. Everything has been collected and it's not officially a crime scene anymore."

"I'll pick you up," he said.

"No, I'll meet you at Highland Park, near the baseball field, in half an hour."

"See you there." He hung up.

Katie turned to Cisco. "I think I'll leave you here to guard the house. Sound good?" She sat for a few moments petting the dog before she jumped up to take a quick shower.

Thirty-five minutes later, Katie parked her Jeep next to the baseball diamond at Highland Park. Chad was already there; this time he was driving his truck instead of the Jeep.

When he saw Katie get out of her vehicle, he leaned inside the truck and retrieved a cup of coffee. "I thought you might need this," he said, smiling.

"Thank you," she said, taking a sip.

"No Cisco?"

"He's protecting the house."

"So, going back to the scene of the crime." Chad gave his signature smile.

"Yes," she said. "I'm at a standstill in the investigation, and waiting for some of the tests to come in from forensics. I'm not sure if that's going to help either."

"What about the other detective? Templeton."

"What about him?"

"Does he have anything to contribute?"

Katie smiled in spite of herself. "Let's just say we aren't on the same page."

"Oh," he said.

"Don't get me wrong. He's fairly competent. It's just that he doesn't follow through, he cuts his interviews too short." Katie stopped herself; she didn't want to discuss the homicide cases with anyone outside the department. "I'm sorry. I really can't say much."

"Of course."

There was a moment of awkwardness. Katie now thought it would have been easier for her to go alone, but it was too late to rescind the invitation.

Chad was the first to speak. "Well, you ready to go?"

"Absolutely," she said, trying to put some positive energy into her voice.

She climbed into the truck and they drove out of the park.

Katie was hypnotized by the landscape streaming by her window, but her thoughts were never very far from the case. She rehashed her interviews, forensics, and what the medical examiner had told her.

"You're very quiet," said Chad. "What is it you hope to find at the crime scene?"

Katie pondered his question for a moment. She wasn't sure exactly what she was looking for. "I guess I've always handled problems I can't solve by going back to the beginning."

Chad took a sharp turn onto a more rural roadway. "That's good advice. It's like infinity."

"What do you mean?" she asked curiously.

"Well, it's the beginning and the end. Infinite. Everything comes back around to the beginning."

"I like that," Katie said. "That's a great way to look at an investigation."

They talked about mundane things. Usually Katie hated idle chat about the weather and who would win the World Series, but today it was relaxing and she found herself enjoying the drive.

Her phone buzzed with a message. She quickly retrieved it and found the text was from John. It was short and extremely interesting: *The ABO test came back from Cisco's swab. It was type O negative blood. Someone has a dog bite.*

She thought about what that meant, her jaw tensed as she rubbed her slightly chapped lips. Was the person who had broken into her house, leaving a message on her wall as well as the letter on her window, the serial killer?

"Everything okay?" asked Chad.

She snapped back into the moment. "Oh, yes. One of the tests came back. Nothing new." She wanted to keep the evidence to herself and include it in the report to her uncle.

She watched Chad as he took the next right turn. His demeanor was relaxed and he seemed genuinely upbeat.

"How's firefighting?" she asked.

"They've been driving me pretty hard during the drills. I wish the budget would come through and they would add me to the full-time roster before they kill me," he laughed.

Katie studied the view through the windshield. The trees seemed more menacing than before. The day was darker and colder than the last time she'd been there, easing into winter with sparse leaves and barbed-looking branches.

"Okay, the second road to the right," she directed. "I know it looks more like a bike path, but you can still see all the tire impressions from the department's emergency vehicles."

Chad eased the truck to the top and parked just a couple of feet from the edge of the cliff. Loose dust floated upwards as he cut the engine.

A chilling feeling permeated Katie's body. She shivered in her jacket but it wouldn't have made any difference if she had worn heavier gear. Something seemed off at the location. Maybe it was just because she knew what had happened there.

The wind gusted outside, rocking the truck slightly.

"Is this it?" asked Chad as he opened the driver's door, allowing a breeze to blow into the cab, swirling around and exiting again.

Katie stepped out and shut the passenger door.

The sun was now hidden behind heavy clouds as the gusts whistled through the trees around them. There was a part of Katie that wanted to get back into the truck and leave. She still had some things to do at the station—namely asking Denise if she was able to run down some information from the three fabric locations. It was a long shot, but she wasn't going to give up and would keep pursuing every clue.

"I'll follow you," said Chad. He made an "after you" gesture with his arm and let Katie lead the way.

Still with the flight feeling, Katie moved toward the tunnel entrance, which was now cut back and heavily trampled. The pathway had been made much bigger, allowing for the easy removal of the two coffins.

The same questions plagued her.

Why here?

What's the significance?

How long did it take the killer to create the graveyard of horror?

Why did he wait so long between murders? Or did he?

She looked up at the sky and wondered how it would look at night-time, with the infinite number of stars.

Infinite.

Staring down, she remembered every second of finding the graves. Those ticking moments of discovery. The horror. Her relief mixed with the tragedy and reality.

She felt the cold gripping her extremities, travelling up her legs and arms, as she walked through the crime-scene memory. She wondered if there was another gravesite carefully planned and tended like this one.

She theorized that the killer had wanted to save the little girls from something. But what? He'd tended them carefully, kept them in the best condition he could, like a garden. Had he planned to dig them up? He'd changed his MO after the first bodies were found. He was angry, no doubt, which was why he'd come after Katie. She was interrupting his carefully laid plans.

"Everything okay?" interrupted Chad. He stood at the entrance to the tunnel, watching her with his hands shoved into his coat pockets. His concerned expression clearly showed his deep sorrow for such a heinous crime.

"I'm fine," she said. "Searching for inspiration."

"That's an interesting way of looking at it," he said.

"The killer's inspiration, not mine," she explained. "What must he have felt here? Why did he choose this location?"

Chad stiffened as he glanced around the area. "Isn't that what psychopaths do? They become what they want you to see. At least that's the way I understand it."

Katie turned and faced him, suddenly seeing him differently. Not just the boy she'd grown up with, but someone who perceived life a certain way. "You're right. He wants us to see only what he wants us to see." She gazed out at the vast view. It had always been beautiful to her, but now it appeared endless, repetitive, isolating, and a bit hopeless.

After a few minutes, she turned to leave. It was clear that Chad was happy to go; he'd been fidgeting with his hands and trying to find something—anything—to focus on. For some, seeing the reality of what a killer did to his victims wasn't something they wanted to acknowledge, much less visit.

He'd become a bit aloof, different from before. Something had changed between the two of them. Maybe it was Katie and her signals. She didn't know what she wanted in a relationship, and everything seemed to indicate that she needed to keep things platonic between her and Chad—at least for now.

She led the way out of the tree tunnel and walked briskly back to the waiting truck. The wind was ratcheting up its speed. Her cell phone rang. She retrieved it from her jacket pocket and answered. Deputy McGaven's voice was rapid and excited.

"There's been a change in the investigation from Detective Templeton's camp," he began.

"What's up?" Katie suspected that the detective had decided to make some bold move.

"I don't know how, but Templeton managed to get a search warrant for the Compton residence and the Haven farm. He wants to close the cases."

"How? Who was the judge?" She felt her pulse rate increase and her chest squeeze like a vice.

"Jeffries."

"Oh," was the only word Katie could muster.

"What do you want to do?" he asked.

"Well, things are going to be different now. I'll meet you at the department in about an hour, an hour and a half. I have to go home first and change."

"Where are you?"

"Just had an errand to do. I'll see you soon." She ended the call.

"Everything okay?" asked Chad.

"I have to get back. Everything has changed."

CHAPTER 43

Police cars arrived at the Haven farm. Detective Templeton exited his vehicle first and headed to the shed where Terrance Price had stayed while he'd worked there. Two other detectives went to the main working area to check out various storage buildings.

Templeton began swiftly tearing the shed apart. He flipped the mattress, dumped out boxes, and kicked around various personal items. In a box filled with basic banking information, he finally found a small piece of paper with the names and addresses of various places Price had worked.

"Got it!" he shouted.

The piece of paper proved that Terrance Price had had contact with the Comptons.

"Let's go," he ordered, and hurried back to the car.

Detective Templeton sped up to the Comptons' residence and parked his dark police sedan half in the street and half in the driveway. Two patrol cars parked in a more respectful manner. A few neighbors came out of their homes to see what the commotion was about.

The detective flung open his car door and immediately barked orders to the neighbors. "Nothing to see, go back inside your homes."

He marched up to the Comptons' front door, followed by another detective, Romano. He shoved his hand in and out of his pocket but didn't pull anything out. Once he reached the door, he knocked loudly four times.

It didn't take long before a slight woman answered. "Yes?" she said.

"Beth-Ann Compton?" stated Templeton, though he knew her already.

"Yes," she said hesitantly.

Reaching into his upper jacket pocket, he said, "I have a warrant to search your home." He handed her the official paperwork.

"I don't understand," she said faintly. It was evident from her frightened expression that she had no idea why the police would want to search her house.

Another patrol car drove up and parked.

Templeton forged into her home, followed by Romano and a couple of deputies. One of the deputies made a gesture for her to wait at the entrance.

The detective went upstairs as the rest of his crew began searching through drawers and closets, working their way to the kitchen. He found one of the bedrooms doubling as a guest room and craft area. Glancing behind him to make sure no one had followed him, he opened a small drawer at the work table, then reached into his pocket and pulled out a small baggie containing a piece of pink fabric with a tiny drop of blood on it. Without hesitating, he dropped the fabric into the drawer with other scraps of material.

"Up here," he yelled.

Within seconds, Romano and the two deputies arrived. Templeton pointed into the drawer. After everyone was satisfied, one of the deputies brought Mrs. Compton upstairs.

"Mrs. Compton, is this your sewing table?" the detective asked.

"Yes," she replied.

"Everything in here belongs to you?" he insisted.

"Yes," she said again.

Templeton made a gesture for one of the deputies to document and properly retrieve the fabric. "Search the entire room and gather any evidence. Keep the chain of custody intact."

"I don't understand," Mrs. Compton said.

"Don't understand what? Why you hid evidence? Or why you killed your daughter?"

"*No!* I didn't kill my daughter. She was taken. I did not kill her…" She turned to run down the stairs but was stopped by the second deputy.

"Mrs. Beth-Ann Compton," he began. "You have the right to remain silent. Anything you say can and will be used against you in a court of law. You have the right to an attorney. If you cannot afford an attorney, one will be provided for you. Do you understand the rights I have just read to you?"

"No," she said. "No, you're wrong. Whatever you found… can't be…"

"Do you understand your rights?" he demanded.

"No, no, please no, please, I didn't kill my daughter…"

"Do you understand your rights?" he said more loudly.

"Yes," she said in a barely audible whisper.

CHAPTER 44

The more Katie wrestled with everything that had happened during the course of the investigation, the suspects, and the evidence, the more convoluted everything became. She had become sidetracked by trying to prove forensic evidence, but there was nothing pointing to any specific suspect yet. In her gut, she knew that the evidence would prove who the killer was only when they had one.

She struggled with the emotion festering throughout her body and gripped the steering wheel harder, trying to will away any bad feelings or sensations trying to control her.

The search warrant acquired by Templeton for the Comptons' house and the Haven farm made her angry. It was wrong. The detective had jumped to a conclusion to try and close the cases. Some might say it was appropriate in order to clear or implicate the Comptons once and for all, but it didn't make sense that they would kill the other girl—unless Templeton was somehow using Terrance Price's involvement to connect the two cases.

There was one killer—Katie would bet her career on that single fact. One killer, three murders. A serial killer; that was where the investigation stood.

Pressing the accelerator as hard as she dared, she sped around the familiar corners along the road leading to her house. She veered too close to the opposite lane and an oncoming driver blew their horn at her. She didn't care. Her first priority was to get home, take care of Cisco and change back into her work clothes. The second priority was to prove Templeton wrong—and to set things straight.

Her cell phone rang.

Taking her foot from the accelerator, she glanced at the screen. It was an incoming call from McGaven. Her stomach churned as she answered.

"Bad news," McGaven said.

Katie didn't respond, but instead braced herself for the worst.

"Templeton arrested Mrs. Compton and they've already transferred her to the jail. She's at booking right now."

"On what charge?"

"Premeditated murder."

Katie shook her head adamantly, her fists clenched. "On what evidence?"

"Apparently they found material from the coffin in her home, and some paperwork that proved she knew Price."

"That's ridiculous. It doesn't fit. This is a disaster." She paused. "What about the Matthews girl? She's still missing."

"What do you want to do?" he asked.

"I'm just about to get to my house right now. I'll meet you at the department in a half-hour."

"See you then," he said.

Katie disconnected the call. This was her fault for not being thorough in her job. There could have been something she had missed, and if she hadn't, things wouldn't be in this mess. It was almost impossible to undo the mistakes once the case began to go through the criminal-justice system.

Damn it.

She took several deep breaths and drove her Jeep slowly up the driveway, noticing that her roses were beginning to bloom. She would be no use if she became emotional—a pitfall of the job. She parked and stepped out, glancing at the roses again. Even though they were yellow, it still made her think about the remnants of red roses in the coffins. She tried to remember where she'd seen some in bloom.

Roses.

Her attention was distracted by her briefcase, which had fallen into the backseat. She stopped and leaned in to retrieve it. As she placed it on the passenger seat to take back to the sheriff's office, Cisco suddenly began barking. It wasn't his happy play greeting; it was a rapid bark that indicated someone was near. It was a warning. Katie could see him at the front window, standing on his hind legs, front paws raised, his nails scraping the glass with a horrible high-pitched sound.

She stood still, stunned by Cisco's behavior, then jogged towards the front door, reaching for her holstered gun underneath her sweatshirt. As she readied herself, she heard a voice behind her say, "Katie."

A shocking blast of electricity hit her torso and reverberated throughout her body, buckling her legs beneath her. She dropped her gun. A strange buzzing sound filled her head, scrambling her rational thoughts. It was the last thing she remembered before hitting the ground.

CHAPTER 45

Deputy McGaven was growing impatient waiting for Katie to meet him at the department. He fidgeted and paced around; nothing kept his attention. He hadn't known her to be late to anything since he had met her; it wasn't in her personality, especially given the current status of the investigation.

"C'mon, Katie, hurry up," he muttered under his breath.

Glancing at his watch again, he realized that more than an hour had passed since he had last spoken with her. Something wasn't right. He called her, but she didn't pick up.

Maybe she'd stopped to take a shower, he thought. Maybe her battery was dead. Maybe she had a problem with her security system. Maybe Cisco had run away. The more he tried to think of reasons why she hadn't shown up to meet him and wasn't answering her phone, the more concerned he became.

Sheriff Scott entered the office with a sour expression on his face. He looked as if he wanted blood.

"Sir," said McGaven.

"Make it quick, Deputy," the sheriff grumbled.

"I know there's a lot going on, but… I can't seem to get a hold of Katie."

"What do you mean? You're partnered with her." The sheriff turned to face him directly.

"Yes, sir. We were supposed to meet here half an hour ago. I wouldn't trouble you, but I think something may be wrong."

Sheriff Scott took a step back to assess what he had heard. It was obvious that he was on his way somewhere important, but this new situation involved a fellow law-enforcement officer, not to mention his niece, at potential risk.

"Sheriff… Sheriff!" Chad hurried into the room, breathless and looking concerned. "It's Katie," he gasped. "I can't find her. I went by her place. Her Jeep is there and Cisco is in the house."

"Take it easy," said the sheriff. "What makes you so concerned?"

"Early this morning, we went up to the graveyard crime-scene area. She wanted to check it out again, but she wouldn't tell me any more than that. I just went along for the ride."

McGaven pushed into the conversation, "Where did you meet her? I talked to her more than an hour ago and she was almost home."

Chad caught his breath and took a step backward. "We met at Highland Park. I drove her to the area, and then we came back and I dropped her off at the park."

A few deputies had gathered in the background, listening to the conversation.

"Why did you go to her house?" asked the sheriff.

"She seemed down after she received that call from McGaven, so I wanted to stop by to see how she was doing."

"I'm not going to stand around debating any longer," said Sheriff Scott. He turned to McGaven. "Try calling her again, and keep calling her on the way to her house."

Two police cars and Chad's truck arrived at Katie's house. The three vehicles blocked the driveway behind her Jeep. The property was quiet and there didn't seem to be anyone around; nothing looked out of place.

Cisco began barking, and Sheriff Scott immediately got out of his unmarked police vehicle. "McGaven, any luck?"

"No, still no answer," the deputy stated with a worried look on his face.

"Check the perimeter," the sheriff ordered. "Chad, come with me."

While McGaven took off to search the grounds and the exterior of the house, Sheriff Scott and Chad ran to the porch, their footsteps pounding on the steps. The sheriff hammered on the front door, causing Cisco to bark even louder. "It's okay, Cisco," yelled the sheriff. "Katie! Katie, you home?" He looked to the left and right. "Katie!" he yelled again.

Nothing.

Peering in the window next to the front door, he couldn't see anyone inside, and the interior didn't look to be disturbed.

McGaven appeared. "Clear," he said breathlessly.

"What do we do now?" asked Chad.

The sheriff glanced up at the front camera and saw that the lens had been covered by some kind of spray paint or adhesive. He immediately reached into his pocket, retrieved a set of keys and inserted one of them into the new lock.

Click.

He waited a moment before he turned the knob and pushed the door open. The alarm went off, waiting for the code to be punched in. The sheriff's jaw clenched. "Cisco, take it easy, boy." He pushed the door open another few inches, and was greeted by a dark nose breathing deeply, followed by canine grumbles. "Easy, boy," the sheriff coaxed as he pushed the door wide, stepping inside and hitting the four-digit code.

Cisco ran around the living room and then moved to the large window. He stood up on his hind legs and pounded his paws against the glass.

"Where's Katie?" the sheriff urged the dog.

McGaven disappeared down the hallway calling out Katie's name. He returned almost immediately, shaking his head.

The sheriff looked around. "Her briefcase and keys aren't here," he said.

McGaven ran out the door, followed closely by Cisco. He opened the unlocked Jeep, where he saw Katie's briefcase on the passenger seat and her keys still in the ignition. He grabbed them up, then returned to the house, where he put the items on the kitchen counter. The three men were quiet for a moment; all of them trying to figure out where Katie was and what could have happened to her.

"Where was the last place you and Katie visited?" the sheriff asked McGaven.

"Today? Nowhere yet. We were meeting back at the department to figure that out. And to find out the details of Mrs. Compton's arrest."

"Yesterday?" he pushed. "Where did you go?"

McGaven stuttered a bit and then recalled the previous day. "I met her at the forensic lab, then we went to talk with the Darren brothers, but they weren't home, so we went to see the medical examiner again and then a couple of carpenters, and to Charles Rey's house to talk about the coffins."

The sheriff spoke in an authoritative tone. "I want to know the whereabouts right now of everyone she had contact with yesterday and the day before. I don't care if it's the waitress at lunch or deputies you passed in the hall. I want to know where *everyone* is now and where they were two hours ago."

He took a moment and then appeared to formulate a plan. "McGaven, pay a visit to both the medical examiner and the forensic lab. Check back in with me as soon as possible. Keep this quiet until there's something to report. Got it?"

McGaven nodded and hurried to the police car.

"Let me help," said Chad. "Please, Sheriff."

The sheriff hesitated. "Okay. Come with me."

"Where are we going?" asked Chad.

"We're going to pay the Darren brothers and Charles Rey a visit," he said. "But you're only here as an observer, and you do as you're told. No argument."

"Got it," said Chad.

CHAPTER 46

A low baritone droning bombarded Katie's eardrums. The sound matched the pain at the back of her head, a relentless, stabbing agony with a pulse. Her body bumped and bounced every once in a while without any sort of rhythm or warning, as if riding in an old-fashioned buckboard wagon. Her breath caught in her throat, pushing down hard on her chest. It was difficult to breathe, and when she tried to gasp for air, it smelled like a musty barn.

She opened her eyes and saw nothing. Turning her head slightly to the left and then to the right, there was just a dark abyss. Even that slight movement made her nauseous, and waves of unconsciousness flowed in and out.

With her eyelids heavy, she slowly raised her right hand and touched her moist face. Clammy and cold, she shivered, her teeth chattering. It made a hollow sound around her, eerie and haunting.

She couldn't remember what had happened.

Where was she?

Why was it so dark?

She bounced again, harder than before, but this time she felt a solid surface next to her. She tried to turn her body to the right, but the obstruction wouldn't let her move in that direction. She tried the same position on the left side, with the same result.

The searing pain at the back of her head pulsed with renewed energy, forcing her to squeeze her eyes shut. When she finally opened them again, she could see a tiny ray of light coming from a faraway corner, like a beacon of hope.

She moved her hands down the sides of her body and realized that the obstruction was wood. Not smooth to the touch, but rough and uneven. Raising them to her face, neck, and upper chest, she felt a cold perspiration that misted her body and chilled her fingertips. She was suddenly aware that she was dressed only in her bra and panties.

Her arms and legs flailed in terror, causing a loud banging all around her as she pounded the wooden walls.

Her fuzzy mind began to clear and her thoughts turned to her predicament. She was lying flat on her back. It was hard and uncomfortable against her spine and the back of her cranium.

The bumping and bouncing resumed.

Her rapid heavy breathing echoed in her ears as the air thinned, making it more difficult to take in oxygen. Her pulse rate accelerated and a panic attack took hold of her, gripping her mind and throwing off any semblance of balance and sanity with a massive dose of adrenalin.

Tears streamed down her face as she realized that she was lying in a sealed wooden coffin. She immediately pictured the dead eyes and perfectly posed bodies of Chelsea Compton and Tammie Myers. The sweet, innocent girls had looked as if they were merely sleeping. The sight was seared into her mind.

Fierce as any warrior, she began to scream with every last ounce of energy, while punching and kicking with her bare hands and feet.

CHAPTER 47

Deputy McGaven sprinted through the department, knocking into a couple of deputies in the process, but kept moving until he rang the buzzer at the forensic lab.

"Open up," he called, waving his hands at the video camera just above his head. His face was pale as he tried to steady his heavy breathing. "Open up," he repeated, knowing he must look crazy.

The door buzzed and unlocked, opening a couple of inches. He pushed it wide.

"Blackburn, you around?" he said as he moved forward.

He peered into several offices and one exam room, but they were all empty.

"Hello?" he said.

Jamie, a forensic tech, emerged from a door to his left.

"Is Blackburn here?" McGaven asked.

"Uh, no, he hasn't come in yet."

"Have you seen Detective Scott today?"

"No, I haven't seen her since the crime scene," Jamie replied with a quizzical expression.

McGaven turned and hurried from the lab.

At the main doors of the morgue, McGaven abruptly stopped. The various cleaning smells and the gurneys shuffling dead people gave him the chills. He hated being inside the building of the dead more than anything, but as a police officer, he knew it was part of the job.

Luck was on his side and he saw the ME leaving one of the exam rooms carrying some file folders.

"Dr. Dean," he said.

"Ah, Deputy McGaven, what can I do for you?" The man always seemed to sound cheerful, even after dissecting a body and weighing human organs.

"Have you seen Detective Scott?"

"You mean since the two of you were here yesterday?"

"Yes."

"Curious question." The doctor studied McGaven closely. "Everything okay?"

"Don't know," said the deputy. "Have you been here all day?"

"Well, yes, and I haven't seen the detective."

"Thanks for your time," McGaven said, and turned to leave.

"Deputy?"

He turned back. "Yes," he said, trying to sound calm.

"Detective Scott has a gift. Whatever you're fretting about, she'll be just fine."

The deputy didn't know what to say. He nodded, then headed out of the morgue to check in with the sheriff.

*

Sheriff Scott decided to park close to the house. It wasn't clear if anyone was home.

As he and Chad walked toward the barn behind the house, the sheriff's cell phone rang. He stopped walking and listened to the caller. "Stay at the department and wait for further instructions."

"What did McGaven find out?" asked Chad.

"Negative."

"Were Blackburn and Dr. Dean there?"

"Blackburn hasn't been at the lab today," said the sheriff, clenching his jaw.

"What does that mean?" Chad persisted.

"Don't know yet."

Chad let out an annoyed sigh.

The sheriff smiled slightly.

"What?"

"Being a detective takes patience. You can't jump to conclusions no matter how tempting it might be, or how hot your emotions are," he said.

"I know." Chad picked up his pace.

When they reached the barn, the doors were closed. The sheriff opened them. "Hello?"

No answer.

The sun shone through the doors, lighting up the tidy interior. It didn't look as if anyone had been working there today.

"No one's here," said Chad, clearly disappointed. He looked at the sheriff, who began to walk around inside the barn. "What are you looking for?"

"Nothing in particular. Just want to be thorough."

"We're wasting time," Chad urged.

"Five minutes won't make a difference one way or another."

Both men examined the work area, looking in drawers and storage areas. Tools were organized and hung in the correct places. Drawers and cubbyholes held nails, screws, and various kinds of adhesives. Everything appeared as it should.

"Satisfied?" asked Chad.

"For now," said the sheriff.

They exited the barn and the sheriff closed the large doors. As they began to walk back to the car, he slowed his pace and looked around the property once again.

"What?" asked Chad.

"Just want to check the house."

They jogged up to the front door and the sheriff knocked. They waited. He knocked again. Still no answer. He put his hand on the doorknob, twisted it, and pushed the door slightly ajar. "Hello? It's the sheriff," he called.

Silence.

They stepped over the threshold and listened. A stark silence greeted them, making the sheriff uneasy. His hand brushed against his sidearm, his fingertips stretching and gripping the handle.

"Stay here," he said in a whisper.

Chad nodded.

The sheriff moved deeper into the house.

Like the barn, it was tidy and organized. The furniture and decor were worn but in good condition and comfortable. The pillows on the couch were arranged symmetrically, and a blue-and-yellow crocheted blanket was draped neatly over the back.

He scanned the living room and moved to the kitchen. The trashcan was filled with empty beer bottles. There was a coffee mug and a plate in the wooden dish rack. The dish towel was on the counter, efficiently folded.

"Anything?" Chad asked from the entrance.

The sheriff took one last look around and saw nothing that would indicate anything unusual. "No," he said.

There was a squeak from a door on the other side of the kitchen, which caught his attention. Thinking it was a pantry door, he went to close it, but felt a cool breeze blowing through the crack. He pulled it open and saw that it led to the basement.

He hesitated. Then he flipped the light switch and started down the steps.

CHAPTER 48

Katie jerked violently before opening her eyes again, as if abruptly waking from a bad dream only to find out that it was a real-life nightmare. She had passed out for only a few minutes and now found herself in the same predicament.

Trapped.

The words *YOU WILL NEVER FIND ME* resonated through her mind with a chilling realization as she finally understood that they referred not to the killer, but to Katie herself.

"No!" she screamed.

But her breath caught in her throat, and her scream emerged as a desperate strained whisper.

Her survival skills kicked into high gear, and she kept moving her hands and feet around the box trying to find something—anything—that would help her escape. Her heart rate reached a dangerous level, making it impossible to think clearly or breathe in a normal manner.

"No!" she whispered again. More tears fell down the sides of her face, leaving droplets near her ears.

She couldn't get her thoughts in a cohesive order to figure out what she should do. She'd had extensive training in combat, shooting, self-defense, dog training, and how to handle a felon, but nothing had prepared her for being ambushed and trapped inside a coffin.

Defeat crept into her mind and heart, a doomed feeling that she had never experienced before trying to take over her thoughts.

"Damn you!" she yelled. "You're not going to win!"

The jarring bumps began to increase in intensity until the motion became almost unbearable. Her fingers, feet, and shins were numb, emitting a buzzing feeling accompanied by pain.

She realized she needed to figure out how long she had been in the vehicle. She assumed it was a type of truck or SUV, but she needed to be ready if there was going to be an opportunity to surprise the kidnapper.

She gritted her teeth, stopped her silly tears, and focused hard on what had happened back at the house. There was a gap in her memory. Absently she touched her chest; it was sore beneath her fingertips. The hazy memory began to come into focus before slipping away again.

Frustrated, she muttered, "You're… not… going… to… win…"

She began to count the seconds and memorize every stop and turn of the vehicle. As she counted, her pulse calmed and leveled off.

One… two… three…

You're never going to win… I won't let you.

CHAPTER 49

The old wooden stairs creaked as Sheriff Scott descended to the bottom. He walked deeper into the basement and looked around.

There were some shelves holding canning jars filled with vegetables and fruits, most likely from the garden. It would be a great place to store them because the basement kept things cool, though it felt colder, damper here than the sheriff had expected. The place had that musty earth odor that was difficult to avoid.

He was turning to leave when he noticed something shiny in the corner where the sun pierced through a small window high in the wall. Moving toward the large Mason jar, he noticed a single key inside. It was the kind of key that opened padlocks—shiny and well used.

He picked it up and looked around. There was nothing indicating what the key was used for. He looked at the walls and spotted a small gouge at around shoulder height. Slowly he inserted the key. It fit. When he turned it, a locking mechanism clicked and released the door.

He instinctively pushed it inward. It was pitch dark and difficult to ascertain if this was a closet or another room. He fumbled around inside until he found a light switch.

A low motorized noise engaged and set off a well-tuned reaction.

One…

Two…

Three…

Four fluorescent lights clicked on overhead and brightened the room. Every corner was illuminated brightly to reveal an organized compartmentalized room.

One area was a stocked craftsman's workshop where rectangular wooden boxes and bolts of fabric waited. Several small plastic containers containing thread, needles, and ribbon were stacked in the corner. He noticed specially cut lengths of ribbon in all colors and the fabric to make teddy bears like the ones at the crime scenes.

His stomach dropped and his nerves tingled as if he had been stunned with electricity. But it was the stainless-steel gurney that stopped him short. On it, secured with heavy straps, lay a motionless, dark-haired little girl. He sucked in a breath, allowing his mind to catch up with what he was seeing.

"Sheriff," called Chad from upstairs. "What's going on?" His voice moved closer.

The sheriff was careful not to touch anything, but went quickly to the little girl to see if she was alive. There was a weak pulse, but she remained unconscious. He recognized her as the missing girl, Dena Matthews. He immediately loosened the straps from her chest, arms, and legs. Picking up her limp body, he headed out of the killer's lair.

"No…" Chad's voice was choked. He stood in the doorway, his face deathly pale. "How could…?" He couldn't bring himself to finish the sentence. "Is she still alive?"

"She's still breathing. We have to get her to the hospital as soon as possible. Don't touch anything," said the sheriff. He was in charge and had to act like it, no matter how upset and horrified he felt.

"Should I call an ambulance?"

Carrying Dena, the sheriff led Chad to the front door without another word. "No, it will take too long for them to get here. I'm going to drive her directly to the hospital."

After he'd secured Dena in the backseat, he took out his cell phone and quickly placed a call requesting forensics and one of the detectives on duty to come to the ranch.

"Sheriff," said Chad. "What about… what about…"

The sheriff finished the call and turned to him. "What are you saying?"

"Is Katie in danger?"

*

The enemy waits for the perfect moment to attack, when you least expect it.

The counting helped to calm Katie's nerves, and her recollection began to come into focus. She remembered watching Cisco barking like crazy at the front window as she slowly approached the house. She had been worried that the person who had left the messages might be back, hiding somewhere waiting to attack her.

She quickly assessed the profile list for the serial killer. He would be between thirty and fifty, wearing a size twelve shoe, and trained in tech work. Everything seemed personal, organized, with a repeated signature. Her gut told her that it was an older man who had some impulse control. When she got too close, he'd had to do something drastic. He had used a stun gun, which had slammed into her, causing her to pass out and hit her head. The pain was still evident on her chest, where the tiny hooks had attached themselves.

She reached behind her head and felt a wet substance seeping through her fingers from the fall. She estimated she would need a few stitches.

She knew that he'd stripped her down to her underwear in case she had a weapon or means of communication. But there was always something a killer didn't completely count on, a slip-up, or a hasty decision that caused a lapse in judgment. There was always something that could be done to escape; it was a matter of finding out what the killer's weakness was.

"I will never give up," she whispered.

CHAPTER 50

Katie's spirits rose as her heart rate returned to normal. She managed to take her mind through her army training and all the people who had made it possible for her to excel. She told herself that her current situation was just another hazard of the job that she needed to get through. She had been in many predicaments that seemed hopeless, but there was always a way out.

She estimated that she had been travelling for roughly forty-five minutes on mostly uneven roads, but that meant she could be anywhere. Her instincts told her they were headed into the countryside, due to the fact that most serial killers didn't like to deviate from their MO and comfort zone. It was also a perfect place to get rid of a body.

Instant shivers pimpled her arms and down the back of her neck.

Stay focused.

Her hands and feet weren't bound, which meant she could move freely.

She wasn't gagged, so she could scream.

She knew that being stripped down to her undergarments made her more vulnerable, but he hadn't taken into consideration the fact that she had been in the army, where you had no privacy. Modesty didn't play any part in the military.

There wasn't enough time to try and work on prying the lid open or making a hole in the wood. But she had noticed that the coffin was rough and haphazardly put together, which might mean that there was some weak point to the construction.

She estimated that another five minutes had passed. There had been so many left and right turns that she had lost count, but one thing was definite: she was deep in the mountains and no one would ever hear her screams.

She moved her raw fingers in a systematic way, beginning with the area behind her head and searching clockwise. She realized straight away that the coffin was wider than necessary. She took the time to feel for anything that seemed weak or unstable. When she couldn't search with her hands, she had to rely on her feet to feel the lower end of the coffin.

Another ten minutes or so had passed.

Without warning, the vehicle abruptly stopped, causing her to slide and hit the end of the coffin.

Her head was higher than it had been before; she appeared to be at a slight angle, as though the vehicle was no longer on flat ground.

She had to make a conscious effort to breathe quietly as she strained to listen. The low hum had not stopped. The distinct opening and closing of a heavy car door sounded next to her head.

No voices.

No audible footsteps.

The minute of waiting seemed to morph into an hour.

There were no other distinguishing sounds.

Suddenly, the startling crash of a tailgate slamming open reverberated around her. Katie knew what would happen next, and she was still no closer to a plan than when she had first found herself in the coffin.

Her nervousness escalated, her head pounding as her blood pressure steadily rose, which made her body and limbs buzz with a strange energy.

There was a high-pitched screech, and she realized that the coffin was being slowly pulled from its current location. The sound of raw wood scraping against the metal of an SUV or truck continued, causing her to grit her teeth and ball her hands into fists. As the horrendous noise stopped, the coffin hit something hard, smashing her head against the top of the box.

She was on solid ground.

CHAPTER 51

Katie had tensed as the coffin fell. The impact was sudden and violent, slamming and contorting her body. The pain in her head heightened as an unrelenting stabbing discomfort gripped her forehead, blurring her vision, while her elbows were battered and her hips bruised from the force.

She squeezed her eyes shut and waited for the next assault.

After a minute, she opened her eyes, still unable to see anything clearly except for the pinprick of light from the lower left corner. Otherwise, darkness abounded and kept her company, though it could do nothing to repel the impending threat.

Perspiration dappled her skin, causing her to shudder uncontrollably, rattling her bones. Fighting the urge to cry out, she kept silent, gritting down on her teeth and maintaining her position as best she could. Her nerves spiked, warning her body and mind what was about to happen, as the familiar sounds and the smell of dust ignited her memory of the battlefield.

Voices behind her yelled of the threat up ahead. The sour taste never left her mouth. The never-ending jangling of large-caliber gunfire rang in her ears. Her ribcage and skull took the brunt of the reverberation. Heat from the foreign climate turned up the escalating inferno inside her heavy uniform. A large explosion slammed her to the ground as dirt blasted her face. Her thoughts were pity and helplessness. Throughout her momentary misery, a wet nose against her face resuscitated her enough to give her the energy needed to crawl. She felt the lean canine next to her wriggling forward, mimicking her position and movements.

An ear-piercing screeching noise interrupted her memory, tossing her back to reality with a shock as she gripped her fists and held her breath. The noise continued around the perimeter of the coffin, and she realized that someone was removing the screws with an electric screwdriver. She placed her hands in front of her in a shaky fighting stance, ready for anything.

The top of the coffin was ripped away, causing a bright light to temporarily blind her. She couldn't see anything, only a lightning whirlwind of white accompanied by a sharp pain behind her eyes. Unclenching her fists, she covered her face with her hands. Her pulse rate heightened erratically and she could hear her own rapid breathing, but she was paralyzed.

It seemed like minutes but was barely thirty seconds before her vision began to clear. She looked up and the first thing she saw was the blue sky accompanied by a few wispy clouds. A couple of birds flew over. Outdoor colors began to darken and she saw immense green trees towering above her, leaves blowing gently in the wind and branches swaying in unison.

She dropped her hands to her sides and focused on the dark figure standing above her. At first, it was difficult to focus, but as her vision came crashing back, she gasped, remembering where she had seen the red roses.

Charles Rey stood there with a shotgun pointed at her head.

CHAPTER 52

"Everyone listen up. We have a code red involving one of our own." Sheriff Scott was standing in front of a huge computer screen showing an aerial view of the two counties surrounding Pine Valley. It was in a special room at the police department that was primarily used for Homeland Security emergencies or any type of national or state-wide disaster.

All available police officers, volunteer officers, recruits, search-and-rescue personnel, and administrative volunteers were present, including Deputy McGaven and Chad. More volunteers were being co-opted from other departments as the sheriff gave instructions.

"Every second counts, so I'm going to make this brief," he continued, swallowing hard so as not to show his emotions. "Here's what we know. At approximately 1300 hours today, Charles Rey kidnapped Detective Katie Scott from her residence." He cleared his throat. "Rey is believed to be driving his late-model Ford truck, license RWX 32J7. He is six foot one, fifty-six years old, one hundred eighty-nine pounds, and knows his way round various types of weapons. At this time, we have found Dena Matthews, who is in a stable condition, and have enough evidence to connect Rey to all three unsolved murders. Forensic services will be searching and documenting his residence."

One of the deputies asked, "What types of evidence were found?"

"The investigation is under way and I'm not at liberty to discuss this part of the case right now. The main objective is to find Rey as soon as possible. It is unclear what he will do with Detective Scott, but we will not take any chances."

"Sir, do we have any other information as to where he could have gone?" asked one of the volunteers.

Sheriff Scott felt sick to his stomach, his heart skipping a beat, as his imagination took many twisted turns thinking about what might happen to Katie and what she was going through at that exact moment. He pushed onward. "We will divide our teams to search all these vicinities." He gestured to the map behind him. "Rey is attracted to rural areas that are less travelled and could be at any of these locations. I've assigned team captains who will further brief you. In addition, we have secured every available resource to expedite the search, including four-wheel-drive vehicles, motorcycles, ATVs, and other equipment."

Chad studied the maps as he listened intently to the sheriff's instructions. "Sir, I have a request," he said. "I would like your permission to take Cisco and search some of the other remote areas you haven't immediately identified. I know some of these areas are more inaccessible, but I'm capable of making the hike. I will be able to cover more ground with the dog and I have a heavy-duty Jeep that can handle any trail or off-road area."

Sheriff Scott thought for a moment, then agreed. "Okay, but you have to stay in touch with the closest team leader by radio and with me by cell phone. Understand?" He reached into his pocket and took out a key ring. "Here's the key to her house."

"Thank you, sir."

"Be very careful and check in every hour, understand? I don't have enough manpower to send someone with you."

"We'll be fine," Chad said, and left the room.

CHAPTER 53

The search teams assembled at three strategic locations along the trails and rugged roadways leading into the more rural areas of the county. They had accumulated more than one hundred volunteers and would concentrate mostly on the vast unincorporated state-park areas and other uninhabitable regions. Every person had been briefed with the most up-to-date information available.

The first team took off in heavy-duty SUVs and trucks, with motorcycles packed in available cargo areas. They fanned out and worked in a grid system. Each vehicle kept in contact with the others and would provide any assistance necessary. Deputy McGaven was included in the group and was determined to find Katie.

The second team was the largest and consisted of many individual volunteers who were used to searching for missing people, lost hikers, and livestock. They set out on foot in small groups to conduct a slow, meticulous search. A few bloodhounds were also included to follow any scent track that was picked up.

The third team was deployed with ATVs to the forestry areas that had flatter roads. They followed the same protocols as the other two teams and worked in more of a circular grid beginning in a central area. No area would remain unsearched until they found Katie.

*

Chad loaded up Cisco in his Jeep, making sure he had everything he might need, including rescue climbing gear, the police-issue radio the sheriff had given him, his cell phone, battery-operated lights, emergency flares, a shotgun, a Glock handgun, and a first-aid kit—plus a few more odds and ends.

Cisco obeyed his commands, and the dog's low, distressed whines showed that he appeared to have a sixth canine sense that it was an emergency.

Chad took one last look inside Katie's house before leaving. Picking up her hoodie that was draped over a chair, he decided to bring it with him as it had her scent on it. He kept his emotions in check and didn't want to think about what might have happened to her. His prayers were never more real than at that moment.

He found Katie's field notebook on the counter, and after reading some of her entries, he realized that she had systematically described her original searches for Chelsea Compton in painstaking detail. He took several precious moments to study her notes and graphs before slipping the notebook into his pocket.

He now had a revised plan.

He worked out search details as he drove to the area where he and Katie had recently had lunch. According to the maps, many of the trails wound around to other areas with vehicle access. He would use Katie's techniques and search parameters to assist in finding her.

Once he reached the picnic area, he continued on westward and then took a road going north that was known only to locals. The police search parties were at different locations, southwest, which was fine with him. He would work a different type of search, straight out of Katie's own handbook, parking the Jeep and doing a perimeter sweep in a line-strip formation. He wanted to get through the largest amount of ground he could before moving on.

He found a good place to park, and got out of the car carrying just the essentials in order to keep his backpack light.

Cisco leaped out next to him, shook himself, and waited for a command while maintaining his ears alert and forward. He caught wind of something immediately, keeping his nose high and inhaling deeply, but then seemed to lose interest in whatever he had scented.

Chad powered up his cell phone and pulled up an aerial view of the region he was going to search. He divided it up into sections—eight in total. He'd work through them systematically.

"C'mon, boy," he said.

With Cisco at his heels, he hiked down the narrow road, keeping in mind the time and the direction they were travelling. For added security, he set his phone GPS to keep him on target.

As he walked, he remembered the technique that Katie used for her searches. She'd briefly explained it to him at the gravesite, telling him how she used all of her senses. He stopped, closed his eyes, and listened intently. After a few minutes, he opened them again, amazed at how vivid and detailed everything seemed. He then took a slow three-hundred-sixty-degree turn, studying his surroundings. He would use this technique every so often during the search to look for anything out of place, anything that moved, or anything that appeared to have been recently disturbed.

Cisco padded along keeping his head low and his tail down, concentrating on any curious scent. It was clear that the dog had an instinct that this wasn't a fun hike. He obediently kept a few paces behind Chad, waiting for his next command.

Chad walked for forty minutes without finding any indication that Rey had taken this particular road. He was at a high altitude and able to see into the various canyon and trail sections. The whole area seemed deserted and lonely. He stopped to listen and take in the view for any indication of movement, dust rising, or unusual sounds.

The air stood still—no wind blew, which was strange in itself. A couple of sparrows chirped their songs, but nothing else moved, scurried, flew, or sang.

Deep emotions welled up inside Chad, something he had never experienced before. He wasn't sure if he wanted to laugh or cry.

The reality of Katie's predicament was overwhelming and it seemed impossible there would be a happy ending as he looked out at the vast area, searching for answers. He imagined her green eyes gazing at him as her long dark hair blew in the wind. She was a strong, intelligent woman who obviously didn't know how beautiful she was—or maybe she did and it didn't make any difference to her. That thought made Chad smile.

The truth was, she could be anywhere—in another state and not in the rural mountain areas that were currently being searched. But looking for her here was a gamble worth taking.

Cisco bumped his wet nose against Chad's hand as if to remind him he was there with him, that they'd find her.

"What's up?" he said, looking down at the jet-black dog with wolf eyes. "I know, I'm scared too." He looked around and remembered the many times they'd hiked and camped in the area growing up. He'd loved her then and nothing had changed.

Cisco kept his eyes fixed on him.

Chad knew that the dog had seen more combat conditions than most humans. He wondered too if Cisco sensed they were embarking on a fight—a fight to find Katie and save her life.

Looking back at the landscape, he whispered, "Where are you, Katie?"

CHAPTER 54

"You should have left things alone," Charles Rey said, never moving the barrel of the gun away from Katie's face. "I warned you… I warned you to leave these cases alone, but you didn't listen."

Katie blinked a couple of times and then took her eyes away from the gun and watched Charles's face as he spoke. She immediately noticed a white bandage wrapped tightly around his upper right arm, speckled with drops of blood.

Good boy, Cisco.

"Why couldn't you just let them sleep?" he said. He lowered his head and mumbled, "Sleep… sleep, my pretty ones…"

"You know I can't do that," she replied, running through every type of escape scenario she could think of.

"I'm not wasting any more time allowing you to undo everything I've done. You made your decision. You're responsible for your own predicament, right here, right now, and you will have to pay."

"You may not believe this, but I do understand," she said.

"Shut up!" His anger rose and unleashed; he seemed unable to control it. "Shut up!"

"I know how you feel," she gently pushed.

"You don't know anything! Have you seen what's going on in the world, everywhere, even right here? It sickens me."

Katie nodded.

"You know that girl's parents had swinger parties? Abuse. Lust. Greed. What kind of environment is that for children? It gets worse every day. Every time I turn on the news I see children who have been victims, who have seen terrible things."

While he was speaking, Katie tightened her abdominals and tried to sit up.

"Stay right there!"

She slowly leaned back, trying not to bruise her head any more than it already was.

"I know you, Katie. Smart. Capable. Tough. I always liked you. But your smarts have gotten you in this situation. I didn't want to do it. I didn't want to do it…"

"Do what?"

The shotgun wavered slightly. "I didn't want to trap you and that nice deputy in the barn to die. I honestly didn't want to…"

"I believe you. If you let me go, I'll do everything within my power to help you. My uncle will do everything he can to help you—I can promise you that."

Charles laughed, a hearty deep belly laugh.

Katie tried to sit up again, but Charles pushed the barrel of the gun toward her face.

"Stay right there, girlie." Holding the weapon steady, he said, "I think for all your smarts you underestimate me. That's why you couldn't figure out the case. It was staring right at you, I was even helping you." He laughed again. "Get up," he said, waving the gun.

Katie hesitated.

"I said get up."

Katie sat up, very aware that she was only dressed in her bra and panties. She watched Charles as he waited for her to obey him. She used her hands to brace herself and balance as she stood up. A wave of dizziness blanketed her, and she fought to keep her equilibrium. Standing up made the back of her head pound harder, and she realized she was in an extremely weakened state. She fought the rising nausea as she stepped from the coffin, her bare feet pressed against the cold dirt.

"Very nice," he said, looking her up and down. "You are a very pretty girl."

Katie flinched, revolted by this man staring at her, a killer of young, innocent girls.

"It's not too late," she said. She glanced at the open coffin, which had been haphazardly assembled with mismatched pieces of wood and secured by two-inch screws. It was a reminder that she would probably be buried alive if the situation didn't change—and soon.

"Don't worry, I'm not going to bury you," Charles said. There was a slight sarcasm to his voice; it was more morbid than funny. "I have something else in mind for you."

Katie stood her ground. Her physical and emotional strength was creeping back as the dizziness faded. She knew she couldn't overpower him, but there would be a moment—most likely only a second or two—that would prove to be in her favor. She would have to wait patiently and have faith it would come.

"You're not good enough to get a special burial. You are going to fly," he said.

Katie assumed that meant she would be pushed to her death. She remained silent, waiting for her opportunity to arise.

He added, "When you're gone, I'll make sure your dog meets his demise too. There will be nothing left of you."

"You surprise me, Charles," she said. "I expected more from you. This is pitiful, even for you."

"Shut up and walk." He gestured to a narrow path leading to a cliff.

"You know you can't take away the memory or the pain?" She was assuming something terrible had happened to him in the past—she guessed it was the loss of someone close before he came to Pine Valley.

"What are you talking about?"

"You know what I'm talking about," she said.

He stopped abruptly. His chest raised and lowered at an accelerated rate. "You never speak of her. You *never* speak of Dottie."

"Would she have agreed with what you're doing? If I had to wager a guess, my answer would be no." She didn't know who Dottie was, but it didn't matter. She had managed to push Rey's distress button to draw him out.

He shoved the barrel of the gun into her back. "You know nothing of what she went through. What they did to her."

"Would she approve of who you are today?"

"They tortured her, raped her, and left her to die." His voice wavered in grief. "What they did was pure evil."

"What makes you different from them?" She wanted to keep him talking.

"I may not have been in her life, but that still didn't change the fact that I was her daddy."

"You couldn't protect her."

"I never had the chance!" he cried. "Never... ever... Things might've been different. She would be alive today."

As Katie neared the cliff, she knew she had options. She had to keep Charles talking about his daughter; it would give her time to think. The area overall was unfamiliar to her and she didn't think she had visited it before. It was difficult to figure out where she was, but from the position of the sun, she could tell they were moving southeast.

Think, Katie.

Think, dammit.

The cliff kept getting closer... closer... and closer.

Now or never.

She spun around, using her right arm and elbow to smack away the shotgun. The timing was perfect and achieved the exact result she wanted. Charles must've relaxed his grip, and the gun flew sideways and landed several yards away, just out of reach.

He let out a weird strangled yell of dismay.

Not having enough time to grab the shotgun, Katie took the opportunity to run toward the truck. Her feet pounded on the hard-packed ground, and she felt every rock, pebble, and bump against her heel and arch.

She didn't dare to look back, so didn't realize how close Charles was behind her. She took a hard hit from him and catapulted forward, landing face down on the ground. He pounced on top of her, and she struggled to free herself, then twisted around to face him, kicking and scratching like a wild animal and clawing at his face, barely missing his eyes.

He was stronger than she had imagined—he had obviously kept up his strength and physical fitness. She let out a fierce yell as she dodged his fists and the spittle flying from his mouth. Then he slapped her across the face with such force that everything became dull and she actually saw flickering stars. She lay back stunned, unable to move.

Charles, face bloodied, took the opportunity to reach for the bowie knife he carried on his belt.

Katie fought to remain conscious and alert. She began scooting backward as she spotted the glint of the large knife in his right hand. His face showed sheer hatred, and with the blood running down his cheeks, he resembled a demon who wanted her dead at any cost. He began swinging the blade back and forth rhythmically, and with each swipe, the edge of it came dangerously close to her face. She tried to use her arms to block it, but he continued his rampage, kicking her hands, forearms, and shoulders.

Her hand sank into a small hole, causing her to lose her balance. She watched helplessly as the blade neared her neck.

Charles caught his breath and prepared for the final blow.

Katie knew she couldn't fight this monster, but as she prepared for the worst, she became aware of a deep rumbling beneath her. The ground shook and the trees swayed. It was a strange and unfamiliar sensation.

Both Katie and Charles froze, their bodies tense.

Katie had never heard or felt anything like it before. It wasn't an earthquake; like most Californians, she was used to those. It was something much more deadly—something from the evil depths below.

The ground vibrated more violently, accompanied by an escalating roar, as if a machine was set to high and was going to shake them to death.

"What the…?" began Charles, but his voice was drowned out by a huge rumble and an ear-shattering boom.

Katie instinctively moved away, ready to get up and run.

The sound became deafening all around them. The ground buckled, leaving behind a trail as if someone had lit a fuse, igniting a runaway fire. A long channel along the trail plummeted into a sinkhole. She looked at Charles one last time, their eyes locking as the earth beneath them fell away and dropped like a lead weight.

Then she watched in paralyzing horror as he disappeared under the ground.

CHAPTER 55

Chad was moving quietly down a long trail just wide enough for a single vehicle, not wanting to alert anyone to his approach. He was followed closely by Cisco, which helped him to maintain a good pace.

His radio buzzed.

"Chad, location?" came the sheriff's voice.

"Working the upper eastern grid. Negative. Ten-four," he replied.

"There are only a few more hours of usable daylight."

"Copy."

"Keep to your check-in times,"

"Copy. Any word?"

There was a slight pause. "Negative."

"Over and out." The radio went silent. Chad didn't want to hear the chatter from the other volunteers. It would make his search that much more dismal, and he wanted to maintain his optimism.

Cisco whined and trotted a few feet ahead of him.

"Let's keep going," Chad said. "Find me something, boy."

They walked for another forty minutes without anything to indicate that Katie was close. Chad searched for tire tracks, freshly moved dirt, or anything that appeared to have been disturbed in the last few hours.

Every step seemed to make the search for Katie that much larger and unmanageable, impossible for only a hundred or so volunteers.

Chad stopped and leaned against a large tree trunk, one of his rare breaks, and retrieved his water bottle. He drank four full gulps and poured some out for Cisco.

Inside his backpack there were various small hand tools for anything he might encounter or run into. He pulled out a pick and flung it across the trail, where it stuck into a tree. His frustration had become his nemesis, and it began to berate him and tell him to turn back, because finding Katie was impossible.

"No!" he yelled. His voice rang through a valley area and slowly disappeared. The eerie echo melted away through the trees and around the hills. "You can't take her!" he said. It made him feel better as he retrieved the pick.

He pushed away any negative thoughts and began to make his way back to the Jeep. He would drive further into the dense area and hike another grid. This time it might be different.

With every step, Chad felt his energy and optimism begin to fade. It was out of character for him to give up when something became tough, so he pushed onward. He thought of Katie's precise notes and how hard she had searched, refusing to admit defeat on finding the missing girl. Following her lead, he would not abandon the search until there were no areas left to explore.

For the past half-hour, he had thought he heard some low rumbling noises, but he couldn't be certain. The last one had sounded like an earthquake, but the ground hadn't moved.

He grabbed his radio. "Ferguson, section four, anyone copy?"

"Section one copy, McGaven here, go ahead."

Chad was relieved to hear a familiar voice. "Strange noises," he continued. "Sounds like an earthquake. Did you hear or see anything unusual? Over."

"No, nothing unusual. Over."

Chad was disappointed, but felt better that he had contacted one of the other teams. "Ten-four, over and out."

Suddenly a loud rumbling followed by a boom interrupted the silence. Cisco began barking, then whining, and continued to rapid-bark.

Chad looked around to see if he could spot anything unusual. A cluster of trees in the distance appeared to move, and a fine dust rose in the air.

"What the hell?"

Explosion?

Unusual earth movement?

He moved to Cisco to try and calm the dog with gentle pats. "It's okay, boy." Then he sat down on a nearby boulder and waited.

More than fifteen minutes passed without any more noises or earth movements. His first thought was that maybe the military were testing some type of bomb; it had happened before, but this was strangely different.

Looking up at the sky, he knew that it had something to do with Katie. But what?

He waited for another couple of minutes before continuing his search.

CHAPTER 56

Charles Rey had fallen into the unknown depths below the surface of the earth. One moment he had been staring at Katie with the intent to kill her, and the next he had vanished like a magic trick. There was no sign left of him. She couldn't hear his voice yelling for help or any sound at all. After the shifting and booming from beneath the surface stopped, it became completely quiet.

Katie had managed to grab hold of heavy tree roots to stop her own plunge, but she didn't know how much longer she could hold on in her precarious twisted, bent-over position. She pulled herself higher and craned her neck to look up. She estimated she was about six feet below the surface. Dirt kept pouring down, and it was only a matter of time before the entire area would cave in completely.

"Charles!" she yelled, and listened as her voice echoed and bounced around for what seemed like miles. Her mouth tasted of dirt. The utter darkness below her triggered momentary vertigo; she was unable to verify if she was upside down or the right way up as she stared down into the abyss.

When she looked up, she could see parts of the sky, but daylight was dwindling. She had no way of knowing if anyone was searching for her, or what would happen when darkness fell. Her face and body were covered in moldy-smelling dirt. It was in her hair and trickling down her back, combining with her perspiration. Her arms and legs trembled from exertion. Fear had woven its way into her mind, but it was something she needed to push away.

With all the strength she had, she slowly climbed upward and began to claw her way out. At first, the loose dirt was impossible to grip and she couldn't find any hand- or footholds.

An image came into her mind of the picnic she'd had with Chad: the laughter, sharing life stories, and being comfortable together. Those moments were difficult to recreate, and when they happened, it was magical. She had begun building her life again—working cases, meeting new colleagues, and settling in at home.

Home.

She knew her uncle would take care of Cisco if anything happened to her. That thought pulled at her heartstrings.

The sinkhole reminded her of the stories from the early settlers in the mountain area who claimed that during the 1870s, towns completely disappeared, with not a trace remaining of buildings, homes, or livestock. No one knew what had happened to them. Could this have been the answer?

She took a deep breath and stretched up her right hand, trying to grab anything that would be stable.

Slowly, inch by inch, she made progress.

Dirt and miscellaneous debris trickled down into her face.

She tried several more times without success.

"You can do this," she said out loud, remembering how hard it was going through boot camp. Her drill sergeant was one of the toughest, and at times, she had hated him with a passion. She could still hear him yelling at her when she was just about to give up. It was brutal, but she understood why he was so insistent.

Push through, Katie.

She glanced around her and saw an area about three feet away that looked as though it could take her weight. From there, she might be able to pull herself up far enough to climb out.

"Okay, I *can* do this…" Speaking out loud helped her to focus, and gave her the comfort of hearing a human voice. "If I can just reach…" She stretched her right arm across the black hole, her fingertips mere inches away from her target.

Just a little bit closer.

Three inches…

Two inches…

She retracted her arm and rested. Her breathing had become rapid, but her perseverance ran the show and she wasn't going to give up.

Rolling her shoulders and taking a deep breath, she reached out her right arm again. This time, she lengthened her neck and shoulder muscles as her fingertips touched the thick tree root. Without a moment to lose, she grasped the root and leaped across, scrambling for a foothold until she found something in the dark that would hold her weight.

She took a minute to reassess her position, ignoring the fact that she was still in her undergarments; under the circumstances, it really didn't matter. Keeping her focus on the light above and the possibility of seeing the sky and trees again, she reached up once more and pulled herself upward. It was only inches at a time, but she was gradually making her way to the top.

At last her eyes were level with the ground, and she quickly scanned the area before hoisting herself up and out. Exhausted, she lay on her back gazing at the afternoon sky and catching her breath. She was finally safe. She silently thanked her drill sergeant, God, and her determination to survive.

Finally she sat up, and then slowly stood. The wind immediately chilled her and she shivered uncontrollably as she crossed her arms to protect her torso from the cold. There was nothing to shield her bare skin from the elements anymore now she was out of the hole.

Trying to keep her teeth from chattering, she took a step, then stopped instantly. She noticed that the ground looked strange, with uneven anomalies and small holes dotted about. The grains of dirt moved as if a snake slithered underneath. It was like nothing she had ever seen before. Clearly she was standing on extremely unstable ground.

The truck was about twenty yards away, presumably on stable ground. She prayed it would contain keys, a cell phone, clothes, and anything else that might help her to escape the area and contact her uncle. She had to at least warn him of the volatile situation, in case he had anyone searching for her.

She had to move now; she couldn't wait any longer, as the wind picked up in velocity and the temperature dropped. She took one tentative step and put her weight on the area, then another, repeating the process until she was only a few yards from the truck.

Looking up, she gave a long sigh of relief at seeing the truck so close. Hope sparked inside her, relieving some of her heavy burden. She took another step—and something changed. A small section of ground had given way. Standing completely still in mid motion, her breath caught in her throat.

No.

Then before she could move, the ground opened up all around her, like a giant wound, and swallowed her, her body dropping through a circular hole. Her descent ended abruptly as she smacked into a section of packed earth. The impact was like hitting a brick wall, and she moved judiciously to make sure she didn't have any broken bones or serious injuries.

Looking up, she saw that she was at least thirty feet below the surface. There was no way she could climb out this time, no matter how much she talked herself into it. No matter how hard she tried to maintain control and strength. She began to cry in frustration and fear, and for everything she hadn't yet experienced in her life.

No one will hear my pleas.
No one will hear my screams.
I will die alone.

CHAPTER 57

Chad reached his Jeep after completing another quadrant resulting in zero clues to Katie's whereabouts. He was weary and depressed. When he opened the driver's door, Cisco pushed past him and effortlessly leaped inside. The dog sat in the passenger seat, his head directed at the windshield with an unmistakable look of eagerness. It was crystal clear to Chad that Cisco wanted to continue the search.

Chad got behind the wheel, glanced at his watch, and decided to continue to the last grid area he had planned. It might become dark during his search, but that didn't matter to him, because he was prepared. He had a heavy-duty flashlight, a lighted headband, and even a few flares.

He drove along the road, which appeared to be more of a rugged walking trail than a roadway. His SUV bounced back and forth, but continued to climb to an area that he wasn't familiar with. A few times, as he negotiated sections of the road that seemed impassable, he wanted to pull over, but his determination pushed him onward.

His thoughts of spending time with Katie kept him company as he wondered if he would ever see her again. He also questioned whether they would work as a couple. She was so driven and determined, and it wasn't written in stone that she was going to stay in her hometown. He knew that she could go anywhere she wanted.

His cell phone made a bell sound as he drifted in and out of signal range, but the GPS seemed to keep a connection and led him towards the area where he would begin his next search.

After fifteen minutes, the Jeep reached flat ground. Chad quickly parked and checked his backpack to make sure he had everything he needed.

The radio crackled into life and the familiar voice of the sheriff said, "Chad, anything yet? Over."

He took a moment to reply. "Negative, over."

"Everything okay? Over."

"We're fine. Last grid location before dark. Over."

"Check back in an hour. Over and out."

The radio returned to quiet mode.

Chad knew that the other search teams weren't coming up with anything either.

He packed more supplies and another sweatshirt due to the falling temperature. Cisco barked and turned his nose in the direction they were headed.

"I hear ya, buddy," Chad said.

The GPS clicked back on and showed the direction they needed to be heading.

"Well this is it," he told the dog. "Put your extra-sharp canine senses to good use."

This time was different; it felt more lonely and remote, but Chad continued to move forward. His quadriceps and hamstrings were put to the test as he trekked down the trail. He felt as if he had already lost ten pounds of body weight and gained twenty pounds of backpack weight.

The sun moved into its low, late-afternoon position, just waiting before hiding behind the trees and then slipping below the western horizon. The wind picked up velocity with a chilling howl. There were no more loud underground rumbles percolating through the landscape.

Cisco padded ahead in point position along the trail, only stopping once in a while to look back at Chad to make sure he was still following. Chad imagined him doing the same thing in Afghanistan. The danger now wasn't imminent, but the situation was just as critical. The dog's dark coat still shone even in the diminishing light as he trotted effortlessly along, fanning his nose for any familiar scent.

Chad didn't want to think about what would happen when the sun actually set and ended the daylight.

CHAPTER 58

After Katie had weakly examined her surroundings, it was clear that the hole she had fallen into was different from the one that had swallowed Charles. It was narrower, more structured, and seemed likely to be man-made instead of a mass irregularity in the earth. It resembled something that might have been used for a mine, like an emergency ventilation shaft.

Her body was weary after her attempts to climb out of the previous hole. Her hands were raw and two of her fingernails had torn away to the quick. Her self-pity tears had run dry. She hadn't eaten or had a drink in hours, as evidenced by the strained growling noises from her stomach and her parched lips. Fatigue and exhaustion had begun to set in. Soon she wouldn't be able to move, but only shiver in the darkness underground until her body couldn't function anymore. Her organs would slowly begin to shut down.

She leaned back against a wall of packed dirt and listened to her surroundings. The wind and trees were the only noises that kept her company.

Sleep overpowered her and tried to beat her into submission, but she didn't want to give in to its powers—not just yet. Her eyelids grew heavy and her breathing was shallow and slow. The muscles in her legs cramped, especially in her calves. Excessive thirst almost overwhelmed her rational thinking. Her body wouldn't stop shaking, and she knew it was a sign of hypothermia. She had rushes of hot and cold, dizziness, and an almost blinding headache was beginning to obscure her vision.

*

Chad regained some energy due to the flat terrain rather than the sharp inclines on his earlier searches. He marveled at the region he was combing. It was a place that he had never visited, at least not in memory, and under any other circumstances it would have been beautiful and tranquil. The landscape gently swelled and dipped, full of contrasting greens, browns, and golden yellows. It had been moved by centuries of earthquakes and natural weather conditions and had become a masterpiece. The view was an artist's nirvana, worthy of oversized photographs and paintings.

He paid particular attention to the trails and narrow roads. He wasn't completely sure, but it looked as if there were some tire tracks travelling in the same direction he was headed. But whether the impressions were recent, days old, or from three months ago was the question of the hour.

He knew that Katie would be able to deduce when the tracks were made. After she'd found the bodies of the two little girls, there'd been quite a bit of gossip. Some thought she was a genius, while others were locked into the idea that it was just pure luck. Either way, she was the one who had found the missing children, alone, and using the skills outlined in her field notebook.

Chad stopped. He gazed at the sky with its clouds rushing in, trying to pull himself together and make sense of what he was facing—and more importantly, what Katie was facing.

Cisco trotted on towards some seemingly enticing bushes, then suddenly dropped to the ground, crawling slowly on his belly, heading southeast. Chad was about to call to him, but decided to let him do what he knew how to do. He watched the dog with curiosity, his heart pounding in his chest. His breath wavered, leaving behind a lump of angst in his throat.

Cisco growled and the hackles stood up along his backbone, making him appear much larger than his eighty-five pounds. His yellowish-brown eyes were focused, targeted and unrelenting, and his ears pointed straight up.

Still Chad didn't move an inch. His own instincts seemed to jump-start, with prickly feelings up his spine and the back of his neck. Something unnatural had caught his attention too, but he didn't know exactly what it was—enemy or friend.

The dog kept his body low, and gave a half growl and half whine. He moved with the stealth of a snake and the single-mindedness of a predator.

The air cooled another five degrees as the clouds covered the sun, leaving behind a black-and-white landscape.

Chad eased his way forward. Unexpectedly the dog turned and began barking at him, bouncing up and down; not playful, but rather an alarm for something important. He was trying to convey a message.

"What is it, Cisco?" Chad said. "Go, find, search, find Katie…" He didn't know what else to say.

The dog turned away and moved another three feet, then stopped once more. He continued to bark rapidly.

*

Hugging her legs close, eyes tightly shut, Katie tried to keep herself warm with wonderful memories of home, her childhood, her parents. As her teeth chattered, she heard the ensuing echo from down below. For some reason, she thought of someone tap dancing and it made her giggle to herself.

Every ragged breath was difficult, leaving her straining for oxygen. Her shallow heartbeat and labored breathing were the only sounds she could hear.

Then, faintly in the distance, there was a repetitive banging that sounded like a machine of some kind. Katie held her breath and struggled to hear. After a few seconds, she realized that it was a dog barking. It was Cisco's bark—there was no doubt about it.

It was rapid and extremely loud. A purposeful bark, the one he gave when he discovered a specific find or track.

A rush of adrenalin flowed through her body as if someone had ignited her with a new lease on life.

"Cisco," she whispered. Her voice sounded strange and disconnected. "Cisco," she said louder. "I'm here! Help! Please help!"

But even as the chance of rescue presented itself, she remembered the reality of the sinkholes and mine shafts, and the realization filled her with horror. "No! Please stay where you are! It's not safe," she called.

*

Chad stood next to Cisco. The dog continued to bark at him rapidly, showing his white teeth. Chad knew he meant business, but was uncertain what to do next. He looked in the direction the dog was indicating and took off at a steady run, sprinting toward a trail that ran into a back road for vehicles. It was surrounded by trees and low-lying bushes with dead debris underneath.

Stopping to catch his breath, he thought he heard something. A voice? A bird? People at the camp ground?

He continued to move toward the sound until he heard it clearly. It was a faint muffled voice: someone calling out for help? He continued to move with caution, but Cisco ran ahead of him. "Cisco, here!" he yelled, remembering Katie's commands. The dog stopped and looked at him. "Here!" he said again. With some reluctance, the dog returned.

Chad grabbed the dog's collar and said, "Katie?" Barely breathing, he waited for an answer. Cisco panted loudly but had stopped barking. He too was waiting.

The voice said, "Help. Help."

Chad didn't know for sure, but it sounded like Katie. It sounded as if she were underground. The thought made him nauseous and fearful. He started to run, but tripped and fell, releasing the dog's collar. As he scrambled to get to his feet again, Cisco barked uncontrollably and inched forward.

"Cisco, down!"

The dog obediently dropped to his belly, though he clearly wanted to continue. He was panting heavily in canine nervousness.

"Katie!" yelled Chad. "Katie!"

"I'm here!" she replied.

"Where?"

"Don't come any closer! The ground isn't safe!"

Chad didn't understand what she meant, but it gave him pause. He wasn't sure if it was a trap and Charles was making her say certain things.

"Katie, are you alone?"

"Yes." There was a pause, and then she said, "Stay back. Look at the ground."

Chad ordered the dog to stay, then walked carefully toward her voice, expecting to see some type of booby trap set up to impale him or shoot him where he stood.

Examining the area, he saw strange lines of dirt travelling several yards. He had never seen anything like it before and looked closer. The ground seemed to move under his feet, and he stopped immediately. It was as if he had stepped into a funhouse; it was clear the area was completely unstable.

"Stay back!" Katie repeated.

"Where are you?"

"Can you see the truck?"

Chad didn't see any truck, so he moved carefully to the left and stepped across an area between several trees. There it was—Charles Rey's truck.

"I see it!"

He waited with trepidation, nerves raw, yet relieved that he had found her. He glanced behind him; Cisco was still in the down position.

"I'm a few yards from the truck," she said.

Chad hastened to move closer to her voice. He wanted to make sure that she was okay, and that it was really her—to make sure she wasn't a mirage. His survival instincts told him to stay low to the ground. He wasn't entirely sure why, but he obeyed his senses and moved toward her on hands and knees. He saw clearly that there was a long sunken area, in addition to some sort of sinkhole.

"Katie," he said.

"Please, Chad, don't come any closer. It's not safe."

A low rumbling reminiscent of the noises he had heard earlier erupted from underneath him. As he scrambled back, part of the ground in front of him fell inward. He gasped in disbelief; he had never seen anything like it before. The area resembled the collateral damage after a bomb had detonated. He saw Charles's truck bounce from side to side; it would soon be the next thing to disappear.

"Stay still," he ordered. "I'll be back."

*

Katie sobbed quietly as she heard Chad leave, calling Cisco's name. They had found her, but she had sensed the earth moving and shifting again, and she knew that she had mere minutes and not hours before she was buried alive. Despite her terror, hearing Chad's voice had helped to ease some of the emotional pain.

*

Chad ran as fast as he could back to his Jeep. He knew that Katie's time was running out. Out of breath, he put Cisco inside the vehicle, where he would be safe, then retrieved his cell phone and dialed Sheriff Scott.

The sheriff answered on the second ring, "What do you have?" His voice sounded strained.

"I found her," replied Chad. "She's okay right now, but we need to move fast."

"Slow down. What do you mean?"

"She's fallen into some type of cavern or underground cave. The ground is extremely unstable and could drop further at any time. We could lose her."

"What about Rey?"

"I don't know. He's gone… The ground is falling in and it's unclear how far the danger extends."

"Text me your coordinates and I'll send help."

"Sir," Chad began. "I've got a winch on my Jeep and I'm going to try and pull her out. Do I have your permission?"

There was a pause.

"Sir?"

"Do what you need to do," was the reply.

"Thank you. My location is coming to you right now." He ended the phone call and sent a text with his GPS location and specific instructions about the unstable area, then jumped behind the wheel.

He knew that no matter how fast he wanted to drive, he had to watch the ground and go slowly. He stopped the Jeep, then inched forward; stopped and then inched forward again. Cisco seemed to feel his heightened energy and trepidation, which made him bark and pant in turn as they made their halting way toward Katie.

When he calculated that they were approximately twenty-five feet away, Chad got out of the vehicle and ran around to the back, opening the cargo area. Inside, he had several two-by-fours used for fencing. He pulled four of them out and placed them strategically on the ground so that he could drive the Jeep onto them. Then, taking out two more, he wedged them behind his back tires.

Cisco jumped around in the cab, barking every so often as though to encourage him in his efforts.

Chad carefully stepped in front of the Jeep and moved toward Katie as far as he dared, calling her name.

He waited. Then a weak reply: "I'm still here…"

"I'm going to send a rope down to you. Are you strong enough to pull yourself up?"

"I think so…"

There was a rumbling sound beneath Chad's feet, and the dirt on the ground shook and spilled inward. He froze, then looked back at the Jeep, with the engine idling and Cisco inside. It was shaking, moving from side to side.

No…

With nothing to do but wait, he remained in his position. The sound finally stopped, and didn't appear to have caused any more damage to the hole.

"Katie?"

"I'm okay, please hurry."

Chad jumped up and released the winch. The large spool began to unroll and he guided the cable with a hook on the end toward the mouth of the hole. He realized that he was holding his breath as he moved as quickly as possible. The ground turned spongy beneath his feet, so he dropped to his stomach and army-crawled toward the opening, before coming to an abrupt stop. The ground morphed and began to cave in. He couldn't get any closer.

"Katie, you'll have to climb up a little bit. Hurry."

He guided the cable inside the hole, then retraced his path until he was at the Jeep once again.

"Say when!" he yelled.

*

Katie sat immobile, huddled, her body frozen and muscles severely cramped. Pure fear had gripped her chest and throat, making it difficult to breathe. She remembered her mantra, *You're not going to win*, and repeated it out loud, over and over. She knew that Chad was out there, and that he must be scared and worried about her.

Fine dirt began to sift down the sides of her safe haven. It built a momentum of earth, cascading down and covering her in layers. Soon she was finding it almost impossible to breathe, but the dirt kept coming.

Out of fear of being buried alive, she clawed her way upward though she wasn't making any real headway. She heard the sound of an engine in the distance, as well as Cisco's distinct bark. Pushing through her exhaustion, she scrabbled through mounds of dirt, searching for the rope that Chad was trying to get to her.

No lifeline came.

Her dwindling energy was being used up in keeping the dirt from completely immobilizing her. She was fighting an endless barrage of soil; there was no other way of escaping other than to keep pushing it away. It was in her mouth and nose, making her cough and choke.

Still no lifeline came.

Chad, you tried. For that I will always be grateful.

She sat back and waited her fate.

There was so much she was grateful for, and so many people who had made an impact on her life—she loved them all.

Just when she felt at her most bleak and hopeless, a metal hook connected to a cable appeared. It was like a beacon in the darkness. Taking a deep breath and remembering all the past challenges she had faced, Katie pushed her body upward and took hold of the hook.

Her bloody fingers and cold hands somehow held on tight as she yelled with every ounce of her strength, "Okay, pull!"

She wasn't sure if Chad had heard her, but an invisible force began to pull her up and out of the shaft. As she reached the surface, the fading daylight was like heaven to her. The winch continued to pull her across the ground on her belly. She could barely feel her hands, but she gritted her teeth and clung on.

*

As Chad manned the winch, he watched the mouth of the hole, hoping that Katie could hang on long enough to get to safety.

When he saw her emerging from the ground covered in dirt and wearing only panties and a bra, his heart broke for what she must've experienced. She was alone and vulnerable, but she had fought her way back to everything she loved.

She let go of the hook, and stood up, wavering, then started to run toward the Jeep. Cisco had squeezed out through the driver's window and ran to her, knocking her down again. He gently took her wrist in his mouth and began to pull her; Chad met them, helping Katie to her feet and guiding her to the car.

"You okay?" he asked.

She could only nod her answer, but it was clear that she was weak and struggling to maintain control of her body.

"C'mon, Cisco. Get in the car," he ordered. The dog obediently jumped into the back.

Holding Katie tight, Chad helped her into the passenger seat, then gunned the engine into reverse, moving as far away from the unstable area as he could. When he figured they were in a safe place, he stopped the car and got out, running around to the back to search for a sweatshirt and a blanket. He helped Katie put the sweatshirt on and wrapped the blanket around her. He had never felt anyone that cold before—even during rescues with the fire department. She was shivering uncontrollably and her skin was pale; she was obviously suffering from hypothermia.

She looked at Chad in silence, but her dark-green eyes conveyed more than mere words could ever do.

"You're safe now," he said, and kissed her.

She leaned into his arms and wept uncontrollably. He held her for as long as she needed, until they heard the sounds of SUVs and emergency vehicles fast approaching.

CHAPTER 59

Colorful balloons, stuffed animals, and cheerful cards cluttered the small hospital room. The curtains were half drawn as Katie lay peacefully sleeping. She had been in the hospital for three days, recuperating from hypothermia and a mild concussion.

Partially awake, she turned to her left side and drifted back into a wonderful dream. It was the most rest she had had in months, and she was taking full advantage of it.

Her uncle appeared in the doorway, dressed in casual clothes. Seeing that Katie was sleeping, he was just about to leave again.

"You weren't going to say hello," murmured Katie.

"Go back to sleep, sweetheart."

"I haven't talked to anyone in a while." She sat up. "Please come in."

The sheriff entered the room, pulled a chair close to the bed, and sat down. "How are you feeling today?" he asked.

"Better. My head doesn't hurt as much, but the stitches are getting itchy. I want to go back to work, or at least go home to look at better scenery."

"It's only been three days—work will still be there. There are a lot of people wanting to see you, including a certain eager young man."

"Uncle Wayne," she said, embarrassed. The truth was, she didn't know what to do about her relationship with Chad. She didn't want a romantic relationship until she could balance other things in her life first.

"I'm just saying—"

"What's the status on the case?" She quickly changed the subject.

"I think we can wait to talk about that."

"No, please, I need to know. What's going on?"

The sheriff smiled and leaned back in the chair. "We're just about to wrap everything up, but there's a few more things before we put this entire thing behind us. They've identified the third girl, Wendy Stiller, age eleven, and have contacted her mom. It looks like Dena Matthews will make a full recovery. We've put together forensic evidence—including the boot prints at your house, Cisco's bite, and the two notes. Everything is falling into place and points to Charles Rey with everything found at his house. The media has been relentless, but we've managed to keep them away from you."

Katie picked up a cup and sipped some water. "Was Rey the only perp?"

"As far as we can tell, there were no other conspirators. Officially the *Toymaker* is dead and buried."

"What about Terrance Price?" she asked, now wide awake.

The sheriff shook his head.

"Are you sure?"

"There's no indication that he was involved in the kidnappings or the murders."

Katie let out a sigh. "I thought it was possible that Rey had used him, or that he was an accomplice after the fact."

"If he was, then he took that secret to his grave. The case for Price is closed. Rey has been declared officially dead, even though the rescuers couldn't find a body. There's no way he could have survived."

"What about…"

"Detective Templeton?" He finished her sentence.

She nodded.

"He's been fired and stripped of his police-officer status for planting evidence, and the DA is deciding what charges, if any, will be brought against him."

"Oh." She looked away. Everything weighed heavy on her. The extreme tiredness pulled her down, willing her to sleep.

Her uncle leaned forward and squeezed her hand. "I'm so sorry for everything Rey put you through—I don't think anyone saw that coming. It's been a tough time, with all the losses in the town, but we'll survive. And most important, we're here for you."

"Can I have a raise?" She laughed weakly.

Sheriff Scott laughed too. "I'll bring that up at the next union meeting."

Katie stared out the window, remembering the attack, the truck ride in the coffin, and falling into the mine. She knew the experience would make her stronger, and a better detective.

"Everything okay?" he asked.

"Yeah, it's just a little hard to comprehend everything that has happened. So what's the status at the site?"

"Well, they've cordoned off the area so that no one else can accidentally stumble upon it, and now the county and the state, along with the geological and archeological departments at the university, are fighting over who has first rights."

"Why?"

"They want to decide if it's a historical area or just a geological anomaly… something like that. They think it might be part of a town that disappeared during 1863, but the jury is still out on that one."

Katie leaned back, overcome by exhaustion. "Sounds like something the conspiracy theorists will love adding their take on…"

Sheriff Scott rose from the chair, leaned over, and kissed her on the forehead. "Rest. I'll be back tomorrow. Don't worry about Cisco; he's being spoiled by Claire as we speak. You need anything?"

She shook her head.

"See you soon," he said.

"Okay." Katie's voice faded. "I'll talk to you soon…" She was already asleep as her uncle left the hospital room. He paused for a moment watching her sleep, and then he was gone.

CHAPTER 60

Three weeks later

Katie had memorized the swearing-in speech that every law-enforcement officer recited to officially become a part of the police department. There was no doubt as to where she wanted to begin her detective career—it was clear that the Pine Valley Sheriff's Department was her home, and she was eager to get to work.

She stood proud, dressed in her uniform, and placed her right hand on the Bible, with the other raised, as she declared: "I, Katherine Ann Scott, do solemnly swear that I will support and defend the Constitution of the United States and the Constitution of the State of California against all enemies, foreign and domestic; that I will bear true faith and allegiance to the Constitution of the United States and the Constitution of the State of California; that I take this obligation freely, without any mental reservation or purpose of evasion; and that I will well and faithfully discharge the duties upon which I am about to enter."

She smiled, her excitement showing as she turned to her friends witnessing the ceremony.

The crowd of at least a hundred police officers cheered. Most were from the sheriff's department, but there were others from some of the surrounding departments, there to welcome Katie and congratulate her on solving the serial-killer case.

She stood in front of her uncle as he handed her a detective's badge and gave her a hug, saying for everyone to hear, "It's my pleasure to welcome you to our family. You've more than earned it." Then he whispered in her ear, "Your parents would have been extremely proud of you, as I am."

"Thank you."

Turning to the audience with tears in her eyes, Katie saw the friendly faces of Deputy McGaven, Supervisor Blackburn, Denise, Aunt Claire, and Chad with Cisco at his side. They were her friends and true family.

Sheriff Scott spoke to the audience. "You are now looking at the detective who will be in charge of our new cold-case division. Welcome, Detective Scott."

More hoots and hollers rose from the crowd.

Katie smiled, feeling a tremendous sense of pride at belonging somewhere important, doing what she was meant to do. It was great to finally be home.

If Katie's first case had you gripped, sign-up to Jennifer's mailing list to be the first to hear about future releases. Your email address will never be shared, and you can unsubscribe at any time.
www.bookouture.com/jennifer-chase/?title=little-girls-sleeping

A LETTER FROM JENNIFER

I want to say a huge thank you for choosing to read *Little Girls Sleeping*. If you enjoyed it, and want to keep up to date with all my latest releases, just sign up at the following link. Your email address will never be shared and you can unsubscribe at any time.

www.bookouture.com/jennifer-chase

This was a special project and I enjoyed writing it. Forensics and criminal profiling is something that I've studied in depth, and to be able to incorporate it into crime fiction has been a thrilling experience for me.

One of my favourite activities outside of writing is dog training. I'm a dog lover, in case you couldn't tell by reading this book, and have had the incredible opportunity to train with my local police K9 association, which covers several counties in California. My dog is certified in trailing, scent detection, and advanced obedience. I loved creating a supporting canine character for my police detective.

I hope you loved *Little Girls Sleeping*; if you did, I would be very grateful if you could write a review. I'd love to hear what you think, and it makes such a difference helping new readers to discover one of my books for the first time.

I love hearing from my readers—you can get in touch on my Facebook page, through Twitter, Goodreads, or my website.

Thanks,
Jennifer Chase

AuthorJenniferChase

JChaseNovelist

authorjenniferchase.com

ACKNOWLEDGEMENTS

I want to thank my husband Mark for his steadfast support and for being my rock even when I had self-doubt.

A special thank you goes out to my law-enforcement, police K9, forensic, and first-responder friends—there are too many to list. I wouldn't be able to bring my crime-fiction stories to life if it wasn't for all of you.

This has been a truly amazing writing experience and I would like to thank my publisher Bookouture and their fantastic staff for helping me to bring this book and the series to life. A very special thank you to my editor, Abigail Fenton, for her patience and unwavering enthusiasm.

Lightning Source UK Ltd.
Milton Keynes UK
UKHW041220040821
388299UK00002B/201